"And, more and more, a spirit, traitor to God and to His Word, has sprung up in Christendom, a spirit which calls itself 'Tolerance,' 'Charity,' and other kindred words, forgetting that God has declared, *'Hereby know ye the Spirit of God: every spirit that confesseth Jesus Christ is come in the flesh, is of God: And Every spirit that confesseth not that Jesus Christ is come in the flesh, is not of God, and this is the spirit of Antichrist, whereof ye have heard that it should come, and even now, already it is in the world.'"*

Scarlet and Purple will show you how to live each day in readiness for Christ's return.

Scarlet and Purple

SYDNEY WATSON

Power Books

Fleming H. Revell Company
Old Tappan, New Jersey

Printed in the United States of America

CONTENTS

PREFACE

WITHIN a few weeks of the publication of "The Mark of the Beast," two separate correspondents, perfect strangers to me, one in India, and the other in San Francisco, wrote in almost exactly the same strain, namely: "Having read your two books 'In the Twinkling of an Eye,' and 'The Mark of the Beast,' it has been borne in upon me that there should be a third book, dealing mainly, with the passage of a soul from death into life, and also showing more fully the condition of ripeness (or certainly *ripening*), of Christendom for the coming of Antichrist." This book is the result of those suggestions. In point of "matter," it may almost be said to immediately *precede* "In the Twinkling of an Eye," and should supply what the Indian and Californian correspondents (since further emphasized by others) have suggested.

I have called the book "Scarlet and Purple": a story of Souls and "Signs," since the book has attempted to fill the gap suggested by my correspondents. The "Scarlet and Purple" is a reference to Rev. 17:4. "Scarlet is the emblem of human and earthly dignity; purple, the combination of scarlet and blue, is emblematic of authority which unites the heavenly and spiritual with that which is earthly and carnal. False doctrine is, for the most part, a corruption of divine truth—error overlaid with a thin layer of truth, like base metal gilded. The 'precious stones and pearls' are emblematic of spiritual truths, and of those wondrous revelations of the Church's position and prospects made known in the sacred scriptures, but corrupted by the 'Woman.' The cup which she holds in her hand is of gold, for the false church will possess and use, for her own purposes, those ordinances which are of divine origin—Baptism; 'The Lord's Supper;' ministry; worship; all these she employs, but not for the communication of spiritual and divine truth and blessing, but prostituted to the basest of purposes, and used to the diffusion of the most pernicious doctrines."

This comment of Thomas Newberry, will give the key to the thought in the mind of the writer of this book, when dealing with the "Scarlet and Purple" of the present-day growing apostasy.

Of the "story of *Souls*," it becomes more and more imperative that we, to whom God has committed the ambassadorial office, should insist upon the "must" of the New Birth. Hence this book is a message to myriads *in* the churches, as well as to those outside; for the Word of God shows plainly the hideous awakening that awaits those who are blinded by a merely religious life, allied to a church membership that is not linked with the "name written in the Lamb's Book of Life."

The coming of our Lord, *presently*, will discover the mere church professors, who being left on earth to go through the horrors of *"The* Great Tribulation," will cry "What fools! What madmen we have been!"

SYDNEY WATSON

"THE FIRS," VERNHAM DEAN,
    HUNGERFORD, BERKS.

PUBLISHER'S NOTE

WE ARE convinced that this story conveys a vital message to myriads in the churches as well as those outside, for it shows the hideous awaking that awaits those who are depending upon "good works," a merely religious life, or church membership to gain an entrance into God's eternal city.

Written in the same fresh, enthusiastic, interest-compelling manner as "In the Twinkling of An Eye," and "The Mark of the Beast," this book brings the reader face to face with Jesus Christ—as Saviour—and emphasizes the "must" of the New Birth. Every home library should contain a copy of this book. Every Sunday-school library should have several copies. You should buy the book yourself—read it—and keep it in circulation among your unsaved friends and loved ones—it may be the means of their conversion.

SCARLET AND PURPLE

ᏹᏹᏹ

CHAPTER I.

BAFFLED!

JACK QUENTIN paused, the charcoal stick was poised between his thumb and index. A perplexed, baffled look filled his face.

The canvas before him was an immense one, it represented the most ambitious conception he had ever essayed —a "Calvary." The Crucifixion should fill the great canvas.

Twice had he attempted to sketch in the face and form of the Divine Man on the centre cross, and each time he had erased his sketching. Then, for the third time he had attempted to transfix his thought on the canvas, but again he suddenly paused. A sense of impotence swept over him. He could not get a true conception of the face of the great sufferer.

Jack Quentin had seen almost every noted picture of the Christ—ancient and modern—Munkasky's, Doré's, and every other great master's Crucifixion were more or less familiar to him. But he did not care to become, even remotely, a copyist. His picture must be his own. He wanted to get out of the more or less beaten rut— if he could.

But now it was suddenly forced upon him that he was not ready for his subject, though the canvas was ready for him.

Jack had been an artist from his pinafore days. Before he was well out of school—at sixteen, to be correct—those capable of judging had predicted for him, a career. From his earliest studio days he had done some wonderful things, and scores of older men envied his gift.

But, for all this, he had never lost his head, or suffered from swelling of that member. Artist, to the soul, he had always recognized his own shortcomnigs. Today, when we meet him first, he is thirty-five years of age. Tall, fair, with a leonine head, and a mane of curly hair, tawny as a lion's, in colour. He was magnificently proportioned in frame. Not distinctively handsome, he was yet decidedly good-looking, with a marked note of strength in his bronzed face.

Bronzed he certainly was, for he had travelled wide and often. "If I was dark instead of fair," he once confided to a chum, "I could easily believe that I had gipsy blood in me, for ingrained in my very composition is the wander-lust."

As he flung down his charcoal, a curious rush of blood swept hotly through all his veins, and a strange restlessness came over him. He knew the feeling; he knew what it portended.

People who are ignorant of this strange, almost uncanny sense, would fail to understand it, and certainly would fail to excuse it. But those who know it, know it as a driving force—this strange, all-powerful wander-lust, which is only equalled in its compelling by the fatal lust for alcohol.

"But I want to paint my Calvary picture!" He spoke the words aloud, almost petulantly, and almost as though he was addressing some unseen person. Yet, even as

he spoke, his eyes wandered to a brown waterproof—
canvas haver-sack that stood in a corner. The brown
thing had been with him whenever his wanderings had
carried him farther afield than the shores of his native
Britain.

"But I want to paint my picture!" He repeated the
words in an aggrieved, aggressive tone. "I have set my
heart upon it!"

The wander-lust, like some mocking imp, laughed
within him, and, tauntingly, cried: "You can't do it!
you can't do it! It needs an inspiration to paint a Calvary
canvas, and you have not got the inspiration—*Yet.*"

As though he would snap the bindings of the strange
lust that had so suddenly seized upon him, he snatched
his hat from the spear-head of the bronze Pompeiian-
Roman sentinel that guarded his studio door, and went
out into the street. Electric lights were leaping to birth
everywhere. A moment later he almost ran into the arms
of an old friend, Ralph Bastin, a rising young journalist.

The two men had not met for over a year, for Bastin
had been abroad on a special Indian tour for his paper.
Their greetings were mutually glad and hearty.

"Was just coming to hunt you up, Jack," Ralph remarked, adding: "Only arrived in dear old London at
two-thirty this morning. My! It's good to be back in
the *real* hub of the Universe—Boston, for all its brag,
is not in it, as the *"hub."*

"I came out to get some dinner, Ralph. Have you fed
yet, old man?" Jack Quentin had signed to a taxi as he
began his explanation.

A moment later the pair were bowling along to a favourite little Bohemian type of restaurant, little known, and less used, by any but the painting fraternity. They dined well—and *wisely*—for both men were clean-living, and abstemious, as regarded "drinks."

"Where shall we go?" Bastin asked, as they finally rose from the table. "We can't talk out our souls until we smoke the midnight pipe. Have you seen 'The Burma Maid'?" he added.

"No, have heard a lot of talk about it," Jack was lighting a cigar as he replied.

"Shall we toddle round and sample it?" Ralph continued.

"Yes, as well there as anywhere else," Jack laughed. The vision of that brown haversack was dancing before his mental eyes, and he felt that it mattered very little to him what he did or where he went, *pro tem,* since, in his inmost soul he knew that nothing could finally allay the *"wander-lust"* that had come upon him.

They were fortunate in securing a couple of stalls, but the play itself never once gripped either of them. Jack Quentin saw practically nothing of it. Before his wander-lust-held eyes rose the regions around Maulmain, Bassein, Rangoon, Mandalay, etc., filling his mental gaze. Pictures of the camp-fire and elephant pickets; pagodas—small and gleaming white in their shunam coating, and pagodas large and costly with gilded domes flashing in the fierce sunlight—these were the scenes that passed before his vision, and not the painted and musical comedy on the theatre stage.

A woman close to him drew out her handkerchief, and its perfume conjured up another vision of the distant east—for the woman's perfume bore near kinship to the scent which filled a carriage of one of the Indian railways when a Rose and Patchouli perfumed woman had once travelled in the same compartment with him, when bound for the hills.

"Bound for the Hills," how he recalled that journey. The weird crossing of the Ganges by night. The train had pulled up at Damukdia,—that queer river-side sta·tion. Here, everyone had to alight, and tramp that abominable quarter of a mile of sand to the Ferry steamer. A motley gang of coolies "humped" the baggage; the whole scene was luridly illumined with paraffin "flares." Dinner had been served on the Ferry-steamer, and, to-night, with the scent of that Rose and Patchouli perfumed woman by his side, in the theatre "stall," he recalled that the curry, at that steamer-dinner, had been "red," and that there was an excess of cocoa-nut in it. Arriving at the opposite side of the river, there came another sandy tramp to the station at Sara Ghat, where the train was waiting, the engine snorting as if in impatience to be off—rare quality in anything in India. He recalled it all to-night through the cue of his neighbour's perfume.

The two men left the house before the last act was over. Arm in arm they strolled away from the glare of the electric-lit palace. Their talk turned, naturally, on Burma, for the native colouring and general atmosphere of the play had been, to them, the only really arrestive part of the performance. And as Jack Quentin listened to his chum who, like himself, had *"done"* Burma, the wander-lust burned more fiercely than ever within him.

Bastin, only just returned from his year of wandering, seemed, to Jack Quentin, to bear about him, like hunting-Esau of old-time, the "smell of the field."

But, suddenly, another phase of the reminiscent mood swept over the versatile, volatile Ralph, and he said:

"Speaking of Burma, Jack, did you know Charley Sladen?"

"Never *knew* him," Quentin returned, "often heard of him in by-gone days, there was something in connection with Burma, I know, but I can't recall what it was. There's a story, eh?"

"There is, Jack, and that play, tonight, brought it all back as fresh as though it had happened yesterday. I think that is why I got sick of the show. Charley and I were school and college chums, and his death was a big blow to me. Talk of there being no romance in these highly-civilized days—bah, while there are two humans left on this old earth, one of either sex, there's bound to be romance. Care to hear the story, Jack?"

"Please?"

"Right ho! Let's get inside somewhere then, and light-up."

Ten minutes later they were in Jack Quentin's den, a room adjoining his studio.

CHAPTER II.

THE DOUBLE TATOO.

THE Den was a curious admixture of the barbaric and sybaritic. Luxuriantly furnished, the walls and ceiling were yet hung with every known and unknown type of barbaric weapon, with hunting trophies, and more than one relic that was positively ghastly in suggestiveness. Pack-saddles; sleeping-bags; Australian blue camping blankets; wide oriental sleeping rugs; gun-cases; gabardine suits, and a hundred-and-one et cœtera, of foreign travel were piled, or littered in the corners and sides of the great old-fashioned room.

As the eyes of Jack Quentin roved round the room the fierce wander-lust burned fiercer than ever within him.

But he made no sign to his friend. He lit his "corn-cob," and settled himself to listen to the story of his chum's chum.

"Charley Sladen," began Ralph, "was as smart a man as could be found in his day and generation. When he was only twenty-four he was sent out to Rangoon on important business for the firm he was connected with. Forced to wait in Rangoon for nearly three weeks, after his business was concluded—he was waiting certain instructions from his principal—he, in a purely accidental way, had met, and become enamoured with a very beautiful, Europeanized Burma girl. Melia was nursery governess to the two young children of an English resident on the outskirts of Rangoon.

"From the first moment of meeting this beautiful Burman, Charley had become utterly fascinated, infatuated; while she, in turn, learned speedily to love him with a blind idolatrous love. Within a week of his meeting Melia, so great was his infatuation, Charley proposed marriage, and when, in response, she flung herself upon his breast, and told him that her love for him was "all her life," he began to sketch pictures of their life together in the little English nest he would make for his beautiful Burma bird.

"He meant all he said, and she believed him utterly. Like many other Burma girls, Melia was a very clever tatooer, and one day he suggested that she should prick a true lover's knot into his arm, the main design to be in blue, with an M and a C., in red, each in the heart of one of the loops of the fancy design.

"'Draw me a picture of this knot,' she said, 'and I will do it, or at least part of it, to-night, when we meet.'

"That evening, when they were alone together, the work was begun. With skilled hand the girl traced the design in blue upon the fleshy part of the inside of Charley's left arm, well above the wrist. Then she began to ply her needles. She could only do a little over half of the work at the first sitting, for they had wasted much time in love-making before she began.

"'To-morrow my love,' she said, as she bandaged the arm with a soft rag anointed with a clever Eastern salve —'to-morrow, I will finish the picture.'

"They arranged their times of meeting for the next day, then they had parted as only infatuated lovers, such as they were, do part. Again and again Charley looked back at the dainty little figure, until it was quite

out of his sight. Then he turned away with a little sigh
saying to himself: 'Life with her ever at my side,
will be heaven.'

"He little dreamed that he would never see her again
in Burma, and that only after three years, and on the
very eve of his marriage to another girl—English, this
time—would he ever meet sweet little Melia again.

"Half-an-hour after parting with his inamorata, he was
closeted with the agent of his firm, the agent taking him
seriously to task. The two men had become very close
friends, and the agent spoke freely and frankly to Charley
about his infatuation for the little Burman.

" 'I have seen her, Charley,' he said, 'and I am bound
to confess that she is pretty enough to turn the heads
of half a million such fellows as you and me. She is
good, too, that is, as good as the countless centuries of
native blood that flows in her veins, can let her be. But,
after all, my dear fellow, it will not do for you to think
of making her your wife.'

"Charley wanted to protest, but the agent said, 'Let me
finish, then you shall say what you like. I want to tell
you a few facts, and there's no getting over facts, so
here goes for the stories of six marriages, well known
to me, that have come off between European friends of
mine and pretty native girls.'

"For an hour the agent talked on, telling the sordid,
unhappy stories of the six ill-assorted marriages to which
he had referred, ending with: 'The mail, just before you
came in, brought me instructions which make it imperative that you should start for Colombo in the morning by
the boat that is timed to leave at 9:15. Now take my
advice, pack your traps and be off without trying to get

another glimpse of that pretty child's black eyes and laughing face. And when, some day, I come home to the old country, you will tell me that I was a real saviour to you.'

" 'But what of the girl?' Charley said, his conscience pricking him at the idea of his suggested desertion.

" 'The girl?' laughed the agent cynically. 'Oh, you can trust a pretty Burma girl not to break her heart, and Melia will soon make another lover.'

"Charley took the advice given him, and though he felt depressed as the steamer left Rangoon, yet, after calling at Ceylon, though the spell of Melia's fascinations had not been wholly broken, he began to allow to himself that a Burmese wife, in England, might prove a little awkward.

"Two years later, in England, Charley became engaged to a lovely golden-haired girl, Pearl Harper. The engagement was a comparatively short one, six months was to see them married. Two days before the wedding-day, accompanied by two friends—the prospective best man and the leading bridesmaid, who were also an engaged couple—they went to Earl's Court to see one of the great Kiralfy spectacles. After the show, the quartette took their seats at a table outside one of the Refreshment Buffets, and Charley ordered a delicious little meal for the four. The girl who waited upon them was a pretty brunette with an altogether un-English face, and if the party had not been so absorbed in the light, laughing badinage so dear to the heart of the typical, superior Londoner, they must have noticed the startled look that leaped into the eyes of this waitress as she gazed at Charley Sladen.

"There were not half-a-dozen other customers near by, and the waitress had no others at her tables. She kept her stand close to the party and heard every word that passed between them. She stood also just where she could watch every movement, every changing expression of Charley's face.

"Presently the second young fellow of the party, addressing the golden-haired *fiancée* of Charley, laughingly said: 'By this time, the day after tomorrow, Pearl, you will be Mrs. Charles Sladen.'

"With an adoring look at her lover, Pearl replied: 'All well, I shall!'

"For a full half-hour the quartette laughed and talked and jested, ate and drank. Once, Charley wanted to make a note of something, took a letter from his pocket, screwed up the envelope and tossed that aside, and making his notes on the blank fly of the letter-sheet, presently returned the letter to his pocket.

"The waitress, watching every movement, contrived to pick up the screwed-up envelope. With her back to the party she smoothed out the envelope and read the address, then put it into the bosom of her dress.

"Absorbed with his *fiancée,* Charley had never once really looked at the waitress, to notice her. And when, a few minutes later, he called for the 'check' for the supper, she turned her back upon him to use a near-by table to write upon. Having entered the amount, she drew a true lover's knot on the blank foot of the 'check,' rapidly printing a capital M. and a capital C. in each of the two side-loops of the knot, and, underneath, printed: 'MELIA.'

"As she handed him the check, the attention of the other three was engaged with something in the grounds. He glanced at the check; a startled look flashed into his eyes, and, lifting them to her face, he met her sad, reproachful gaze. By a powerful effort he pulled himself together, and turning to the trio, said, quietly:

" 'You three toddle on for a moment or two, I'll pick you up.'

"The trio moved away, and he made as though he was going to the pay-desk, the waitress following him. A moment later he turned, shame-facedly, to meet her gaze again.

" 'Melia !'

"It was all he could say, and there were half-a-dozen different emotions rolled into the tone of his uttering that one word.

" 'Why did you leave me, Charley?' she cried under her breath. 'Why did you not come back to me? The tatoo was never finished.'

" 'No,' he faltered, and there was shame and confusion in his face and voice.

" 'The day after to-morrow you are going to marry the lady with the hair of gold, and the face of marble whiteness !' There was reproach and sorrow in her voice.

" 'Yes,' he replied.

"She drew the folded envelope from its hiding, opened it out, and said: 'This is your address?'

" 'Yes, Melia !'

" 'I will be there at a quarter to twelve to-night,' she went on, 'for I *must* see you once before the maiden has you, and I lose you for ever.'

"With another of her sad, reproachful looks, she turned sharply away, and he passed on to the pay-desk, and a minute later he had joined his friends. But the world to him had seemingly changed in four short minutes.

"Perhaps no one would ever have known all this but for the curious fact that I called on Charley that night about half-past ten, while he was waiting for the coming of the Burma girl, and he told me the story. Just all that happened after I left, and she arrived, no one will ever know in absolute detail, but with my journalistic instinct and habit I can roughly picture what followed.

"Melia would sink her reproaches in new love-words. and Charley (he was always very impressionable where a woman was in the case) would again fall under the spell of her fascinations. Melia had spoken of the unfinished tatoo, when she had met him at Earl's Court, now she would ask to see it. Charley would bare his arm, and she, bringing out her needles, etc., would ask him, as a last favour, to let her finish it, and he—poor old Charley—would readily agree. Besides the ordinary items of India ink, red pigment, etc., found next day, there was also a small bottle of clear liquid, which she evidently used as an opiate against the pain of the pricking, dipping her needles into it. The opiate mingling with his blood, as the tatooing went on, Charley would drift into a more or less dreamy state.

"The pair would be lovers again, for the time, and, doubtless, poor infatuated Charley would take full toll of the rich full red lips of the Burman beauty.

"The tatoo of Charley was finished, and Melia had doubtless said, 'It is now my turn,' and swiftly tatooed upon the satin-like flesh of her own right fore-arm a crimson heart, pierced with a long blue arrow.

"The work finished, she flung her arms about her lover's neck. They were found, next morning, locked in each others arms, cheek resting against cheek, as if they slept. It was the sleep of Death, for Melia had purposely chosen an opiate that was also a powerful eastern poison.

"They were buried together, and golden-haired Pearl Harper, who is always robed in mourning garb, keeps the double grave bright with the flower-tributes which she carries twice a week to the cemetery."

As Ralph Bastin finished his story, the little French drummer boy on the mantel clock, played a tatoo on his tiny kettledrum. Both men glanced at the clock. It was eleven.

"Poor Charley Sladen!" came softly from Jack Quentin's lips, as he rose slowly to his feet.

"Aye, poor Charley," returned Ralph, "but I fancy Pearl Harper is most to be pitied. The boy-god gives more pain than joy, I believe, take his work altogether!"

There was silence for the fraction of a second between the two men, then Ralph said:

"What about supper, Jack?"

"I'm ready, Ralph!"

"Right ho, boy! But before we go out let me see what you've got on your easel."

There was a moment's hesitancy on Quentin's part, then he moved to the door of the study, with a "Come along, then!"

"My! old man, you've gone in for acreage!" Bastin laughed, as his eyes lit upon the great canvas. There was enough of the three crosses sketched to tell him what the subject was to be.

"Just beginning, Jack?" he said.

"As a matter of fact I can't begin, Ralph. Got to a dead-lock. Sketched in the Christ three times, but neither the face nor form will *begin* to satisfy me. I have an ideal in my mind, and until I can realize that ideal on the canvas, I shall not begin to paint in. I shall wait until it comes to me before I touch it again."

"'When will that be?' says the bells of Stepney," laughed Ralph.

"'I do not know!' says the Great Bell of Bow," Quentin replied, entering into the boyish mood of his chum.

It seemed but an easy transition for the talk to turn upon Christ, and the meaning of the Cross.

"That He was God manifest in the flesh," Ralph remarked, "cannot be well gainsaid. If He was not that He was the basest imposter the world has ever seen. But if He had been an imposter, the imposture would have died with Him, or, at most, have fizzled out a few years after His decease, as almost all the other impostures of the world have done.

"I have heard my dear old dad tell how that even in *his* boyhood's days, there were a few believers in Johanna Southcott, who held their strange, wild, mystic meetings in an old stable in a street leading out of the Walworth Road. You know the Johanna Southcott imposture, Jack?"

"No! don't seem to recall anything about the lady, Ralph!"

"Well, the woman prophesied that Christ would come again, *via* an immaculate *re*-incarnation, and that it had

been revealed to her that she had been chosen to be His
mother. It is amazing the number of dupes she found,
and among them people of wealth and more than ordinary
intelligence. Then, when all the world of 'Southcott'
believers were daily expecting the re-birth of the Christ,
and some of the simple idiots spent hundreds of pounds
on a marvellous swinging cot, the poor wretched woman-
imposter succumbed to dropsy.

"No, no, a thousand times no! Jesus Christ was no
imposter. He *was God*. That was attested by His
power over Death, for though modern preachers rarely
dwell upon the Resurrection, save at Easter, yet the
Resurrection is the great fundamental truth on which His
Deity must ever rest—or so it seems to me. Then, as
though the Resurrection were not enough, the Deity and
Divinity of His work is being ever attested by the *real*
triumphs that follow the preaching of His Gospel.

"Mark you, Jack, I do not say that the much-vaunted
Christendom of today represents the triumph of the
Gospel, for the vast bulk of *professing* Christians, to-day,
are but the products of an advanced civilization which
practically demands the nominal acceptance of this or
that creed of what has become little better than a *psuedo-*
christianity."

Jack Quentin looked keenly at his friend, but did not
interrupt him by word or gesture.

"I don't know, Jack, if ever you have studied the
Epistles of Paul?" Ralph went on. "For the Pauline
Epistles are, without doubt, written to be the actual text-
books for the life of a real Christian!"

Quentin shook his head. The Bible, altogether, was
largely a sealed book to him, sealed by ignorant neglect.

"I leave out the 'Sermon on the Mount,' in Matthew's gospel," Ralph went on, "because, outsider as I confess I am, I believe Arch-bishop Magee was right when he said that it was impossible to conduct the affairs of the British, or any other nation, on the basis of the 'Sermon on the Mount.' He was criticized and condemned on every hand for saying such a thing, but he was right, and as that prince of expositors and fearless teacher, Campbell Morgan, of Westminster Chapel, said, '*Arch-bishop Magee was quite right, you cannot govern the British nation on the basis of the "Sermon on the Mount"* —because the nation is not loyal to THE KING. If you have any doubt about it, you have only to get a seat in Parliament, and endeavour to introduce half-a-dozen principles from the Sermon on the Mount, in a short bill, and see if you can get them carried. You will find that to be the surest test of the accuracy of what the Archbishop said. You cannot do it, because you are dealing with a people who are not prepared to obey.'

"And, Jack, I endorse every word of that statement of Campbell Morgan's. For the *ordinary professing* Christian neither obeys the commands of Christ, nor *attempts* to obey them. The very leaders of our Churches —conformist and non-conformist alike,—save in a very few cases, make no attempt to live out the commands of God, either as uttered by Christ, or written by His chosen servant Paul, in the real text-book for Christians —the Epistles."

He broke off suddenly, and with a mirthless laugh said, "The fact is, Jack, as a nation we are a pack of hypocrites, if, I mean, we call ourselves a *'Christian Nation.'* But I'm running the journalist into the parson (if that is not paying a compliment to the *average* parson, who would no more preach what I've been preaching than he'd attempt to fly from the steeple of his 'place of worship,' to Heaven). So come along and let us get our supper."

Ralph Bastin's religious talk had sprung mainly from the thoughtful journalistic *mind*, it was not *heart*-talk; and, like an extra wrap, when unwanted, was lightly cast aside.

The two men made a merry meal; but not even when he parted from his friend, did Jack Quentin allude to the wander-lust that was consuming him. Twenty-four hours later he was missing from all his old haunts, and gradually it became known that, as often before, he had been lured from London to——none knew where—by the "call of the wild."

CHAPTER III.

A JAPANESE "CHIEL TAKIN' NOTES."

THE very moment that Jack Quentin's train left Euston for Liverpool, the travel-fever that had been coursing through his veins for days, stilled. Like a coursing hound that has been with difficulty held in leash until the starter's signal has been given, so the soul of Jack had fretted until he had started. But now he was off, his soul was eager as before, for the wilds beyond, only, *now*, the fret and impatience were gone.

He was hardly sure, yet, where he would finally steer for, though, at the back of his mind, not yet expressed even to himself, New Mexico hovered. Twice before in his life, New Mexico had been his objective in travel, but each time curious and unforseen incidents had arisen to block the way.

To himself, as he settled into his cabin, it was a bit puzzling that the talk of Ralph Bastin, as to the Christ, should have so strangely affected him. Again and again it returned to him.

Lying in his bunk on the first night of the voyage to New York, the question suddenly came to him: "Why was the face of the Christ so elusive to me? Why was it that, try as I would, I could not satisfy myself with my sketching? Was it, is it, because He *himself* is unfamiliar to me? I am not even *au fait* with the records of the Christ."

It was strange that, even in that quiet moment of thought, it did not occur to him that the sooner he secured a copy of the records of Christ the sooner he would become familiar with the God-man whom he had assayed to sketch.

The second day out of Liverpool there was a religious
service being conducted on the third-class deck. A boy's
voice of surpassing power and beauty was soloing, and
almost every first-class passenger who was not *hors de
combat* with *mal de mer,* gathered to listen to the marvellous voice as it sang, with rare power and feeling:

> "Years I spent in vanity and pride,
> Caring not my Lord was crucified,
> Knowing not it was for me He died
>   On Calvary.
>
> Mercy there was great, and grace was free;
> Pardon there was multiplied to me;
> There my burden'd soul found liberty
>   At Calvary.
>
> By God's word at last my sin I learn'd
> Then I trembled at the law I'd spurn'd,
> Till my guilty soul imploring turn'd
>   To Calvary."

The singer had just begun the chorus again, "Mercy
there was great, etc.," when someone next to Jack Quentin, in low, clear tones, asked a by-standing steward:
"Who is the wonderful boy?"

Jack caught the reply: "He's one of a party of boys
from an English Home for Waifs and Strays, who
are going out West to be distributed among fruit-
growers."

That was all, no one wanted to talk then, for the boy's
pure, rich voice was ringing out in the next verse:

> "Now I've given to Jesus ev'rything;
> Now I gladly own Him as my King;
> Now my raptured soul can only sing
>   Of Calvary.
>
> Oh, the Love that drew salvation's plan!
> Oh, the grace that brought it down to man!
> Oh, the mighty gulf that God did span
>   At Calvary."

The leader of the party of boys, an ex-soldier, taking the theme of the boy's song for a text, gave a short, crisp, moving address on every man's need of the work of Calvary.

He followed with an impassioned appeal, to all who listened, to give their purchased lives to the Christ of Calvary. Then he called upon "our little lad Victor, to sing to us again."

The lad was small and slender, his very fair face was of ethereal type. His blue eyes filled with a rare spiritual light, as he sang:

"I stand all amazed at the love Jesus offers me,
    Confused at the grace, that so freely He proffers me;
I tremble to know that for me He was crucified—
    That for me, a sinner, He suffer'd, He bled, and died.

    Oh, it is wonderful that He should care for me!
        Enough to die for me!
    Oh, it is wonderful, wonderful to me!

Jack Quentin missed the second verse, for his mind became absorbed with thought arising out of the first verse. He came back to the present, with a start, just as the bird-like voice rang out again:

"I think of His hands pierced and bleeding to pay the debt!
    Such mercy, such love and devotion can I forget?
No, no! I will praise and adore at the mercy-seat,
    Until at the glorified throne I kneel at His feet.

    Oh, it is wonderful that He should care for me!
        Enough to die for me!
    Oh, it is wonderful, wonderful to me!"

The service closed with prayer, and the people dispersed.

As Jack Quentin slowly turned back, to regain the "*first-class*" territory, he found himself side by side with a young Japanese man, whom he had noticed leave the cabin next to his own, that morning. The pair now exchanged a remark on the wonderful voice of the boy whose singing had so delighted them.

Within five minutes each of the two men had discovered that the other was an artist, and they shook hands on the strength of the comaradarie that attaches to the "profession." The Jap* spoke splendid English, having being educated at Oxford. His manners were perfect, and he was not niggardly in his expressed admiration of the English, and of English painters in particular.

"Nearly all that I know of true perspective," he said, "and of the *technique* of art, in general, I owe to the tuition of your English painters, whom I have found to be the very essence of kindness."

"But I have my own art, as regards atmosphere and effects," he explained.

At Jack's request he showed him the contents of a small portfolio of his water colours. Jack was amazed at the daintiness of the exquisite things. One especially captivated him—a bit of the Surrey side of the Thames, in the fading after-glow of a sunset. The whole producing of the special atmospheric effect was a mystery to Quentin.

Friendships, acquaintanceships are more quickly formed on board a ship, than any where ashore, and Jack and the Jap soon became close friends.

---

* Should these pages ever be read by a Japanese, will he or she please believe that the Author uses the abbreviation "Jap," in kindly unconventionality of speech, just as he would abbreviate names of his own special friends—The Author.

"We must not lose sight of each other, when we return to England," Jack said. "When I am back in London, you must run me down."

"When will that be?" the Jap asked.

Jack smiled a little ambiguously, and a curious far-away look crept into his eyes, as he replied:

"Ah, when? I cannot tell. It may be only three months or it may easily be a year——or two years."

The night before the liner reached New York, the pair were walking the deck. For a while neither of them spoke, for the spell of the wondrous sea at night, was upon them. The deep violet sky was glorious with a myriad brilliant stars. The mighty, heaving ocean waste, lifting itself in long, deep rollers, flashed with the phosphorus lighting. The moon was too young to give much light, but the port side-light sent a ruddy gleam on the roller crests—for the two men were on the port side of the vessel. For awhile, the artist soul in each was absorbed by the beauty of the scene—alow and aloft. Presently they began to talk, and the conversation turned to question on Jack's part.

"Tell me frankly, Tom," (Jack had long since anglicised his new friend's Japanese name, and boiled it down to Tom.) "Tell me, Tom, how has England really impressed you?"

"As a race, Jack, I have the profoundest admiration for their might, and power, their resourcefulness, grit, bull-dog tenacity of purpose, the prosperousness of all the classes as compared with those of my own land. Then their habitual kindness to myself as a foreigner, and—oh many, many other things."

Jack laughed merrily as he said: "Have you then found no blots on our escutcheon?"

"Oh, yes, but not many from my Japanese standpoint. The chief fault I find with you is that, religiously as a nation, you are a nation of hypocrites."

Jack looked a little startled, then suddenly burst into a ringing laugh, he enjoyed the frankness of the Jap.

"Now we're coming to the point," he said, "so come on, Tom, prove your statement."

"I may be perfectly frank, eh, Jack?" the Jap returned.

"By all means, Tom. Do you know our Scotch poet's way of putting things?

> "Oh wad some power
> The giftie gi'e us,
> To see oursels
> As ithers see us."

The Jap laughed lightly, then his face and voice alike grew grave, as he went on:

"What I meant, Jack, was this. You have your sacred books, as we have, as all we Eastern peoples have. *We* fashion our *lives* by the direction of our religious books, but you English do not, at least, I never met but one man (to know him and to be able to watch him) who ever *began* to live the life laid down in your Bible—in the New Testament, of course, I mean; and more especially the Pauline Letters, which are, professedly, the guide to the *Christian* life.

"I do not think I am what your wonderful English language calls an egotist—a wonderful word that, Jack— Yet I am bound to confess that my own life is an infinitely purer one than that of hundreds of men whom I met at Oxford, many of whom propose to practice as ministers of your religion, presently. I need not tell you, Jack, the kind of lives many of the fellows live, at your colleges, and *away* from your colleges. So that I have often said, to myself, that all I should have to do to become a *better* Christian than these men, would be to give my *mental* assent to the creed which they profess (negatively only, I admit.)

"I have carefully studied your New Testament—the professed text-book for the Christian—(remember, Jack, I have studied as an *outsider*, and that I have been un-hampered in my study by any traditions or prejudices, any preconceived ideas. I approached it as I approached your English History, as part of my curriculum.) Well, as I was going to say, that, studying what is revealed in the 'Pauline Letters' about Christianity, I find, first, that it teaches that the whole human race has become involved in the recorded Fall, involved in the sin of the world's first pair of parents. They were created in innocency, they sinned, and sin thus entered the world and has been perpetuated in the Race. I remember, when I was reading your book of Genesis, that your God is said to have created the first man 'in His Own image,' but, after the Fall (as your theologians term the entrance of sin into the world) that Adam *'begat a son in* HIS OWN *likeness after* HIS *image.'* Thus, according to your own Scrip-utres, the GOD-image and likeness was lost.

"You have *two* Adams in your Bible, the *first* man Adam, the *earthy*, the *last* Adam, heavenly, a God-man. And, as your great apostle Paul says: *'The* FIRST *man Adam became a living soul; the* LAST *Adam a quickening spirit.'* Ah, Jack, my friend, that is a very great word, and if I was an Englishman and a Christian, I should prize it greatly. As it is I am only what your missionary Societies would call *'a poor heathen;'* but I am a heathen who has closely studied Christianity as revealed in your Bible.

"Yes, first I find the 'Fall,' and after that, every soul of man is dead in *natural* sin. But Jesus Christ, God's last Adam, (according to your Bible,) came to die in the stead of the fallen man. He died the shameful death of Crucifixion.

("I want to paint the crucifixion, someday, if I can only come to grasp the mighty subject, fully.")

Jack did not interrupt him, to tell him of his own projected Calvary picture.

"Now, Jack," the eager Jap went on, *"theoretically,* the *professing* Christians of your land, believe they are sinners. But, *actually* and in practical, every day life, if you tried to bring this fact home to them, they would resent it. I remember, when I was up at Oxford, I heard one of the fellows talking of an American-Irishman, who said he 'was as good as any man, only a great deal better.' Now that is the actual pose which your *ordinary* Christian professor takes up. Yet I find that the great Paul of your Scriptures, during the last five or six years of his life, (I go, of course, by the latest generally accepted chronology of your New Testament) grew to feel himself increasingly a sinner. *First,* I find him saying (holy man that he was) that he was *'less than the least of the* APOSTLES.' A year or so later, he says he is *'less than the least of all* SAINTS.' And, just before his death he calls himself the *'Chief of Sinners.'*

"Now, Jack, no one who knows you English people, (perhaps I should say the *ordinary* professing Christian among you) would attempt to maintain that such professors realized the Pauline epistle condition of the depravity of the human heart."

In a slow; meditative fashion, almost as though he was speaking to himself, he went on:

"I feel that there must be *depths* of teaching on these points that I, a merely educated heathen, cannot possibly fathom, or demonstrate. But, there, on the very surface of the teaching of your wonderful book, by which you English professors of Christianity *profess* to fashion your lives, there, I say, on the very surface of its teaching, in fact evident that you do not *live* what you profess, you do not even *attempt* to do it. Why, is there one in five thousand of your people who has ever *actually* (I leave out, of course, the *theoretical* side) taken his or her place as a lost sinner? And yet—(ah, why are your *professors* of Christianity so blind to this *first* fundamental?) until a man takes his true place before God as a sinner, *realizes* that it was *his* sin that crucified the Christ, he cannot *begin* to be a Christian. Mark you, Jack, my friend, I am taking up the teaching of your Book, I am arguing from the stand-point of the English *profession* of Christianity, for, theoretically, your nation *professes* to fashion its life by the New Testament teaching.

"Now if some newspaper editor asked me to write my impressions of you, as a nation of professing Christians, and I wrote my real impression of your church and chapel-goers, I should write: 'After seven years residence and close study of the British nation, I am bound to confess that, *religiously*, they are *not* Christian, if, as I presume, the standard by which they are to be judged is that of their Christian exposition—The New Testament—. The

ordinary *professing* Christian is *religious* but *not* Christian. And if I have rightly read their New Testament
(and I have made a closer study of that book than of
any other in this land) if, then, I have rightly read their
Book, to be *religious* without being a Christian, is to damn
the soul to all eternity as much as though the puny human
fist was flung defiantly, rebelliously into the face of God,
and the soul openly denied and defied Him.'

"This, Jack, my good friend is the teaching of your
New Testament, and you cannot get away from it. And
if I believed in your creed, and in your Bible, I should
be in a state of abject terror until, by taking the lost
sinner's place before God, I had been 'Born Again' from
above, as your Evangelist John taught: 'For' said he,
quoting the actual words of his Master, Jesus Christ, in
an interview with a leading religious man of the day,
'except a man be born again he cannot see* (let alone
enter) *the Kingdom of God,'* not even if he be as *religious*
and as *true* a man as that Nicodemus was.

"No, Jack, if I have read your Holy Book aright, it
does not teach that religiousness saves the soul, any
more than it teaches Reformation as soul-saving. No,
the teaching of your Book is that nothing less than a
new life, the outcome of a new *birth* can save the soul.
It teaches that that *new life* is the Eternal life of Christ
Himself, because, at this wondrous change which your
Book calls the New Birth, Christ Himself enters the
human soul with *His* life, and thus is Himself the New
life. For that same evangelist of yours, John, says:
'*To as many as received Him*(Jesus) *gave He power to
become Sons of God.'* And he further says: '*I* (Christ)
give unto my sheep ETERNAL *life.'*

"Ah, friend, Jack, believe me, heathen as I should be considered by your Missionaries and other teachers, I can, I do see more in your beautiful, your wonderful New Testament revelations, than the majority of your *ordinary professors* of Christianity do."

Jack Quentin never once interrupted his eager companion. He was learning more of the Bible demands upon the professors of its creed, than he had ever dreamed. He could not stay the argument of the Jap by any counter-argument, for he was positively ignorant of even the terms of the Pauline Epistles, which the Jap had declared to be the true text book of the Christian.

The Jap had paused for the briefest moment, evidently to give Jack an opportunity of saying anything in reply. Then, as no reply came, he went on:

"But the inconsistency of you English people who *profess* to be Christians does not end with your failure to apprehend the *real beginning* of the Christian career as laid down in your New Testament, but also in all the *after* life of the career. If there is one principle more enforced than any other in the New Testament, as regards the life of the follower of your Christ, it is that of utter, absolute renunciation of this present world—that is, as I understand it, not a *withdrawal from* the world itself, the monastic idea, but a withdrawal from the worldly spirit of the populations of the world, the *spirit of which is wholly, utterly, absolutely* ANTI-*Christian,* and not Christian. (Please, Jack, good friend, don't forget that it is not I, myself, who am laying down these lines, it is your own Holy Book, I am only repeating what your Book says.")

For the first time Jack now interrupted with the question: "What would you define as worldliness, Tom?"

Jack Quentin spoke quietly. His voice was utterly even, perfectly calm, yet his whole soul was aflame with an intense interest.

"It is not for me to define," the Jap answered. "It is what does your New Testament say, how does your Holy Book define it? Over and over again your New Testament declares that to be Christ's true follower, to live the *saint*-life to which every Christian is called, is to have no pleasure, no joy other than that which is born of fellowship and communion with God, by His Spirit, in Christ Jesus. Over and over again it teaches absolutely that 'in Him,' Christ Jesus, *'all fullness dwells.'* Your professing Christian congregation sing:

> "O rest at Jesus' feet!
> There toil is pleasure, my wants a treasure,
> And pain for Him is sweet:"

"Your Book enforces this command upon you, that you don the whole armour of God, that you may fight against everything that partakes of the *worldly,* the *Anti-*Christ spirit. Yet I find that you English Christians—that is the ordinary members of your so-called Christian Churches,—never dream of going to God, and to their Holy Book for their *joy,* for their pleasure. In your churches, on the week-nights, you are lucky if you get *ten* at a Prayer-meeting, but you can get five hundred or even a thousand (according to the building accommodation) to a concert, a soiree, amateur theatricals, or whatnot. And your concerts, etc., season by season grow more and more worldly, more and more like the Variety

theatre program. Yet the Prayer-meeting has the imme-
diate, definite promise and fact of the actual presence of
Christ. Eh O, you are queer folk, you *professed* English
Christians.

"I stood outside a big ring of people at an open-air
service, one night in Islington, and a young man, on the
outskirts of the crowd, asked if he might say a word.
The leaders of the meeting did not like to refuse him,
and he passed through the people, and stood in the very
heart of the ring. Very jauntily he said: 'I don't profess
to be a Christian, but if I did I'd get my pleasure from
the same source that I professed to get my safety. The
chap that's just spoken professes to be a Christian, he
has just told us that he's "saved." He said that salvation
was like an Insurance ticket for Heaven, and that the
Christ who saves satisfies.

"'Now, if Christ satisfies, how is it that the chap
that has just told us this, is obliged to go to the Islington
Music Halls to get his pleasure? I know he does, for
he sat by my side the other night, and we chatted together
between the "turns," and he talked (he's got the gift of
the gab, mind, we'll all admit that after the "spout" he's
treated us to-night) he talked to me about everything,
except Christianity.

"'I'm a grocer's assistant (I shan't tell you where or
you'll think I'm only doing what I am to-night, by way
of an advert), and my governor has had a draw-line of
sugar in his window, for a week or more—lump sugar
a penny-farthing a pound. The other morning a swellish
sort of woman came in and ordered twenty-five pounds
of that penny-farthing lump, but nothing else. My governor said: "Where do you purchase your tea, ma'am?"

She told him she had it from a city house, and my
governor said: "Then you must get your sugar from your
city house, ma'am, my cheap line of sugar is for customers
for my tea."

" 'Now then, it seems to me that a lot of the Christians
—if they *really are* Christians—who come out here and
spout like that last chap has been spouting, want to get
their sugar (their *pleasure*) from the world (the devil)
and their strength and their safety from Hell, from Jesus
Christ. That's not sound logic, and it ain't Bible, either.'

"The fellow laughed aloud, Jack, as he went back out
of the ring, and I felt that he had a right to laugh. That,
Jack, is of a piece with what I have found in your ordinary
professor of Christianity. He does not practice what he
professes. I have been utterly astounded to find that the
ordinary church book of members, includes Brewers, dis-
tillers, publicans—all of whom, by dispensing what more
than one of your best English statesmen has called 'liquid
damnation,' 'the Devil in solution,' etc., have done more
to curse the bodies and souls of the people of your beautiful country than everything else that is evil, put together;
—yet your churches hold these men on their books, as
professedly in communion with Christ. On those same
church books there are the names of bankrupts who have
screened themselves behind some technical flaw in the
Bankruptcy law, or behind some tissue of lies which they
have marshalled as evidence.

"And besides these more flagrant cases, who are unfit
for membership in the Christian church, there are whole
hosts of men and women who know no more, personally,
of the New Birth, than your cottager's pig knows of
stenography.

"Talking of those bankrupt members of the Church rolls, I happen to have come across several cases myself, quite recently. Here is one: I knew a builder, in the Midlands, who speculated largely, over-built, had sixty thousand pounds worth of property; he bankrupted, but had somehow juggled with nearly forty thousand pounds worth of his property, so that it was in his wife's name. He got through somehow, and in another part of the country, lives in a swell house, drives a swagger motor-car, and all this on the tens of thousands he has swindled his creditors of. Yet he is a member of a Christian church—*and preaches.*

"Now my point is, Jack, that this man *cannot* be living the Christian life according to your New Testament standard of a Christian, though he is accepted as such, and allowed to preach, by churches that are so lax in their discipline as almost to merit the name Apostate. If that man was *truly* Christian, truly Christ's man, he would have handed over every pennyworth of his possessions, unreservedly to his creditors, for the God and Saviour whom he professed, has undertaken that he should not starve or be wholly destitute, for your Book says: '*Seek* FIRST *my kingdom, and all these things*—eating, and drinking, and clothing—*shall be added unto you, for your Heavenly Father knoweth that ye have need of these things.*'

"I remember once, Jack, tackling a minister of your religion, as to his inconsistency in certain things in his life, and he replied that the *conventionalities of life* demanded that he should do this and that, as others did. I asked him of what *life* did he speak? He stammered a bit, then said: 'Why the *ordinary life of the world.*'

'But,' I replied, 'as a Christian, your life is *in Christ,* your *citizenship,* your *conventionalities,* are in Heaven, are of a Heavenly, a Christly character. You are supposed to have utterly renounced the world.' He snapped me up sharply, saying: 'As a foreigner you do not understand, it is absurd to talk as you do, the world could not go on at all if every one acted as you seem to suppose they ought to do.'

"I told him that he made two great mistakes, first, 'I did not speak of *"every one,"* but those who professed themselves *"Christian."* And *secondly,'* I continued, 'You have nothing to do with keeping the world going, the Devil, who your Christian Book declares, is the prince of the world, will see to the running of his own business. Beside,' I said to him, 'from all that I can see in this *professedly* Christian nation, there are so very, very few who are really Christ's men and women, that if they were all taken out of the world to-morrow, the world would not miss them, for the *true* Christian (according to your Book) "is not of the world." '

"He got very angry with me, said some very foolish things, among others, he said: 'I have two sons, heads of two separate large commercial concerns in London, do you mean then to tell me that, because they are members of Christian churches, they must not keep pace with the usual commercial code, in their business transactions?'

" 'No,' I said, 'I do not mean to say that if they are simply members of a Christian church (so-called) but that if they were *Christians,* members of Christ's body, they must keep their hands and consciences clear and clean from *all* questionable practices, even though those practices were labelled "commercial." '

"Again he grew very angry with me, and declared that it would be impossible for Christians to *'get on'* in life if they adopted such ultra ideas in business, in the twentieth century.

"I replied that *'getting on'* was nowhere laid down in the New Testament, as a necessity for the Christian life, but that the fundamental principle everywhere enforced was that of getting *up*. *'Grow in Grace'* was the command, *'Seek God's Kingdom and Righteousness,' 'Be not conformed to this world, but be transformed by the renewing of your mind.'* The man would not listen to me any more, and his face was purple with passion when he turned and left me."

Something that sounded almost like a sigh broke from Jack, as he said: "What a marvellous knowledge you have of your Bible, Tom."

There was light enough for Jack to see the quiet smile on his friend's face, as he replied:

"Of *your* Bible, you mean, Jack, not mine. I have studied your New Testament for years, therefore I ought to know its words. I believe I could repeat the whole of the Epistles, they are so, so wonderful! But, say, Jack, my friend, what an extraordinary thing it is, that so few of your professing Christians know their Bibles, their New Testament Epistles, especially. I do not wonder that their lives are inconsistent from the New Testament standpoint. I have been invited into many of your English homes,—the homes of people who went to their churches on the Sunday——but I have seen no Bible lying around, there has never been one in my bedroom:

and I have, over and over again, searched the shelves
of their libraries, but have found no Bible. The people
themselves have never talked from the Bible, they have
quoted Shakespeare, Shelley, Campbell, Burns, Browning.
Swinburne, William Watson, Kipling, and dozens of
others, and they knew their favourite poets so well that
they could go blindfold, almost, into the room and pluck
their copy from the shelf, and could turn up to this or
that passage which they had quoted, but the Bible——
which is supposed to be the text-book of their lives, the
food of their souls, the order for their warfare—they are
as foreign and as ignorant of that Book as 'a cat in a
strange garret,' as one of your proverbs has it. No, no,
Jack, good friend, England is *not* Christian, because she
has a State Church, and *professes* to live by the Bible,
nor yet because other churches and creeds—their name
is 'Legion'—beside your State Church, also have a more
or less large following. She is *not* Christian because, for
all that she *professes,* she does not practise the teaching of
her God—Christ Jesus—as laid down in the New Testament.

"I said something like that to an English friend once,
and he told me that *within every* section of the Evangelical
church (that was the term he used) there was a little band
of people ('Believers' he called them) who *did* live the
Pauline Epistle life, and that even outside all the recognized communions there were others who did the same.
This I could not deny, because I did not know, I could
only say 'A foreigner, like myself, a heathen as he would
be considered, has no means of knowing these little
genuine bands of people, and no *entree* into their homes,
so that such an one cannot judge.

"Then again, Jack, there is another most wonderful thing about your Christian churches.—I have been into hundreds, for I usually go *twice* on a Sunday, to some of your churches.—That is, that, though your New Testament, as I read it, has more to say about a future *return* of Jesus Christ, than about any other subject, yet, never once have I heard the fact mentioned in a sermon or——."

" 'Coming again'? Christ returning to this earth again, Tom." There was a ring of amaze in Jack Quentin's voice. "What, in the name of Fortune, do you mean, old boy?"

"I did not say 'coming to the earth,' Jack, though, as a matter of fact, He is to do that according to your Old and New Testament. But first, He is to come *'into the air,'* and from thence He will call all the dead, who have been true Christians, to meet Him up there, then all the living Christians. Following this wonderful event, there would appear to be an awful time on earth, when all the Christians are taken away—they will, up to that time have been acting as salt amid the growing foulness of the world. There will appear, after the Christians are gone, a special agent of the Devil's, (Remember, Jack, I am only quoting your Christian New Testament, for, as a Heathen, so called, I do not accept your creed or your Book—at least, *not as yet*) he will be raised up, and your Book calls him the Anti-Christ. He will lead the whole world astray, the world will grow worse and worse, until your Christ, (with all those saints of His, who have been 'caught up to meet Him in the air') will come down on the Earth and destroy every rebel unbeliever. Ah, Jack, Jack, my friend! I tell you, that if I were a Christian, if I believed all that you Christians *profess* to

believe, I should be looking for Christ to come any hour.
I should never dream of expecting to die.

"And, again, if I were a Christian, I should accept all
your New Testament revelations, and thus accepting them
I should see, all around me, the *signs* that He might
return at any moment."

"Signs! Signs!" Jack echoed vaguely, "Signs of
Christ's return? Where, Tom?"

"Everywhere, Jack! The condition of the world
is absolutely ripe for His return according to your
Scriptures. And the world, nay more, the *professed*
Christian Church, is as blind to its near-coming fate.
(I am, of course, as you understand, Jack, taking
the stand-point of your own Scriptures.) Your professing Church, I say, Jack, is as blind to the judgments
coming upon it, as are the wood and stone idols of
the Heathen temples which your church so much
scorns. The vast bulk of your professing Christians
are not 'Born Again,' hence, according to your Scriptures, they are under the wrath of God, and *must*
come under the judgments that belong to the Great
Tribulation that accompanies the coming of Anti-
Christ, *after* the true 'Born Again' ones have been
'caught up into the air' to be with their Lord for
ever.

"I wonder, exceedingly, Jack, that the very language
in which all this is portrayed in the New Testament,
does not arrest the *professed* Christian—for it is the
most marvellously convincing language under the
Sun, is the language of the New Testament. The
fact is. Jack. as I said before, the mere professing

Christian is as ignorant of his own scriptures, as is
the school-dunce of mathematics."

At this moment there came an interruption. Some
of the men of the middle watch were preparing to
wash the promenade deck. Jack and his friend were
amazed to find that it was nearly two a. m. They
were almost compelled to go to their cabins.

Next morning they slept late, and found, on going
on deck after breakfast, that they were nearing their
shore berthing. There was no opportunity of resuming
their talk of the previous night, for all was bustle
and confusion preparatory to landing.

The excitement, etc., partially, but not wholly
drove from Jack Quentin's mind the great truths
given utterance to by his clever little Japanese friend.
"He's a very wonderful little chap!" Jack told himself, adding: "And I should say nearer being a true
Christian than any fellow whom I ever met before."

CHAPTER IV.
THE PASSION PLAY.

TOMASSI ITOI, the Japanese artist, in whom Jack Quentin had grown so intensely interested, could only remain one day and night in New York. He had come to America on important business in Ohio state. On his return from Ohio, he hoped to make a longer stay in the City. Meanwhile the two men had arranged to put up at the same hotel for the one night that the Jap would spend in New York.

There had been no clear opportunity for the resumption of their talk on Christianity versus mere Religion. They dined together on the evening of their landing, and over the table discussed what they should do, where they should go after dinner.

"The whole city, I find, is talking of a most wonderful production of the Ober-Ammergau Passion Play, by kinematograph," Jack remarked. "Would you care to go, Tom?"

The Jap saw how keen his friend was, on going, so instantly agreed to the suggestion that they should see the play. Jack arranged with the waiter to 'phone for seats for the pair. They were only just secured in time.

"I had just been reading about the preparations for the production of the films," the Jap went on. "The cost of production exceeds twelve thousand pounds, and every Holy site in Palestine has been visited to ensure that the atmosphere and natural surroundings of the pictures should be as perfect as possible.

The Flight into Egypt of Joseph and Mary, and
the young child, has been pictured with the Sphinx
and the Pyramids for a setting. Bethlehem, Olivet,
Nazareth, Galilee—its sea and fishing boats and fish-
ermen have all been laid under tribute. The scene
with the returning caravan, to which Joseph and
Mary were attached on their departure from the
Temple, when they missed the child Jesus, is said
to have occupied a whole day in the taking, while
a great crowd of Easterns, and forty camels were
employed. The Temple scenes were enacted in a
building put up specially, and though the scenes will
occupy but a few minutes on the screen, the building
took a month to erect."

Jack smiled across the table as he said:

"What an enthusiast you are, Tom! If ever you
become a Christian you'll want to go for a Missionary."

"If," replied the Jap, "such a thing ever happened
—and it might have been, if I had found your professing Christian nation, or even your church professors, practising the Christ whom they *profess* to
follow—if, I say, such a thing as you suggest, happened, and I became a Missionary, I would elect to
go to my own country-men. I would, I think, follow
my profession, and paint Bible subjects, especially
from the life of your Christ, and would seek to
preach through my art. as well as by my life and
lips."

There was something so very extraordinary to Jack
Quentin, in the fascination which the things of Christianity evidently exercised over this Japanese comrade

of his, that as in their long talk on board the liner,
so now, he found it difficult to reply in any way.

Half-an-hour later the pair were in the gloom of
the great House where the Passion Play was passing
over the screen. The only lights possible in the
place were those which passed through dull ruby
glass bulbs, the ruby hue not interfering with the
clearness of the pictures.

Both men sat silent and fascinated with the displayed scenes. Presently there came the actual
Passion scenes. The agony in the garden of Geth-
semene; the Arrest of Jesus; the mock trials during the night; Pilate's "kitchen" with the brazier of
burning charcoal; Peter's denial; the *Ecce Homo*;
Pilate's hand-washing, with every other important
detail. Then, amid an awed hush, Christ, bearing
His cross, was seen descending from the Judgment
Hall. Suddenly he sank beneath the weight of the
cross; the *fabled* St. Veronica leaped forward and
with her kerchief, wiped the sweat from the face of
the Divine Man.

Yes, there it was, every item of the precious story
even to the Crucifixion and entombment, and Res-
surrection, in a living, moving picture show. And
no one appeared to see any impiety in it, there
was not one note of dissent from the mighty crowd
of on-lookers.

As Jack Quentin and the Japanese presently emerged
into the street, Jack asked:

"What do you think of it all, Tom?"

The face and voice of the Japanese were very
grave as he replied: "As a spectacle, it is a triumph

of the kinematograph art. But if I were a Christian, Jack—a *Christian*, I say, not a mere professor, but one who loved the Christ, and *therefore* sought to serve Him—I should condemn the spectacle root and branch, and say 'How dare they make a theatrical performance of the Passion of my Lord? How dare they exploit the things of God for mere money-making? I should enter my public protest, through the Press, against an actor posing for and person-ating the Saviour Himself—for you know, Jack, the whole thing was produced (according to what I read to-day) under the direction of theatricals, and it was an actor who personated the Christ. Your Picture Palaces will become utterly degraded if this thing be permitted, and no true, self-respecting Christian will ever pass the doors. Oh, I could, Jack, *if I were a Christian*, denounce that wonderful show on many grounds."

"Upon my word, Tom," Jack cried, "I begin to think that without any profession of Christianity, you are already a better Christian than any man whom *I* ever met."

The Jap flashed a quick look back into his friend's face, as in a surprised tone, he said:

"Do you not *yet* understand, Jack, that no man or woman can be a Christian, unless they be *in* Christ Jesus. And that before any one can be *in* Christ Jesus, they *must* have taken the place in which your God, in the Bible, places them, that of lost, undone, hell-deserving sinners, with absolutely *nothing* good in them. Why your great Apostle says of Himself: '*For I know that in me (that is, in my flesh*) *dwelleth no good thing.'* Yes, yes, this is the great truth which you Britons need to learn, that unless you have been born again, God is not your Father, but (what says your Scriptures) *'Ye are of your father, the Devil.'* If I rightly understand this word of Christ's, it refers not to the world, so much, if at all, as it does to professors who are not saved."

Jack gave vent to a sharp exclamation, but the Japanese arguer stopped him as, smilingly, he said: "Don't be angry with me, good friend, Jack, *I* am not saying these things, I am only repeating what your own scriptures say."

They were at the Hotel by this time. A telegram was waiting the Japanese. He had to start off, at once, on the first lap of his journey.

Jack accompanied him to the depot, they had only a few moments margin of time. No time for much interchange, but they parted with the understanding that they were to renew their acquaintance as soon as ever Jack returned to London.

Jack walked back to the Hotel strangely quiet. The amazing talk of the Jap, his wonderful knowledge of the Bible, his unanswerable arguments, had all strangely gripped him.

Before he went to bed that night he had decided as to his next move. He would go to New Mexico. Twice before he had been on the point of going thither, but had been hindered.

"The wilderness and solitude of some of those prairies will do me good," he told himself.

CHAPTER V.

THE CAPTAIN OF THE "SCHOONER."

JACK QUENTIN rode alone and unattended over the beautiful, western wild—for there was a realness of beauty in the wonderful wild. It suited his mood, if not actually to court danger, at least to be supremely indifferent to it. He had ridden thirty miles since early morn. His way had led through luxuriant grasses, and wild growths of wonderful clovers; across acres and acres of Verbenas of every hue, and of Vervain of blazing scarlet. And as he had ridden he found a sense of pleasure in the solitude.

At the moment that we meet him again he is traversing an immense tract of the variegated-thistle. The crest of the thistle-field—it reached for miles every way—was one sea of rose-purple flower. The cattle had made innumerable well-defined tracks through the dense growth of purple bosses that tossed themselves ten feet from the ground.

Away to his left, one of the cattle-tracks, broader than the others, stretched in an ever-widening way. Left to his own devices the horse took this path. Jack rode on for another hour, and came out to a spot where the thistle jungle grew thinner, and where, from his vantage point in the saddle, he could see signs of another country altogether. Tall pine trees waved their topmost branches, a hundred feet in the air, while beyond, again, against the distant foothills, the forests of cedar and oak-scrub showed dark and cool-looking. Behind all this, and at a still greater distance, were the rugged sides and summits of the mighty mountains.

Once or twice Jack raised his head, came out of his silent reverie, and looked around upon the strange panorama. As now, again, he looked up, and sent a long, sweeping comprehensive glance around, his eye took in a huge, cumbrous, moving mass in the distance. He knew, at a glance, what it was, and smiled at the strange irony of thought, in christening such a lumbering affair a "Schooner"—a "Prairie Schooner."

The giant cart, with its eighteen-feet by fourteen-feet bed; and its canvas cave-body nearly ten feet high, creaked on its slow tedious way. It was drawn by sixteen oxen, and would presently cross the line of path that Jack was pursuing.

The driver had evidently not seen him, and was beguiling the way with song. The voice was strong but not unmusical, and as Jack got nearer he was a little surprised to recognize a most pronounced Milesian brogue. True to his nationality, the singer's song proved to be "The Last Rose of Summer."

Suddenly, in the middle of a verse, he stopped singing. He had caught sight of Jack, and fired off a long-shot greeting in richest Irish.

At the sound of the driver's voice, two villanous-looking, Mexican half-breeds, showed their faces from somewhere out of the "schooner's" cargo. The oxen needed no great amount of persuasion to stop; a few words were exchanged between Jack

and the Irish driver, with the result that they agreed
to camp together for the night.

The Sun was near setting, and night would soon
draw down. A convenient camping spot was chosen;
one of the half-breeds outspanned the oxen, while
the other made a fire.

Jack enjoyed the novelty of the situation, and the
merry mood of the Irishman had something so in-
fectious, that the laughter-spirit caught himself.
The fellow was full of the drollest sayings and
similes that Jack had ever listened to.

"A foine country is this, sur," he remarked as he
turned the frizzling beans about with a queer old-time
Mexican prong. "The childer in Ould Ireland used
to say that the schulemaster's gape was as big as
all outdoors. But, bedad, an' I dunno what they'd
say to the Prairies, fur shure they're bigger than all
outdoors an' indoors put together. Mighty power-
fu' places are these same Prairies an' Plains, an'
mighty dang'rous, too, sometimes, shure. A man 'ud
need to be as sharp as the little end o' nuthin' to
keep topsides wi' everythink here about."

He paused a moment to lift a bacon rasher with
his prong, and to admire the browning beans. Then,
lifting his eyes again to Jack's face, he said more
soberly, "An' bedad, its mony a good bhoy has gone
under in these pairts fur the want o' a dish o' these
same banes, or somethink else, to kape the body an'
soul ov him together at all. When they've traveled
a week, wi' no more meal than 'ud make porridge fur
a sick mosquita—ah, them's hard dues, fur shure, sur.
But thank all the Holy Saints we aint put to the like

o' that to-night, sur. Fur shure the banes are done
to a turn, the rashers are frizzled to perfiction, an'
the sooner we begin jaw-waggin', the better."

Intensely amused with his companion, Jack found
himself positively enjoying the rough *al fresco* meal.
When the last spoonful of beans had been cleared,
and the Irishman had successfully "fired up the
dudeen"—as he described his pipe-lighting, he puffed
away in silence for a few minutes. Then, evidently
going back, mentally, to the subject discussed before
supper, he presently said:

"Sure then, it's many's the broth o' a bhoy that
ha' missed the number o' his cabin on these same
Prairies, an' died wi'out a prayer fro' a praist or a
shrive to help him through purgatory. Och, but its
a grate land, is this, to the man who loses his
thrack."

"Do you think then, Mike," (the Irishman had told
Jack his name was Mike Doolan) "that the prayers
or blessings of a priest can help a man in the great
unknown world beyond Death?"

"Is it my rale, *inside*, honest opinion yer wantin',
sir?" There was a merry twinkle in the Irishman's
eyes as he asked his question.

"Yes, Mike," returned Jack, "your real honest, inside opinion."

"Then shure I'm boun' to say, sir," (he lowered
his voice here) "its meeself that feels that no mortal
man—praist or Pope—can do this. Only God can
do it, shure. Its very little sinse that Mickey Doolan
is supposed to hev, sur, an' a sight less 'ligion, but
I've enuff sinse to know that much."

With a sudden wild uproarious laugh, he continued: "Bedad, sur, but I'll tell yer what happened between Father McCarthy an' meeself, six months afore I left ould Limerick. 'Mike, said he, one day when he met me, an' me jist afther comin' away fro seein' me swatheheart, Kitty Kelly, as was—but by the same token she's changed her name now sin' she married that thafe o' a Patsy Ryan, an' is brakin' her heart for meeself twenty-five hours ivery day. Well, as I was sayin', sur, Father McCarthy met me an' sez he to me, (an he lookin' as melancholy as a suicide's burial at midnight, as he spake) sez he, 'Mike, I've not seen yer at confession fur a very long time!'

" 'That's thrue fur yer, Father McCarthy, sez I, 'an' I'm thinkin' it's a very long time to come afore yer see meesel' there again.'

" 'An' why's that for?' sez he, sharp as the snap o' rat-trap.

"So I ups an' tells him the same as I telled ye, sur, awhile since. Then he begins to quote the Blessed Book, an' sez he, 'Mike, listen to what the Holy Apostle James, o' blessed memory, an' a true saint as well as an apostle sez, "Confess yer faults *one to another."* '

"Then he stops an' looks at me, like a new wife 'ud look at her mate who'd let a little man whack him in a fair fight, an' that the first glorious scrimmage he'd been in afther the weddin'. Well, the priest looked at me an' waited a moment, then sez he agin, 'Now, Mike, what hev yer got to say to that Blessed Scripture.' 'What I sez, Father Mc-

Carthy,' sez I, 'is this; that the 'postle James had more sinse in his little finger than the Pope has in his whole body, an' I b'lieves in the varse ye've jist put out.'

"He grinned like a beggar afore a dish o' tateys an' butter-milk. But afore himself could say another word I chips in wi' ' "Confess yer faults *one to another*," aye, Father McCarthy, I believes in that, an' as I've confessed hundreds o' times to you, suppose you ups an' confesses to me now, an' that'll be *"one to another."* '

Jack Quentin laughed as he had not done for a long time, as Mike told this old chestnut of table-turning. The Irishman's eyes twinkled with fun over the old-time memory, and went on:

"Bedad, sur, but if ye'd seen the praist then, sure its yerself that 'ud ha' laughed all the buttons off yer best weskitt, fur he looked as wild as the exciseman who's missed the still he'd thought he'd diskivered, and jes' about as helpless as the man as tried to lift himself over the fence by the sthraps o' his boots.

"Och, but it's meeself that enjoyed the ghoke at the time. But shure the praist niver forgave me an' worried me about like a terrier 'ud worry a rat. I couldn't live at all fur his pirsicution, an' I got as thin as moonshine, an' as wake as the bubbles the childer blow on a washin'-day. That's why I immi-grated, an' it's meeself that is almost as much in love wid this beautifu' counthry as I was wid Kitty Kelly —an' she, by the same token, is a widdy now, an' is afther comin' out next month from the ould counthry, to marry me."

More and more interested in his companion, Jack
Quentin led him on to talk of where he had been.
and what he had seen in the land of his adoption.
They smoked and talked until midnight. The conversation had, strangely enough, taken a religious
turn, and the Irishman had told Jack a story that
amazed him.

"It isn't every one, yer honour," Mike had said,
"who knows that in this blessed counthry, where we
are, there's a sex o' 'ligious people as b'lieves as
they'll git to Heaven all right, if only they crucifies
theyselves, as the blessed Son o' Mary wur crucified."

Jack looked in amaze at the Irishman.

"It's facks, sur," Mike went on. "Away up in
Northern New Mexico, there's lots o' little out-o-the-
way places where they still crucifies one another. A
mate o' mine told me he seed it done hisself one
time, at a place called Taos, an'—."

The Irishman was obliged to yawn, it momentarily
stopped his speech, and it gave Jack warning to let
his companion "up," and go to rest. He asked a few
more particulars, however, about this surprising religious rite, then the pair rolled themselves in their
blankets.

As might readily be expected, Jack failed to sleep
at first. His mind was full of many new topics.
His last waking thoughts found expression in an
inward determination to visit Taos, and its neighbourhood, and see for himself something of this
reported up-to-date crucifixion. He was glad it was
April, and so near Good Friday.

CHAPTER VI.

"EL CALVARIO."

IT was twelve, noon. The Calendars of civilization called the day "Good Friday." Jack Quentin had been two days in the neighbourhood where we now find him. The wonders of the bare but beautiful valley had grown upon him every hour. Its situation was among the Rockies of Northern New Mexico, and for quiet and solitude could hardly be matched anywhere in the world—that is, for a partially-peopled place.

It was the words of Mike Doolan, the Prairie Schooner driver that had led the restless-hearted Jack to this place. In a tiny clearing in a small wood close by—where he had camped for two nights,—Jack had left his horse securely hobbled, but free to graze the short herbage nourished by the forest shade.

Jack himself had been ensconced for two hours in a safe and comfortable nook from whence he would be able to see all that should transpire in the little rugged vale just beneath him.

During his two hours of watching there had been a considerable amount of quiet excitement apparent among the dwellers of the place. Just at the moment that we come upon the watching Jack, things were evidently culminating towards some supreme point.

A procession was being formed. Men, women and children took their places in a rude kind of order. An aged man, with a keen, sharp face, and a tough wiry frame, which the years of a long life had failed, apparently, to weaken, read aloud some prayers. His voice was clear, distinct, far-reaching. The eyes of the people were turned towards the open door of the "Morada." A moment later several men emerged bearing crosses of immense weight upon their backs. Silence fell upon the gathered people, and again the voice of the old prayer-reader rang out strong and clear.

The responses of the gathered religionists had scarcely escaped their lips before the shrill, piercing notes of a high-pitched fife gave the signal to march. Over the pathway, made painful to the bare feet of the cross-bearers by the sharp stones and cruel cactus, the procession toiled upward to a hillock a little way off. On the side of the hillock a huge cross was rudely painted, to suggest Calvary. At certain intervals the procession paused while the people made "the Stations of the Cross."

Jack Quentin watched everything with an ever-increasing interest. The procession again resumed its march. Arrived at the hillock, he watched the bearers of the crosses prostrate themselves, face downwards on the ground, the ponderous crosses being laid upon their backs. Then the whole company formed a semi-circle about the prostrate figures, while, led by the fifer, a sad, weird hymn was sung. Once more the procession re-formed in its original order, and returned to the Morada, only to repeat again and again the same manoeuvres.

Nearly two hours had been thus occupied when the watching Jack saw that some change in the

tactics was contemplated. **The leader of the procession** bent his head and spoke quietly to the man
on the right, who, leaving the ranks, followed the
leader into the Morada. The silence during the
absence of the pair was more profound than ever.
Every eye was fixed upon that open doorway. Presently the two emerged from the Morada, and walking between them was a man with eyes cast down,
clothed simply in a pair of thin cotton drawers.
The trio headed the procession, the "pitero" piped,
and the march recommenced. This time there was
a change in the route. They passed on to a spot a
hundred yards to the south of the hillock with the
painted cross.

From his vantage point Jack looked right down
upon the people, where they halted. A huge cross
lay upon the ground, and at its base was a large exca-
vation. The semi-naked victim walked firmly to the
cross, gazed fearlessly, smilingly, all around upon the
gathered people, then laid himself down with his
back to the long standard of the cross, and stretched
his arms upon the cross-piece.

Four attendants then took thick hempen ropes
and began to lash the limbs of the victim to the
cross. Amid the deathly silence, the infatuated
man's voice rose in almost agonized tones as he
cried:

"*Nail* me! Do not rope me! Do not disgrace
me with ropes; but for the love of God, nail me!"

Jack, eagerly watching, saw that the lashings were
quickly cast off, and that spikes and hammer were

taken from a bag, while the holders of them knelt
on one knee preparatory to nailing their victim to
the cross.

Jack held his breath, as he asked himself the
question, "Will they really nail him? or is this only
a rude, realistic play?"

Before he could imagine a reply, the clink of the
hammers on the heads of the nails reached his ears.
He shuddered, thrust his fingers in his ears, and
closed his eyes. But he could not wholly shut out
the sound.

Presently the sounds ceased. He opened his eyes.
There was an awesome silence. The cross, with its
impaled victim, was being raised. The base of the
centre-piece was in a line with the deep hole that
had been dug. Nearer and nearer the structure approached the perpendicular, and presently dropped
into the hole with a dull, sickening thud.

Horrified, yet fascinated, Jack gazed upon the
awful scene. The upreared victim's face was almost
in a line with his own. He saw the awful agony
written upon it; but no sound escaped the lips of
the poor wretch.

The blazing sun of that southern sky poured
down upon this modern Calvary. No sounds of
Nature's life broke the intense stillness—for birds
and insects, there were none. Upon this band of
strange religionists—"Los Hermanos Penitentes" (The
Penitent Brothers) as they are called—hardened as
they are to such scenes, there had fallen a solemn
hush. Every eye was lifted to that solitary, suffering

figure. No one paid the slightest attention to two other "Penitentes," who had cast their naked bodies upon a bed of cactus a little way off.

Some of the officers of this strange order had crowned themselves with cactus, and their gaunt faces were streaked with the trickling blood that oozed from the wounds of the stinging thorns.

If an absolute silence can be said to deepen, it deepened now, as the minutes dragged on. To the watching Jack, the time that the crucified man hung upon that cross, appeared to be many hours. He found after consulting his watch that it was not more than twenty-five minutes.

Suddenly, the chief of the "Penitentes" gave a sign. Ready hands sprang forward. The cross was lowered. The bleeding, swooning victim was released and he was borne, with marked, reverent tenderness back to the Morada.*

Jack Quentin passed his hand across his forehead, and flung off the great drops of perspiration that had gathered there, like a heavy dew. "Am I dreaming? Am I the subject of some optical delusion?" he asked himself. But no, he knew that all that he had seen was real; and he fell into a train of profound thought.

At first, the question "Why did that man willingly give himself as a victim for that hideous crucifixion?" occupied his mind only. Then slowly his

---

*This Mexican Crucifixion is as literal a reproduction of an actual scene and fact, as is possible to a writer. S. W.

thoughts travelled to the great scene of the Crucifixion of the World's Redeemer more than nineteen hundred years before.

Presently securing his horse he rode away to the spot he had camped on. the night before. He slept but little, and was early astir in the morning.

CHAPTER VII

THE CARGADOR'S PACK.

IT was noon of the day after the "crucifixion." Jack was resting his horse, and eating a snack of food. His mind was a turmoil of many thoughts.

"If only I had a New Testament!" he said softly to himself. "I would read it over and over again as my good little Jap has done."

A far-off look came into his eyes as he gazed into space. His brows knit in pain and perplexity, as he muttered: "'Ye are of your father the Devil.' Under the wrath of God!' How those two words stick to me! How solemnly the little Jap used them. And well he might, if they actually mean all he declared they meant."

A soft sigh escaped him as he added: "It's strange how we all—every one whom I know intimately—live as though we were to live here for ever, instead of here a few, uncertain years, all told, and elsewhere, in Heaven, or Hell (they are very vague terms to me, but they stand, I suppose, for eternal bliss or eternal loss) for ever and ever. I wish—yes, I wish I had a Bible, or a New Testament, I'd——"

His horse lifted its head sharply and looked away beyond him. He turned his head to look in the direction his horse's startled gaze had travelled.

A man was coming towards him bearing an immense wicker basket on his back. As he drew nearer, Jack saw that a wide leather strap went round his forehead, so that the great muscular neck practically took the burden of the heavy pack.

Jack recognized the type, the man was a Cargador. His name (official), he knew came from "*Carga*" a measure of weight of 300 pounds, which every Cargador was supposed to be able to carry on the roughest steepest mountain side, as well as upon the level plain.

The man halted as he came abreast of Jack, and slipped the leather strap from his forehead, and showing all his discoloured teeth in a broad grin, gave Jack a "Good-day, senor," in the vile patois common to the district.

By race, the Cargador was evidently an "Indios." He was of dark brown complexion. His height about five feet six inches. His face was long and thin; he stooped forward (the result of his arduous carrying). He looked anything but a giant in strength until one took note of his muscles. His white cotton pants were rolled up to the groins. He wore no shirt. A long-bladed knife was stuck in the waistband of his cotton pants. A wide brimmed, high-crown straw hat covered the thick mat of black hair that thatched his head. On his feet he wore "guaraches" (light sandals), and he carried in his hands a kind of alpenstock, long and stout—he needed this to negotiate the steep mountain ascents, made increasingly dangerous by the weight he bore on his back.

So scantily robed, the muscles of the man were seen to advantage. The muscles of his calves, and thighs were abnormally developed, some of them as thick as an inch and a quarter rope—and quite as hard. The muscles in the neck were equally huge and hard.

This man's pack weighed fully a hundred and ninety pounds, as Jack discovered. It had weighed two hundred and fifty when he started, but he had done business everywhere he went.

He gladly unpacked for Jack to see, though Jack protested that he wanted nothing. About a quarter of the way down the great packet, the fellow pulled out a small oblong package, done up in strong Manilla paper. Opening the packet he held a book out to Jack, explaining that it was a sacred book of the "Protestants." It had been ordered by a customer some time before, but when the cargador took it to the house on his next round, he found that the man had died, and it was thus thrown as dead stock on the trader's hands.

The book proved to be a handsomely bound, limp cloth, New Testament, in Spanish. Jack bought it instantly, for he was as much at home with Spanish, French, and Italian, as he was with English.

Day after day, and night after night, he now read the precious volume. It was all new and strange to him, but he speedily, easily came to endorse the words of the Jap, that "the very language of the New Testament carried force with it, and that the book had a quality all its own, a quality unlike any other book."

The soul, the mind of Jack Quentin, like those of the little Jap, became fascinated with the wondrous story of the Christ life. Somehow Mark XV., 15 to

39, and the first, the tenth, and last six chapters of
John became his favorite gospel portions, while the
Epistles so fascinated him that he, unconsciously
almost, became nearly letter-perfect in them.

Again and again he found references to other
parts of a book which was not bound up with his
Testament, and from the mention of such words as,
"as Esaias, the prophet, saith,"—"as it is written in
the Psalms,"—"of whom Moses and the prophets
wrote," and other similar references, he knew that in
some way the book called "The Old Testament,"
found its companion part in the "New."

By the time he had read his Testament right
through, his discerning mind saw clearly that everything in it bore the same intimate relation to the
great central facts of the Book—The Death and
Resurrection of Jesus Christ.

During the last forty-eight hours the Spirit of God
had been leading his soul into increased light. Some
impulse had led him back to the eyrie where he had
watched the Crucifixion of the "Penitent Brother."
At the back of his mind, the real thought in his
returning, was to find out the fate of the man whom
he had seen impaled.

Now perched in his old hiding place, and while
he softly repeated the words of his favorite twenty-
four verses of Mark XV, like an object lesson, the
awful imitation of the Calvary scene he had witnessed
from the eyrie where he now sat, passed before him.

Absorbed in thought he forgot time and place
and all else until he began to feel cramped in his
limbs, and a trifle chilled. He had almost decided

to return to where he had left his horse, and where he purposed camping for the night, when the beauty of the little rugged valley, now lit by the rising moon, arrested him for a moment. There was something almost weird and uncanny in the moonlit appearance of the rude huts and Morada of the little settlement.

His eyes became fixed upon the hillock-side to which the processionists had *first* marched, and he seemed to see a figure stretched upon the painted cross.

The moonlight flooded the hillock. He knew that the figure he seemed to gaze upon, was but a mental illusion. Yet it held his eyes in a strange fascination. Slowly, as the illusion took clearer shape he realized that the features were not those of the Mexican whom he had seen crucified, but that of the Christ of the many pictures which he had seen in continental and other galleries.

His mind full of the actual words of the Gospel story, he seemed to see the brow of the murdered Jesus, crowned with thorns. Like the soft-breathing music of an Æolian harp; like the whispered words of a dying one; like a spirit-voice to his soul, there seemed borne to him those wondrous last words of the Atoning Christ—"It is Finished!"

His thought had just begun to fix itself on the solving of those five syllables, when a faint sound in the vale below attracted his attention. A black-robed form passed close to the Morada. A moment later a single deep note of a bell sounded out. Six seconds and a second note sounded. Again six seconds and another note. It was a funeral knell.

Slow, sonorous, weird, the knell rang out. Then, suddenly, a slow, grim, silent procession began to issue from the Morada. Slowly the people marched into the broad glare of the brilliant moonlight. Six men bore a bier between them. It told its own story, and Jack Quentin knew that the crucified man had died in his self-imposed act of religiousness.

With slow, wearisome steps the procession toiled up that steep rugged path. Presently it halted before a kind of flat ledge. The bearers of the bier deposited their burden. Picks and shovels were brought forth, and, in rapid silence, a shallow grave was dug.

Reverently, the body was laid in the hole. A slow, weird song in a minor key was chanted over the open grave. Then, amid audible sobs from the women, and the sharp-voiced utterance of a short prayer from the reader of the exercises, who had officiated in the processions of the afternoon of the crucifixion, the grave was filled in.

A huge slab of rock stood leaning against the wall of the ledge, where the grave had been made. The whole body of men gathered round this slab, one of them uttered a low, clear, ringing—"One—two—three," and with an united effort at the sound of "three," the great slab fell upon the newly-covered grave with a dull thud.

All was over. The procession almost raced down the hill. Jack even thought he caught the sounds of some laughter. Full of deep thought he returned to his camping place.

CHAPTER VIII.

IN THE SHADOW OF A ROCK.

JACK QUENTIN could not sleep. The events of the past days; the *result* of the crucifixion, as seen by him that night in that weird, moonlit funeral; the tumult of his thoughts; all these things combined to render him sleepless. Yet the hours of that night did not appear long, for the grave *personal* questions of Salvation so occupied his mind as to render him oblivious to Time's flight.

When the sun finally rose, he got up, made up his blanket, secured his horse, "packed" his camp impediment, and rode rapidly away from the neighbourhood of the valley of ghastly associations.

A gallop of a couple of hours brought him to a retired spot where a wide stream ran brawling down towards the far distant sea. Here he dismounted, hobbled his horse, and enjoyed the luxury of a good bath before preparing his simple breakfast.

There was something exceedingly pleasant to Jack Quentin, in the lonely, do-for-yourself, rough, open life he was just now living. The actual dangers of travelling quite alone scarcely ever crossed his mind; if they did, they rather added piquancy to the situation, than otherwise.

His breakfast over, he chose a shady spot and with an unconscious, deep-drawn sigh, he opened his Spanish Testament.

"Strange!" he mused, "how this crucifixion of Jesus Christ, The Nazareth Jew of nineteen hundred years ago, has coloured the thoughts and influenced the lives of hundreds of thousands of rich and poor learned and ignorant, of every time, clime, and race, since His Death."

The leaves of his New Testament were slowly, aimlessly slipping through his fingers. His eye lit upon a pencil mark—one of many which he had made in reading through the chapters. He laid the Book open at the marked page, and read: *"Be it known unto* you * * * *that through this Man is preached unto* you *forgiveness of sins, and by Him all that believe are justified from all things, from which ye could not be justified by the law of Moses."*

"There it is again," he murmured, "Forgiveness of sins through this Man, Jesus."

Again the leaves slipped through his fingers, his eyes vaguely watching the falling pages, while his heart pondered over the truths that had filled his soul with a greater unrest than the wander-lust that had driven him from his studio. One of the falling leaves of his Book had become creased, in some-way, in his pocket. He laid the Book open on a flat piece of rock at his side, and with his thumbnail he pressed out the crease. The words immediately beneath his thumb arrested his attention, and he read, *"It is written, there is none righteous, no not one."*

Down through the next fourteen verses of that wonderful third of Romans, he read eagerly and attentively. He paused upon the twenty-third verse and re-read it, *"For all have sinned and come short of the glory of God."*

For a few moments he gazed fixedly across the wild scene that faced his resting place. Then, half-audibly, he said: "Yes, *'all have sinned'*, I have sinned, and it is the knowledge of this, which has been borne in upon me with such crushing force, that fills me with an unrest that holds in it an element of fear. Had anyone, a year ago, tried to convince me that I was a sinner (in the sense in which those verses I have just read, puts it) I believe they would have failed utterly. But when I read this Book, some strange, unseen, outside-of-myself influence—I cannot explain what it is—make the words fairly *rake* my soul until, now this morning, I know that *I am* a sinner, and that what I need to calm my unrest, is pardon of my sin."

He smiled to himself as he continued, "I am confident that no priest, pope, or any other man, can give me this pardon. No, it must be God, and my heart tells me that the secret of how to obtain pardon and peace lies within these pages."

A sudden look of determination came into his face, as, sitting bolt upright, he said, aloud: "Yes! Pardon and peace are here, and, God helping me, I will find them before the sun sets."

He did not kneel and offer a formal prayer, but that "God helping me" which had leaped devoutly from his yearning heart was understood by God.

Again he sought the passage in Acts xiii., and he saw the words in a new and more convincing light. *"Through this Man is preached unto* YOU *the forgiveness of sins."*

"I believe it!" he cried. "But *how,* how does it
come to pass that through this death of Christ upon
the cross, I can go free?"

For a moment or two his eyes held perplexity.
Then he murmured: "What was that I was reading
the other evening which I could not then understand? I put two crosses, I remember, against the
passage, it was on one of the left hand pages."

Slowly, carefully, he let the pages of the Book
fall through his fingers until he came to Galatians iii.
There, against the 10th verse, he saw his double cross-
mark, and read, *"Cursed is everyone that continueth
not in all things which are written in the Book of the
Law to do them."*

"That," he said, aloud, "fits in with the last statement of that verse in the Acts," he murmured.
"And," (he sighed heavily) "I feel that no form or
ceremony can justify me before God."

His eyes fell again on his marked page, and he
went on: "And here is the same thought emphasized again: *'But that no man is justified by the Law,
in the sight of God, it is evident for the just shall live
BY FAITH'."*

The old deep, longing, far-away look crept once
more into his eyes as he sat thinking a moment.
His thoughts found expression in the half-audible
words: "*'Live by faith.'* On, in what, is my faith to
be exercised, and to *rest?*"

Once more he scanned the printed page before
him, and he read aloud:

"Christ hath Redeemed us from the curse of the Law, being made a curse for us: for it is written, 'Cursed is every one that hangeth on a tree'."

Again and again he read the words. His heart was full of unuttered prayer, and in response to all his unexpressed prayer the light of God's Spirit revealed Jesus to him.

With a sudden burst of joy, he leaped to his feet. He turned his eyes—glistening with tears—upwards to the glorious light of the physical sun, as the Sun of Righteousness arose in his soul, and he cried: "I see it! I see the whole thing! All have sinned—*I* have sinned, my whole nature is corrupt and sinful— the curse of God rested upon me—it merited death —Justice demanded death—Jesus died on the Cross He died a death of shame and of curse, a death that only the *cursed of God* could die—He was buried— God raised Him from the dead, and that Resurrection was a witness that He was satisfied with the Atonement made for sin. Jesus *'died for my sins and rose again for my Justification.'* He bore my curse and shame, and now, God, here, in this Word, calls to me and says: '*Through this Man—Jesus—is preached unto you, Jack Quentin, the forgiveness of sins.'* And '*The just shall live by faith.'* I believe it! All my soul believes it, and my weary heart rests upon it, and——"

He had been talking rapidly, and talking aloud. Suddenly he paused, and his face was well-nigh transfigured by the glory of God's new thought that came to him. His voice rang with an exultant gladness as he gave utterance to his thought: "And—*he that believeth*, HATH *everlasting life.*"

"*Everlasting life! 'Justified!'* Hallelujah! I understand now. Now I understand what I could not understand the other evening, about that Publican, in the Temple. He asked for '*Mercy*'—'*God be* MERCIFUL *to me, a sinner!*' But Jesus said: '*He went down to his house* JUSTIFIED!' Oh how much beyond mercy, is Justification!"

A look of new amaze came into his eyes, as they peered into space, yet seeing nothing of the scenery before him. What he saw, by inward vision, was a scene in Central South Africa, a reproduction of an event that had transpired five years before, when the wander-lust had led him into the African wild.

He had been travelling alone, save for his "boys." He had just halted for the night, the oxen were outspanned from his store-waggon, and he had walked to the edge of a ravine, near by.

Jem, his faithful kaffir henchman, crept up to him, and with his nose uplifted in the air, sniffing as he walked, he whispered: "Baas, 'noder white man camp. A—h smell 'em white man, an' a—h smell strange to-bac!"

"Which way, Jem?" he had asked, and the Kaffir had pointed the way.

He, Jack Quentin, had strode away in the direction Jem had indicated, and in a few minutes came upon a crazy old waggon, six oxen, two kaffirs—and a white man sitting over a small camp-fire smoking.

A dog leaped from under the waggon, and gave tongue. The white man sprang sharply to his feet, and faced Jack.

"Jack Quentin!" he cried.

Amazed at the recognition, Jack took a pace nearer, and searched the other's face. The solitary stranger did not speak, but suffered the keen scrutiny. Jack suddenly started, held out his hand, and cried, excitedly:

"Frank Salter! Can it be—is it you, Frank?"

It was his old, long-lost friend Frank Salter. The story was a common one, but none the less sad because of its commonness. Frank Salter, young, inexperienced, had fallen in with a fast set; gone the pace; "over-ran the constable;" had made himself a criminal in his efforts to recover his hopeless condition; was bowled out, and had fled the country. He would never have got clear of the country, but that the man whom he had robbed, in a fit of good nature, had said, "I'll show you mercy. I will put the police off the scent for twenty-four hours, that will give you time to be clear of the country."

Frank had fled. No one had ever heard of him or seen him from that day until Jack Quentin had so strangely met him.

Over their pipes (for they made one camp that night) Frank had cried out, bitterly, "Would to God I'd stayed in England, Jack, and faced the music. Forestier's Mercy to me was meant in kindness. But what is the use of Mercy, when the Law is after you, and when Justice demands punishment?"

Like a vision linking itself onto his new spiritual experience, Jack Quentin saw that far-distant African scene, and heard again Frank Salter's cry. And thinking of the exile's cry, he murmured: "No, no, of course, Mercy would have been useless to that poor Publican, he needed to be *justified*.

"And Mercy would not have helped *me*, for the Law would still have been against me. But Jesus satisfied the Law's demands by His death in my place, and rose again for my Justification."

In a deep, quiet ecstasy he rose to his feet and poured out his soul in praise.

In after days, when the whole Bible was well-known to him, and when he sometimes told the story of this eventful day, he would say: "It was a literal experience with me, that 'The wilderness and solitary place was glad, and the desert blossomed as a rose,' for that wild, dry, desert-like country, where I found God, seemed suddenly to be filled with the most exquisite beauty!"

When he broke camp an hour later, the wanderlust had died out of him, and he turned his face once more towards civilization and to home.

Ten days later he was in New York. He had been down to the great berthing places of the mighty Atlantic liners, inspecting the cabins previous to choosing one for the homeward voyage. He was coming off the liner, on the landing-stage, when he was amazed to see his whilom camp-mate—Mike Doolan, sitting on a bollard-head on the quay. The Irishman was regarding him with the broadest of grins, and saluted him, as he drew near, with the characteristic greeting, "The tip-top o' the mornin' to ye, yer honour, an' may every day o' yer life be a St. Patrick's Day an' a Fourth o' July rolled inter one. How are yer, yer honour?"

Jack Quentin replied heartily to the greeting, then asked Mike how he came to be in New York.

"Sure then, yer honour, it's Kitty, God bless her, as is at the two ends an' the middle o' this thrip. It's meeself that was after havin' a letter fro' her sayin' as she'd be here by the Lucania, an' perposin' as I should come to the city an' meet her, an' we'd git married at onct. 'Fur,' says she in that same letter, 'I missed havin' yer the fust toime, Micky, my darlint, an' I dont want ter miss havin' yer the second toime; as I would to my sorrer, ef someone else bothered me inter weddin' him afore I got up inter the wilderness o' a place where yer lives.' Now, by the same token, sur, its meeself, Micky Doolan, as is agreed wi' Kitty this time, fur I'll look out no ither spalpeen marries her. So here I am on watch fur her beautiful face, an' shure I'll niver budge away till I sees her, an' gits a rale grip on her. May all the Holy Saints bless her han'some face."

For half-an-hour, Jack Quentin talked with the merry Irishman, and, full of his new-born life and love, he told him of his conversion, and sought to direct the heart of Micky into the way of Life.

Twenty-four hours later Jack was en-route for England.

CHAPTER IX.

"WITHOUT THE CAMP."

JACK QUENTIN'S friends were mostly men, (a few women) of the same craft as himself. Personal relatives he had none, he was alone in the world. He was welcomed with open arms on his return to London, for, strong man that he was, he was withal a loveable man.

But his friends found him changed. They told him so, and strong and loveable man that he was, he told them the story of the change. He was with a little crowd of men in an atelier where they had often foregathered. His voice was not only fearless in its tones, as he told the wondrous story, but there was a ring of rapturous gladness in it. And there was a new light in his face as he spoke.

"But you don't mean, Jack," cried one of his special cronies, "that you've gone in for a 'Moody and Sankey' religion?"

Jack smiled at the description. "There is no Moody and Sankey religion in God's sight, Bob," he replied. "God recognizes only one religion, that is the religion of Jesus Christ, which means, if it means anything, eternal life in Christ, by the 'New Birth.' If a man is 'Born Again' by the Spirit of God, that New Birth means a new creation, old things are passed away, and all things become new."

His eager eyes swept the faces of friends, as he went on: "Mark you, friends all, best of chums as you have all been, and, I trust, ever will be—mark you, I do not say that it is impossible to have this Eternal life, except by a *sudden* and wonderful change such as came to me, as I have just told you. Some times it is a slower, and even an imperceptible process, but the change *must* come, or the soul has no life in God, and, without life in God, we are 'dead *in trespasses* and sin,' '*the wrath of God abideth upon us,*' and to die thus must, inevitably mean, eternal separation from God."

No one spoke, so he went on: "Coming over in the liner, from New York, I got chummy with an English clergyman, a man of exceptionally fine parts, who exchanged stories with me. He had always been a *good* lad—not '*goody-goody*' he was careful to explain to me, not weak or milk soppy, but with a very distinct spice of the devil about him ('original sin,') he called it. He was confirmed when he was fifteen, took the Sacrament every Sunday; went up to college, took honours; was afterwards ordained in the Church of England; was a curate two years; then had a living, in a large parish in North London, presented to him. He was popular as a vicar, and as a preacher, and his church was always filled. Then, eight years after he became a vicar, he was called to visit a young railway porter, who was dying. He took out his prayer-book, but before he read the prayers fitting, as he conceived, for the occasion, he began to utter a few of the usual religious platitudes. But the young fellow stopped him, crying almost in anguish: 'I know all those *general* things, parson, what I want now is to know how I may be saved. I know I've got to meet God soon, my heart is in that condition, the doctor says, that I may go off at any moment, and I want to meet God as a saved man. How can I be converted?'

"The clergyman was non-plussed for a moment, and could find no answer. The man spoke again: 'How were you converted, sir? Tell me that, and perhaps it will help me!'

"But the clergyman had never been converted. He was in a worse fix than ever, contrived to put the poor fellow off, by saying he must go, but he would come again next morning. When he went next morning the young man was dead. But he had been visited, an hour after the vicar left, by a godly, converted young curate, who led the soul of the dying man to Christ, and remained with him until the breath left the body.

"The vicar told me that from that day he never rested until he too, knew that he was converted. It was many months before he realized fully that he was 'Born Again,' for the process was so slow with him. But one day, alone in his study, he was reading *'One thing I know, whereas I was blind, now I see.'* He could not put his finger upon the day, the hour, the moment, but he *was* 'Born Again' he knew.

"'Since then,' he told me, 'I have had the joy of leading hundreds to Christ, the majority of whom have been converted in a moment, as we say, that is there had been a distinct sense, a point of time, when they realized that in virtue of having *"believed God"*—what God said about His Son's finished work, and His (God's) acceptance of that work—that they had passed from the *natural* death of sin, *into* the Life of Christ—Eternal life in Christ Jesus.

"'Because,' the vicar went on, 'there are a *few* genuine cases of men and women being born again without being able to point to the time or place when the actual change took place, I sometimes quote, an exquisite bit of Spiritual poetry, to help such people'."

Jack's eye flashed round on the little circle of astonished, interested faces, as he added:

"The thing gripped me so, that I learned it, listen:

"You ask me, *how* I gave my heart to Christ?
                I do not know.
I found earth's flowerets would fade and die;
I wept for something that would satisfy:
And then—and there—somehow I seemed to dare
    To lift my broken heart to Him in prayer
        I do not know—I cannot tell you *how*—
I only know, He is my Saviour now.

"You ask me, *when* I gave my heart to Christ?
                I cannot tell,
The day or just the hour I do not now
                Remember well;
It must have been when I was all alone,
The light of His forgiving spirit shone
Into my heart, so clouded o'er with sin;
    I think—I think—'twas then I let Him in.
        I do not know—I cannot tell you *when*;
I only know, He is so dear since then.

"You ask me *where* I gave my heart to Christ?
                I cannot say.
That sacred place has faded from my sight
                As yesterday;

Perhaps He thought it better I should not
Remember *where*. How I should love that spot!
I think I could not tear myself away
For I should want for ever there to stay.
                    I do not know——
I only know *He* came and *blessed* me *there*.

"You ask me, *why* I gave my heart to Christ?
                    I can reply——
It is a wondrous story, listen! While
                    I tell you *why*.
My heart was drawn at length to seek His face,
I was alone—I had no resting place:
I heard of One who loved me—with a love
    Of depth so great—of height so far above
                    All human ken,——
    I longed such love to share;
And sought it then upon my knees in prayer.

"You ask me—*why* I thought this Christ
                    Would heed my prayer?
I knew He died upon the Cross for me:
                    I nailed Him there!
I heard His dying cry——'Father, forgive!'
I saw Him drink death's cup, that I might live,
My head was bowed upon my breast in shame,
    He called me, and in penitence I came;
                    He heard my prayer!
    I cannot tell you *how*—nor *when*—nor *where!*
                    Why—I have told you now."

The lines had fallen from Jack's lips, filled with
a strange unction. A silence that was almost an
awe had fallen upon the little band of careless-hearted
Bohemians. The silence lasted a full half-minute.
Jack broke it at last, saying:

"A new Birth means a new life, there must
necessarily be a severance, on my part, from some of
the things we once enjoyed together, but I trust it
will make no difference to our actual friendship, for,
believe me, my love for everyone of you is a deeper,
truer thing than ever before, and my hope is—"

At that instant the door of the *atelier* opened hurriedly, and a young fellow, known to them all, entered. Almost breathless with haste, and evident intense excitement, he cried:

"I say, you fellows, Jack M'clure has shot himself!"

"Shot himself!" The words leaped simultaneously from several lips. Then came hurried, eager enquiries, with equally hurried, excited replies, and in three minutes the whole party had rushed off to the house of their shot comrade and friend.

*   *   *   *   *

It did not take Jack Quentin many days to realize that if he would live a Christian life (as he had learned Christ from the New Testament) he would have to be utterly misunderstood even as His Master had been misunderstood. Reading, one morning, the prophecy of Simeon, that Christ should be for *"a sign which shall be spoken against,"* Jack smiled as he read the words. *"Shall be spoken against,"* he repeated again to himself; and he realized, at once, that he must expect the same treatment himself.

He had looked up Ralph Bastin, only to find that he had sailed for South America a week before his own return.

"I wonder where my little Jap friend is?" he asked himself. He smiled quietly as he murmured:

"How strange! Almost to a man, my friends, if they were tackled on the subject, would maintain that they were Christians, even though they live like polished heathens (the life which I myself, lived, until I learned Christ,) while my Jap chum calls himself a heathen and lives a better life than the average professing Christian."

He mused quietly for a moment or two, then, speaking to himself again, he went on:

"Of course I am only a 'babe in Christ,' to use Paul's term, and as a 'babe' I cannot expect to know a great deal, spiritually, yet, but I do know, as a late, utter worldling, what a worldling is like, what he does, what he says, how he thinks, and how he acts. Such an one would be indignant if he was told he was not a Christian, yet he lives utterly without God. His very attendances at a Sunday morning service—the sum total of all the religion he ever practises—is actually a blasphemy. How well I know the matter, for I read myself into the description the other morning: *They come unto Thee as the people cometh, and they sit before Thee as My people, and they hear Thy words, but they will not do them: for with their mouth they show much love, but their heart goeth after their covetousness.'* What a picture of the ordinary worshipper in the churches of to-day! God help me to learn more and more the true inwardness of spiritual life, to learn more and more what it means to be a 'CHRISTIAN'—to be *in* Christ. For, surely, Christ never came from heaven to earth, lived a suffering, misunderstood life for thirty odd years, and then died a cruel, shameful, ignominious death, to save the fallen race, if that race, by education, culture, polish, correct living, and all else that passes current, to-day, for Christianity, could thus fit itself for Heaven. No, No, No! There must be a new nature implanted from somewhere. That new nature,

God's word definitely states, must be the result of the
New Birth. For *'that which is born of the flesh'*—however good and kind, and cultured, and correct, the
life may be, by nature, is, after all—*'flesh,'* and the
flesh is synonymous with natural sin, and natural sin,
is the state of death, and we must be born of the
Spirit, before we can be linked on to God. *'They
that are* IN THE FLESH *cannot please God'."*

Jack drew himself up as though he was literally
bracing himself for a battle, as he murmured:

"I thank God I've been called out of nature's
death *into* the life of Christ—and, by His grace, I'll
play the game, I'll live out the life of Christ that is
within me."

He had a few small commissions to perform out-
of-doors. He put on his hat and coat and passed
out of the house, his inward soul chiming:

"Though Christ a thousand times in Bethlehem be born,
If He's not born *in thee*, thy soul is all forlorn.
God's spirit falls on me, as dewdrops on a rose,
If I but, like a rose, my heart to Him disclose.
In all eternity no tone can be so sweet,
As when man's heart with God's in unison doth beat,
Whate'er thou lovest, man, that, too, become thou must—
God, if thou lovest God; dust, if thou lovest dust."

CHAPTER X.

"MANY WATERS CANNOT QUENCH LOVE."

OCCUPYING a prominent place in Jack Quentin's studio, was a picture painted when he was not more than twenty-two. It was a portrait of a girl of barely eighteen years, and was probably one of the choicest bits of work he had ever done.

There was a romance connected with it, and he had painted the portrait when bathed in the glowing splendour of a first and only love.

Within a few hours of his making that full confession of his new-found faith, to his artist friends, he had gone over to where the portrait of Maggie McInnes hung, and standing before it, and apostrophising the absent original, he said softly, tenderly:

"Maggie, dear heart! After all these years I am in a condition to meet you again, I can honestly declare that I have fulfilled the condition you imposed upon me, and I'm starting to-morrow to see you."

Just for one instant the thought came to him, "Shall I, after fourteen years, find her free to listen to my suit?"

The query was only for an instant. He looked up again at the sweet face, and the blue eyes seemed to answer him back:

"My hand is lonely for your clasping, dear,
  My ear is tired waiting for your call;
 I want your strength to help, your laugh to cheer;
  Heart, soul, and senses need you, one and all,
 I droop without your full, frank sympathy—
  We ought to be together, You and I.

> "We want each other so, to comprehend
>   The dream, the hope, things planned or seen or wrought;
> Companion, comforter, and guide, and friend,
>   As much as love asks love, does thought need thought,
> Life is so short, so fast the lone hours fly—
>   We ought to be together, You and I."

He dropped into a chair where he could feast his eyes on the pictured face. His mind swept back in a reverie which was as real as the actual.

At seventeen-and-a-half, Maggie McInnes would have been raved over as a singular Beauty even if she had lived in the smallest village in the kingdom, in a town or city the raving would have been stronger. She was tall, for a girl—she came of Scottish Highland stock. Some of Raphael's saints were limned by him, with faces like hers. Her eyes were wide, blue, questioning. Simple and innocent as a two-year-old babe's in their questioning expression, deep and unfathomable as those of a *savant,* in their more thoughtful moods. Her form was one of wondrous grace, and no trained woman athlete was ever more graceful, or more healthily strong.

She was cultured, too, with that best of all culture —that of the mind rather than the merely superficial culture of conventionality. She was steeped in the best poetry, and the best literature in the English language, and from her wide poetic and other reading, was fully conversant with "Love's strange, sweet tale," though no lover had as yet come within her ken.

Sometimes, in the gaiety of her heart, and with her *book* knowledge of Love, she sang:

> "*Two* in a boat on the turn of the tide;
>   *Two* in the sight of the leaf and the land;
>   *Two* on the breast of the waves that are wide;

Two on the narrow gold strip of the sand.
But *one* on the ocean of love and at rest;
  One midst the rush, and *one* in the roar;
One like a bird winging home to its nest:
  Who asks as much, or dare hunger for more?

"*Two* in the gold of the Sun as it sets;
  Two close together at the death of the day;
Two in the world that forgives and forgets;
  Two in the joy of the beach and the bay.
But *one* in the faith, and one in the prayer;
  One in the Heaven, and one in the blue;
One in the light, and the life and the air:
  Who can ask more? O! my darling can you?"

Then as her face grew graver she would murmur softly to herself:

"Love-songs, so called, are all very well in their way, but all other love must pale before the Love of God in Christ Jesus."

Her face was the face of a saint as she would softly chant:

"O Love Divine, how sweet Thou art!
When shall I find my willing heart
  All taken up by Thee?
I thirst, I faint, I die to prove
The greatness of Redeeming Love,
  The Love of Christ to me."

Her soul soared to wondrous heights of longing as she moved homewards, after a pleasant afternoon spent in the woods, and when she had sung thus of Love. Her head was as erect as some girl Egyptian water pot carrier, her step was the step of a Queen.

While she had been absent from home that afternoon something had happened—anything beyond the ordinary, hourly, daily routine scarcely ever occurred.

Her father, John McInnes—a typical Scotchman, tall, big-boned, with a shrewd, honest, kindly face, and eyes the colour of his daughter's—had been fitting a new well-rope to the drum of the well, which his own hands had dug and fashioned, nearly forty years before. Suddenly, as he lifted his eyes a moment, he saw a sun-bronzed young man, with a knapsack on his shoulders, and a fold-up easel in his hand.

One glance at the face of the new-comer, when they came to closer quarters, was sufficient to assure good old John McInnes of two things, *first,* that the young man was clever, *second,* that he was honest. He was very young, not more than twenty-two, so John surmised, and there was an almost boyish frankness and unconventionality in his manner and speech, as he said:

"I wonder, friend, if you could let me have the use of a bedroom, and a place at your board—I do not mind how simple it is, the simpler the better, for me—just for a week or two. I am a painter, and want to make some sketches of this beautiful neighbourhood. Can you, will you take me in?"

A fair, sweet-faced woman, with a gentle voice, and winning manner, had come quietly from the house, and now stood by her husband's side. He turned to her as the young artist preferred his request.

"Jessie, lass, what's thee say, for—"

He looked up at the new-comer as, with a quizzical little smile, he added:

"It's the wummen o' our hooses on whom the heft o' these like things fa'. If Jessie, my gude wife, thinks she kin tak' yer, frien', I'm perfectly

willin' to ha'e ye, fur I ken an honest lad when I
looks him in the een."

"I'm weel agreed, John," the wife replied, "if oor
Maggie agrees 't."

She lifted her eyes to the young man's face, as
she explained:

'Maggie's our daughter, jus' our on'y chiel. She's
awa' the noo, in the wood, I'm thinkin', but she'll no
be long the noo. Till then, come ye in, an' tak' a
sup o' milk an' a scone. Or may-be ye'd lik' a wash,
the first."

She laughed lightly as she added: "yer shall ha'
yer own accommodation fur washin', in yer ain room,
when Maggie has arranged yer room, Mr. —— er—
what will I be callin' yer, sir?"

"My name is Jack Quentin," the stranger replied,
"but for pity's sake don't call me, 'Quentin,' call
me, Jack. I hate surnames, and Mr., and all that
kind of thing. But you were speaking of washing.
I don't mind where I wash, I'm used to camping out,
a bucket, down at the burn's side, there, will suit me
splendidly. But, by the bye, what am I to call you
two friends?"

"Our names are John and Jessie McInnes," the
man replied, "but if we're no to mister you, may-be
you'd like best to call us John an' Jessie?"

Jack Quentin had gladly agreed to the simple arrangement.

It was close upon an hour before Maggie arrived
home, by which time Jack had freshened up his
whole appearance, and had become quite intimate
with his host and hostess, had heard, in outline, the

story of their settling on that lonely moor, while
Jack had, in return, given to the honest, loving
couple, a brief resume of his own career.

Jack had been amazed at the many signs of culture
and refinement in the house, and equally so by a
certain measure of culture in his host and hostess.

"You are musical," he remarked, as, beside a
splendid piano, he noticed two violins, a guitar, a
mandoline, and in a smaller room at the side of the
main room where they were sitting, a large American
organ.

"I play the feedle, a lettle," his host replied,
modestly, "but to Maggie, our lassie, no instrument
comes amiss. Ah, she's comin' the noo, hearken to
her.—

From across the moor there came the sound of a
girl's pure, rich voice, singing:

> "Lo, the soul Thy love hast bought,
>   Through the ages, Lord, am I,
>   Knowing nought, and willing nought,
>   Thine alone, eternally————.
>   Thine the Bride Thy love has won,
>   Gift of God to Christ His Son."

"We'll keep back, an' no let her see you, Jack,"
McInnes said, and the trio kept just inside the
door-way. Jack listened in delighted wonder at the
pure, rich, liquid notes of the oncoming girl's voice,
as it rang out,

> "In Thy strength my soul is still
>   Clay within the potter's hands,
>   Moulded by Thy tender will,
>   Mightier than all commands;
>   Shaped and moved by Thee alone,
>   Now, and evermore Thine own."

The song ceased. The singer was within twenty yards of the house. McInnes signed to Jack to follow him. The father stepped out to meet his "lassie," but Jack gave a moment's pause to give the man an opportunity to speak to the girl. When, an instant later, Jack stepped clear of the porch, he was held motionless by the striking personality of the beautiful girl.

A moment or two later he was being introduced to Maggie McInnes. As their hands touched in greeting, and they gazed into each other's eyes, one of those strange, instantaneous love-fires, sometimes kindled at first sight, leaped to birth in each of their hearts.

From that moment a new life began for each of them. The new revelation of life was doubtless greater to Maggie than to Jack, since her life's environment had been peculiarly isolated and secluded.

She had been infinitely happy every hour of her life. But it had been a happiness of mind. Her heart; save to her God, had never yet been opened to Love's touch.

One curious thing about her instant—as well as her *after*—influence upon Jack Quentin, was the fact that she was absolutely ignorant of the power of her own beauty and charm.

Before the sun set that night, the quartette might have lived together all their lives, so perfectly intimate had they become. Quentin called his host and hostess, "John" and "Jessie;" and the girl, "Maggie;" they each, in their turn, calling him, Jack, though

Maggie's use of the name was a trifle shy, but that was only natural.

They spent the evening with music. Jack had not told them that he was musical, but the moment he touched the keys of the organ and the piano, they all knew that he was a master of them.

Behind a screen was a very beautiful harp. Jack had not seen it, or had any idea of the presence of such an instrument, until his host brought it out, when the evening was half over. The moment that Maggie's fingers touched the strings, her soul became so absolutely absorbed that she appeared to forget the very presence of the others. It was a wonderful evening to them all.

When the clock warned for ten, Mrs. McInnes, said, in her gentle way: "Maggie, lassie, get the buke."

Maggie placed a large Bible on the table in front of her father, and he read the 91st Psalm, read it as Jack Quentin had never heard the Bible read before. Then the household knelt. Jack kneeled with them, though it was the first time he ever remembered doing such a thing.

John McInnes prayed, and again the whole thing was a revelation to Jack Quentin. Once, Jack turned his face towards the petitioner, for it seemed to him almost as if the elder man was speaking to some one actually present. It was all as strange and incomprehensible to Jack Quentin, as it was moving and wondrous.

It was nearly ten-thirty before they actually parted for the night—a late hour for the moor-land household. When Maggie and Jack shook hands—

romantic as it may sound to some—each knew that the love of a life-time had been born within their hearts.

They were early risers on that moor, and the quartette met at six o'clock next morning. In the eyes of Jack Quentin, Maggie looked even more beautiful than she had done over-night. A pleased light came into her eyes, and a little tender blush into her cheeks, as their eyes met, and their hands clasped.

The table was already laid for breakfast. But, as if by arrangement, the same instinct led the feet of the pair through the open door until they stood outside on the moor.

"It is an hour too late to see and feel the richest charm of a moor morning in its fulness," Maggie remarked. "But, still, what could be fresher and sweeter than this?"

Her great, liquid eyes, full of a momentary wordless admiration, swept the scene, and, with a faint sigh, she added:

"I sometimes think that I should pine and die if cooped up in some city slum."

She caught her breath quickly, almost as though she would call back that last sentence, then said, softly, reverently:

"Of course, I spoke from the purely human standpoint. As a follower of Jesus, I would *gladly* go, and stay, where He would have me go, and have me stay."

Jack was staring in amaze at her. Such trust in the Christ of whom he knew practically nothing even by letter, let alone Spirit, was utterly new to him, as had been the "worship" of the evening before.

The girl did not see his face, hence missed the amaze in it, and before either of them had time to speak again, Mrs. McInnes called to them from the door to come to breakfast.

Jack Quentin had been eight days with the McInnes'. Maggie and he were alone together. The father and mother had driven off, an hour before, to a market, thirteen miles away.

Suddenly Jack's love broke loose and he began, with the hot impetuosity of love, and of youth, to pour out all that had been pent-up in his heart during the past eight days.

"You love me, Maggie, as I love you, dear lassie!" he cried confidently.

She could only confess that she did, and for one blissful moment she suffered herself to be gathered to his breast, and gave him the kiss he asked for, in return for those he rained on her.

Then in the hot impetuosity of his love, he cried: "Tell me, Maggie, darling, how soon will you marry me, how soon will you come into my life and marry me?"

Then she remembered Whose she was, and Whom she served. Quietly, resolutely she drew herself out of his arms, and said:

"Listen to me, dear Jack. I do love you. I never loved before—perhaps I'm over young, even now, to love as I do—and I know in my deepest soul that I shall never love any other man; but, dear one, even though I have to go sorrowing for you all my days, I'll never, never be able to wed you until you love the Lord Jesus, until your life is given up to serve Him. We should never be happy if I was to play traitor to my Lord, Who says 'Be ye not unequally yoked with unbelievers'——."

Jack tried to interrupt her, tried to take her back into his arms again, but she would not let him do either, she would finish what she had to say, even if it broke her heart.

"Satan whispers to me, dear," she went on, "Marry your lover, and win him to your Lord. That is like Satan to tempt me first to disobey God, then expect me to be successful in disobedience. No, my darling, though my heart breaks as I say it, nothing could ever tempt me to disobey my Lord's command, even though I lose you—"

Her voice broke, and she turned and fled to her room. She had barely reached its shelter before she heard the sound of wheels. Her room faced the front, and looking out of the window she saw a neighbour who lived only six miles away, driving up to the house.

With one glance into the looking-glass, to see that her tears had left no trace, she raced down the stairs. Jack was already by the side of the trap; he was holding a telegram in his hand, the terra-cotta envelope lying at his feet.

"I met the gillie, Maggie," the farmer explained, "one o' Archie McTavish's laddies, comin' hither, an' as I was comin' wi' in a wee o' yer hoose, I offered to bring the message along."

Maggie's eyes were fixed upon her lover's face.
He lifted his eyes, their glances met.

"No bad news, I hope, Jack?" she said, and her
voice was gentle, almost caressing.

"Not *bad* news, Maggie, only important business,
and I ought to leave at once."

"Is it to the station ye'll be wanting to go, laddie?" the farmer asked, "because yer could drive wi'
me, an'——."

Jack accepted the offer. It took him only a few
minutes to pack his things, then there was a bitter-
sweet parting between the lovers, in the house, and
beyond the ken of the farmer.

"I'll wait for you, dear Jack, even until I am old,
and silver-haired," she sobbed. "For, oh, my dear,
dear love, I am sure God will find you, and we shall
yet be together. God bless you, my own, own laddie,
my dear love. Good-bye!"

His voice was choked. He could only clasp her
to himself, and bid her good-bye.

Suddenly she broke from him, and ran sobbing to
her room.

That was the memory that had swept over Jack
Quentin, as he gazed on the picture face. He had
never seen the *living* face of his love since. He had
always known, deep, deep in his heart, that it would
be worse than useless ever to attempt to see her,
until her God was his God.

He had known, too, as surely as though an angel
from Heaven had come to assure him of the fact,
that Maggie *would* wait for him.

On his return to London at that time, he had
made a round of many of the churches. He heard
some of the most interesting sermons, compositions built
up most cleverly, and delivered with more or less
oratory—but they all lacked the wonderful quality
of unction which charactised the words and prayers
of good old John McInnes.

He heard, too, some of the most vapid, empty,
essay sort of talk, that ever disgraced the name of
" preaching." But the one thing he did not hear,
the one thing he wanted to hear, was the real message of salvation by Christ Jesus. Had he only
known *where* to go, he could have heard what he
most needed, but then he supposed, as any outsider
naturally would suppose, that every clergyman and
minister preached the *Gospel*, even if some of them
failed to *live* it.

We have seen how, at last, he found God.

No woman had, in the lapsed years, ever had
power to stir in Jack Quentin the faintest affection,
other than that of ordinary friendship or comrade-
ship. His heart's fullest *love* had been given to
Maggie McInnes. Now, he determined to seek her,
and at the very earliest moment possible, he started
North.

CHAPTER XI.

LOVE TRIUMPHANT.

THE longest day which Maggie McInnes ever lived, was the day that Jack Quentin departed. But she did not falter for one second in her fealty to her Lord, and, deep in her soul, she had the chime of His own personal message " *There hath no one left (lover), for My sake, and the Gospels, but shall in this life receive a hundred-fold.*" And Hope fed her heart, and her soul was kept in perfect peace, her feet, even, were kept from growing leaden.

Sometimes she sang:

> "'Tis mystery all! but God is Love,
>   And Love must triumph soon or late.
> Thus through our griefs we ever prove
>   That love is stronger than our fate."

The years dealt kindly with Maggie McInnes. At thirty-one she was infinitely more beautiful than she had been at seventeen. The very sorrow of her life had served to give an added grace and sweetness to her face.

This same sorrow had moulded and fashioned her soul, even more wondrously than it had done her face. Soul and face alike are very beautiful, to-day, as, standing in the doorway of the house on the moor, she gives vent in song to her soul's experience:

"How good it is, when weaned from all beside,
With God alone the soul is satisfied,
        Deep hidden in His heart!
How good it is, redeemed, and washed, and shriven,
To dwell, a cloistered soul, with Christ in Heaven,
        Joined never more to part!
How good the heart's still chamber thus to close
        On all but God alone——
There in the sweetness of His love repose,
        His love unknown!
All else for ever lost—forgotten all
        That else can be;
In rapture undisturbed, O Lord, to fall
        And worship Thee."

In all the years since that day when Jack Quentin
had left her side, she had lived in that attitude towards her Lord. And, for all those years she had
waited for her lover.   Surely the old world had
never seen a constancy more wondrous, for never
once had she doubted that he would come again to
her, and come as a Christian, as one with her in
Christ Jesus. "He *will* come!" she told herself,
"and God is '*Mizpah*,' I'm sure, watching between
us."

She would not have been human if she had not
sorrowed sometimes over his delay. But through all
the years she had stanched the bleeding of her heart
with the balm of God's promises, and bandaged it
with Hope.

A dozen or more men had found her out during
the years of her waiting, some of them very rich,
two were titled. But all alike received the same
treatment, the same answer. Not one of them ever
won an answering smile from her.

Her father and mother were laid to rest, and
she was now living alone. Yesterday had been the

anniversary of the parting between Jack and herself. She never forgot the date, and each succeeding year found her, on the same special day, expecting her lover to come.

When the sun had set, and he had not come, and she had turned back into her living-room, and sat down once again to her lonely meal, the food had suddenly choked her, and she had turned and buried her face in the cushions of the couch and wept.

When the new day had dawned, the day when once more we meet her, a strange new hope had suddenly leaped to birth within her, a new, glad expectancy that bordered upon assurance. She could not have defined this new sense, but she was more and more powerfully conscious of it as the hours of the day moved on.

It was within half-an-hour of sunset, she had been sitting by the window sewing. Suddenly she dropped her sewing—too restless to stitch—and went out into the porch.

Her eyes travelled in the same direction they always took. But there was nothing in sight, save the wide, wild moor "baring its breast to heaven, health-breathing, bright."

She caught her breath in a deep sigh. Then in that same instant of disappointment, a sound reached her ear. It was the throb and rush of a motor. It was coming from the opposite direction to that in which she had been peering.

Turning swiftly about, she instantly recognized the man sitting next to the chauffeur—it was her lover.

In a moment the car was abreast of the door.
Jack had leaped from it as it slowed down, and the
lovers were locked in each other's arms, before the
car, five yards ahead of them, had actually stopped.

"My love, my love!" she cried. "I knew you would
come some day. And, *to-day*, I *felt* you coming!"

With the rest of that wonderful re-union we need
not concern ourselves, other than to say that it was
midnight before they had each, in turn, touched even
the fringe of their respective stories.

Forty-eight hours later they were married by
Scottish law, and by special license, as well. The
next twenty-four hours saw them in London. They
were en-route to the Continent, but spent three days
first in the Metropolis.

Love's wondrous link had bound their hearts to
each other, through all the years they had been
separated, but now the bond of Divine Love made
stronger the link of the human love.

The month they had spent on the Continent together
was the most wonderful time Maggie had ever known.
All that she had read of the various places, had not
prepared her for half the delight she experienced,
but then there was one thing she did not, at first,
take into account, that was that everything she saw,
she saw through the glamour of her deep, deep love
for the man with whom she companioned.

They had reached Calais, on their return journey,
and were passing down to the Dover boat, when
Jack suddenly spied his Japanese friend. At the
same moment, the latter caught sight of Jack, and
raced across to meet him.

The greetings on both sides were very warm. Then came the introduction to Maggie. "She has heard a great deal about you, Tom," Jack explained, "for I tell her that I believed God suffered you to be the instrument of my first quickening towards Him—for you must know, Tom, old boy, that I am *now* a Christian—such a Christian, I hope, as you once sketched to me as the Pauline ideal of such a man."

He broke off shortly, then said, "But we must hurry if we're going to save this boat. You are England-bound, Tom?"

The Jap said, "Yes," and the trio hurried on board. The passage was a splendid one. The boat never shipped a drop of water, and the three friends sat together, facing each other, while their respective stories were begun. Only begun, because they were continued, and barely finished, during, the train run to Charing-Cross.

The Jap, too, no longer claimed "heathen," as his designation, but "Christian." The story was a very wonderful one.

"I had returned to Japan," he explained, after my business in Ohio was completed. I went to my brother's house to stay. He lives in Yokohama. As you know, dear friend, Jack, last year was a very critical time with us, as a nation. Our victory over the Russians was a costly victory, for it has drained our national resources to the dregs almost. But, as one of your English newspapers said, in a paragraph that reflected the Japanese character, perfectly: 'Every Japanese is a patriot. There is not a man, woman, or child, who would not sell his or her soul, (if there was a market for such commodities,) and gladly give the price of the sale to the National War Chest. As a matter of fact, many of the wealthy men are gladly disposing of their collections of native curios. In many cases these collections are priceless. More than one wealthy curio-hunter from America, we understand, is on the way to the "Land of the Chrysanthemum," hoping to profit by this national spirit of self-sacrifice.'

"The day after I reached my brother at Yoko-hama, he came home very excited, and told me a wonderful story. He had been to the great figure of Buddha, (my brother is a maker of rikishas, and loans out, to coolies, and others, a hundred or two of those light carriages of ours.)

"My brother was quietly resting on one of the steps of the Buddha-flight, watching a man who looked like one of our countrymen. His features were very like ours, his hair and complexion were also like ours, and, when it suited his purpose, he passed himself off as one of our land—for he spoke our language like a native. But he was an imposter, a bad villian, whom those of my countrymen, who knew him, hated. He was a low-life Londoner, and came from Goldsmith's Row, Hackney, (wherever that may be.)

"My brother guessed that this man was where he was for no good, and determined to watch him. Presently one of my brother's rikishas was raced up to the steps, by a coolie, and the passenger alighted. The man in front of my brother, the

cockney rascal who had, even in his boyhood, at
home, in London, been called ' Japan Joe,' because
of his likeness to our race, got up from where he
was sitting, as the new arrival got out of his rikisha.

"The new-comer was an American, that was
written upon him from head to foot—for we Japanese, as a people, soon learn to know the various
nationalities, by certain distinctive marks about them.
As the American came up the steps, that fellow,
'Japan Joe,' nodded, smiled, and remarked: 'A
glorious morning, sir!'

"'That's so, stranger!' the other replied. He was
evidently gregarious by nature, voluble by habit,
unsuspicious and trustful through ignorance and
self-conceit. In five minutes, the pair were sitting
on a step about half-way up the great flight chat-
ting like old friends. My brother was sitting on
a step above, not directly behind, but within easy
earshot.

"'My name,' said the American, 'is Thaddeus K.
Bilk,' and he handed that blackguard Joe his card.

"'Awm 'Mexican, aw guess,' he went on, in a
spread-eagle kind of way, 'an' aw've kum d'reckt fro'
Chicago ter buy up all the hull lot o' curios, that
yer nation hev got ter trade off!'

"He half-turned to Joe, as he said: 'Awm per-
soomin,' by yer features, sir, that yer air a Jap.'

"That fellow, Joe, smiled very speciously as he
replied: 'I am a *Japanese*, sir, though, as a race, a
rising race, sir, a nation which must henceforth be

counted among the leading powers of the world, **we** object to the term *"Jap"*.'

" With an even more specious smile than before, and with an airy wave of the hand, he added:

" 'But people do not, generally, know our objection to the abbreviation, so we pass over it.'

"The American was not particularly interested in the Buddha, but began to talk of curios, and his desire to buy up some.

" 'It is fortunate that you met me, sir,' Joe said, 'for it is so easy for a stranger to the curios of our land, to be taken in by imitations. Now, sir, I happen to have entrusted to me, the sale of half-a-dozen or more large cases of the most wonderful curios that Japan has ever produced. Old lacquer, sir, six hundred years old. Some of it was originally bought by weighing its own weight, in gold, in the opposite scale. Some real Ritsuo, too, none of your Osaka imitations. Satsuma ware, and Basske ware, too, the genuine article, sir.'

"The fellow laughed softly, with the quiet assumption of the real connoisseur, as he went on:

" 'You see, sir, a foreigner may easily be deceived by imitations; but you cannot deceive a real Japanese.'

"The American tried to get a word in here, but Joe was too much for him.

" 'Old Kioto,' he went on, 'Eraku, Seidji, and other minor sorts. As to the wonderful metallurgic curios in real Syakfdo stuff, there is, among the collection, of which I speak, some specimens so rare and beautiful that the Mikado himself tried to induce

the old count—for whom I am acting—to sell. But
he would not. Ah! there had been no war then,
the nation did not need funds, and the count's *hobby*
was a greater thing *then* than his patriotism. Now
the handsome old man has gone to Korea on business of state for his Emperor, and he discovers that
his patriotism is mightier than his hobby, and all
that is made by the sale of the curios I am to hand
over to the National Fund.'

"For half an hour longer the pair talked on,
seemingly utterly oblivious of the possibility of being overheard. The confab ended with Joe bargain-
ing for the payment (on the American's approval of
and receipt for the various articles) of thirty thousand pounds sterling. 'I will meet you here at nine,
to-morrow morning,' he said; as they went down to
their waiting rikishas. 'I will bring the *Government* receipt with me, and we will ride the six miles
out to the place where the curios were packed, ready
for shipment—for I was going with them myself, to
sell them to the great English Museum at Kensing-
ton, London.'

"The pair shook hands, and parted, each going a
different way.   As the American rode away, my
brother, jumped into a rikisha and told the coolie
to keep up with the one in front.   When the
American alighted, at his hotel, he went on to the
verandah, and a moment or two later my brother
followed him, and asked if he could speak to him,
privately. The American looked surprised, and said:
'Privately?'

" 'I would save you from being swindled by the man with whom you bargained, just now, sir,' my brother replied, keeping his voice low.

"What my brother said 'fetched' the American, as they say, and he jumped to his feet, and said, 'Come with me into the grounds.'

"Once in the grounds, and assured that they could not be overheard, my brother said: 'The man you are dealing with, sir, is a rogue and a mean scoundrel. He is not a Japanese, but an Englishman, a Londoner. I know all his history, so do hundreds of others in this city, who scorn him for a rogue, and a scoundrel, sir.'

" 'You speak English,' the American said suddenly, interrupting my brother, 'speak it almost like an Englishman.'

" 'I have lived long with the English-speaking peoples, sir,' my brother explained, 'in America, Australia, and England.'

"Then, for a full half-hour, my brother and the American, held close confab. Then, before my brother left, he said, 'You have not yet parted with any money sir?'

" 'Not a cent!'

" 'Good! I will be with you early in the morning, sir, and will bring you a roll of *imitation* notes, so cleverly imitated that not even that cunning rascal would know the difference. The money must pass from you to him, sir, to make the case perfect. After that, sir, leave all to me, and you shall see how we sons of Japan can maintain the honour of our race.'

"All that happened afterwards, my friends, would read like a bit of one of your magazine stories. Let me tell it as I would tell it for one of your Editors.

"The village was six miles from the city. It was not a large village, but it was noted for its temple, which was very handsome and spacious.

"Many tourists and travellers came to see the rows of fine - grained, richly - coloured, exquisitely - carved Retinospora which supported a most gloriously-worked panelled ceiling.

"My brother led a score of my countrymen, in whom he had confided—they all belonged to the city—into the temple, where they paid their morning votive-offering to the image of the great lord, Buddha. Their worship over, my brother led them to a hiding-place.

"A quarter of an hour later two rikishas arrived, and the American, and 'Japan Joe,' walked together to a shed. Here, Joe began to unpack a number of cases of the veriest shoddy of imitation Japanese curios.

"The American had caught his cue properly from my brother, and pretended to be dazzled by the stuff shewn him, and closed with the 'wonderful bargain,' at once, handing over the roll of imitation notes which he had, earlier that morning, received from my brother.

"Just as 'Joe,' put the notes in his pocket, and handed the American the promised 'Government' receipt, my brother and his crowd suddenly appeared, and, at a sign from my brother, Joe was gagged

and his arms bound behind his back, and he was
marched out.

"Behind the shed was a thick patch of bamboo.
Beyond the bamboo was an open bit of rough
uncultivated ground.   Here the whole party were
halted by my brother, and formed in a semi-circle
around the scoundrelly prisoner.

"The fellow was greeny-grey with fear. My brother
turned to his fellow-countrymen, and speaking in our
tongue, said: 'Brothers! This mean-souled, lying
dog, has posed as one of our race. He has taken
advantage of a certain likeness of face to us, to call
himself one of our august race.   He has professed
to be acting for our government, to sell some wonderful Japanese curios——.'

"A scornful laugh rang out from my countrymen.

"'You saw,' my brother went on, 'the trash that
he would have traded off as genuine Ritsuo, Satsuma,
Banko, Kioto, Syakfdo, and the rest. He trusted to
the credulity of this American gentleman, and cared
not that we, as a race, should be branded as swind-
lers, when the fraud should be discovered. He has
traded on the best feelings of our race, to brand
us with disloyalty and traitorship.   What shall be
his doom?'

"Every voice of the little crowd of my countrymen, sounded as one, as they cried: 'The sword!'

"The American did not, of course, understand
what was said, for all this had been in the tongue
of my dear land.

"'You have heard,' my brother said, addressing
Joe, 'for you know our tongue.'

"The bulging eyes of the scoundrel acknowledged that he had heard, though his gagged mouth prevented his speaking.

" 'You have often boasted that you belonged to "No WHERE",' my brother went on.

"He nodded to the four men who held the prisoner. They forced him down on his knees.

" 'If you belong to *"No where"*,' my brother continued, 'then go where you belong!'

"He nodded again, and Japan Joe's head rolled in the dust, severed by a sword by one of the four who guarded him.

"The story has, (from the English standpoint) a gruesome ending, and you would have to know my countrymen well, and their pride in the virtues of their race, to be able to understand their summary dealing with a traitor.

"I was not present at the execution, of course, but Otis, my brother gave me all the particulars, and how they dug a hole and buried 'the body of the thing they had sent to *"No where"*,' as my brother put it.

"Somehow, friends, that word *'No where'* troubled me. I had long before lost faith in my own, the native religion of my country, and though I knew your Christian religion by 'the *letter*,' as Paul puts it, yet I had never seen my way to adopt it for myself, because of the seeming infidelity of those of your countrymen whom I had met, who, while calling themselves—or at least *counting* themselves—Christians, yet lived lives utterly at variance with the commands of Christ."

The train, at that moment, began to slow up. The
journey to London was not half performed. Jack
looked out of the window to ascertain the cause of
the stopping—for they had finally stopped. Drawing
his head back, a moment later, he said:

"It's all right! The signal was against us, but it
has dropped again, and—here we go again."

The train moved on, and the Jap resumed his
story.

"For three days, that word, 'Go to Nowhere,'
haunted me, and again and again I said to myself,
'The spirit of a man must go *somewhere*. You can't
destroy a spirit, though you can a body. Now, where
has the spirit of 'Japan Joe' gone?'

"Almost instantly my mind darted from the soul
of the scoundrel to my own, and I asked myself the
question, 'If death overtook *me*, where would my
soul go?'

"Now it was a curious thing, friends, but my
mind never suggested the Buddhist answer to my
question, but the answer of the Christian Bible, and
I found myself saying: *'After death the judgement,'*
'and I saw the (wicked) dead, small and great, stand
before God; and the books were opened: and another
book was opened, which is the book of Life, and the
dead were judged out of those things which were writ-
*ten in the books, according to their works * * * and*
whosoever was not found written in the book of Life was
cast into the lake of fire.'

"I remember how it struck me as so curious that
I should recall only the *Christian* scriptures, as
answer to the question of my mind.

"I remember how often I had read the words of John, the Evangelist, *'He that believeth not is judged already, because he hath not believed in the name of the only begotten Son of God'*—Judged, condemned, not for an unclean or vicious life, but because he had not believed *in*, had not accepted Jesus Christ, the Son of God, as Saviour of his soul."

The Jap turned his eyes, eloquent with the theme that possessed him, to Jack, as he said: "You remember, Jack, my love for, and knowledge of the Bible, the New Testament especially. I am not sure that I was not just a little bit conceited over my knowledge of the Scriptures, I hardly dare call it Pharisaic because, to be that, I should have had to trust for my salvation in my knowledge; whereas my soul's salvation had never (in the days when I knew you first, Jack) become a factor in my thought, or in my study of the scriptures. But it pleased me, as one whom your missionaries would regard a heathen, to be more conversant with your Bible, than any of the professed Christians whom I met.

"But in those days of my first conviction of sin in Yokohama—for I know, now, that it *was* conviction of sin—passage after passage of the New Testament came up before me condemning me as a sinner. Yes, condemning me, a heathen, a Buddhist. *'Dead in sins,' 'under wrath,'* thundered in my soul. *'Loving darkness,' 'loving the world,' 'children of disobedience,' 'of your father the Devil,' 'without Christ,' 'Having no hope, and without God in the world.'*

"I felt as if the burden of my sin would crush me. Men talk about there being no hell. I knew there was a hell in those days of darkness and misery before the light of God came to me.

"I was tempted to destroy myself, then the thought came to me that that would but hurry me into the judgement presence of Christ. In my misery I recalled something which Otis, my brother, had told me. I had asked him about a mutual friend, who had been at school with us, as boys, and he had astounded me by telling me that Ito had become a Christian, had been saved among the strange people 'The Salvation Army.' Otis had told me that, the first night I was home. Now, as I recalled it, I determined to go and find Ito, tell him all my trouble, and get him to help me.

"There was a meeting at the Salvation Army Hall that night, and Ito (who was now an officer) was leading the meeting. When I went into the great place I found it nearly full. Half-a-dozen girls of my own city—I recognised two whom I had known, years before—were standing up on the platform, each with a timbrel, and singing in beautiful harmony:

"We're bound for the land of the pure and the holy,
The home of the happy, the kingdom of love.
Ye wanderers from God in the broad road of folly,
Oh, say, will you go to the Eden above?"

"Three times over, as they swayed their bodies to the rhythm of the music, they sang the chorus:

"Will you go, will you go, will you go, will you go,
Oh, say, will you go to the Eden above?"

"The question of the verse and chorus seemed like a veritable message of God to me, and in my soul I groaned out, 'If only I knew how to go, how to apprehend this great salvation!'

"A very short scripture lesson was read, by a mere lad, who was acting the part of lieutenant to my old friend Ito.   Then all the people sang again, sang out of the Japanese 'War Cry,' (as the 'Salvation Army' paper, is called.) I confess, friends, I was quite staggered as my eyes followed the printed lines of the hymn—I bought one of the papers. How the people sang! I hardly knew how heartily, and well my own people *could* sing, until I heard them sing that wonderful hymn, which seemed to have been written for me:

> *"With a sorrow for sin must Repentance begin,*
> *Then salvation, of course, will draw nigh;*
> *But till washed in the Blood of the crucified Lord,*
> *You will never be ready to die."*

"There was a wonderful chorus to the hymn which only the saved were supposed to sing:

> *"Oh, I'm happy all the day, now my Saviour I obey,*
> *And I never want to grieve Him any more;*
> *For my Saviour He has washed me in His all-atoning Blood,*
> *And I hope to see Him washing many more."*

"How I longed to be able to say, '*He has washed* ME *in His all-atoning Blood,*' but could not then.

"The next verse was sung:

> *"We've His word and His oath, and His Blood seals them both—*
> *And we're sure the Almighty can't lie——*
> *If you do not delay, but repent while you may,*
> *He will soon make you ready to die."*

" 'And when a man is ready to die,' interpolated Ito, 'he is ready to live.'

"From that thought he drifted into a talk on Salvation. But somehow it did not grip me, and I sat bowed in my soul-misery.

"After his little talk he said, 'My soul assures me there are some here to-night who are longing for pardon and peace. Now, while we are singing, very softly, the third verse of the hymn we were singing just now, let every seeking soul come out here to the front. They tell me, that in England, from whence the Salvation first came to our country, that some people are very shy to kneel down to confess their sins. But we, of grand old Japan, have been accustomed to kneel in our temples, and if we want Jesus Christ, the Sinner's Pardoner, *we* shall not mind coming out to the front, here to kneel, and to seek Salvation. Now, the saved souls only sing, sing it for the unsaved:'

"And that you may succeed, come along with all speed
To a Saviour who will not deny; so kneel down at His feet,
At the blest Mercy Seat, and He'll soon make you ready to die."

"And as they sang, I made my way forward. Ito recognised me, and gripped my hand with friendship's great joy, and with the joy of a Salvation teacher welcoming a convert.

"Others came and knelt near me, but the noise of the Salvationists hindered me. I told Ito this, and he arranged that I should go home with him, and learn God's way in the quiet of his house.

"We were leaving the Hall together, when a man came to urge him to come to the dying bed of a woman. Ito turned to me, saying, 'I cannot, of course, tell how long I shall be, I may have to stay the night, or a large part of it—you see, time is everything in the case of a dying person, and it would never do for me to leave this poor soul until I was assured that she was fully trusting in Jesus Christ. When shall I see you, Tomassi?'

"I told him I would come in the forenoon of the morrow and we parted. I went home, but I could not sleep. All that passed through my mind it is beyond me to recall, I only know that I grew more and more alarmed at my unsaved condition.

"At nine o'clock in the morning, I went to the house of Ito. I found him at work on an exquisite piece of carving. He explained to me that, rather than be a source of expense upon the work of the Salvation Army, he worked at his trade during the first half of the day; spent his afternoons in visiting and 'War Cry,' selling, and his evenings, as I had found him occupied the evening before.

"I asked him about the dying woman he had been sent for to visit, overnight. He told me that about midnight she had entered into God's rest of perfect Peace in Christ Jesus, and that half-an-hour later she died.

"Then turning to me, he said: 'But now, dear old friend, let us get your soul-sickness healed.' He asked me many questions, that he might not only see where I was, as regarded spiritual things but the processes of heart that had led me to the point of inquiry.

"When he heard of my long, deep study of the scriptures, he turned quickly to me, and said: 'Did you never, while thus studying the New Testament, feel the drawing of the Unseen, feel the power of God's Holy Spirit leading you to accept this wonderful gift of Eternal Life in Christ Jesus?'

"I told him I had felt drawn to Chist, as He was revealed to me in the New Testament, but that the lives of the English, who were supposed to be Christians, had thwarted me in seeking Christ for myself.

"He looked at me very sadly, very pityingly, as he said: 'Ah, my friend, it has been with you as it was with the people of old, when Jesus Himself walked among men, so that He was obliged to say to *them, "Ye will not come unto* ME, that ye might have life." And there was another thing which Jesus saw happening to them, that was, that, coming and going, without accepting Him, it became more and more difficult for them to accept.'

"He turned with his sunny smile to me, as he said: 'Do you remember, the night before you sailed for England, years ago, you came to me?'

"I nodded assent. 'Do you remember what I was doing when you came in?' he asked again.

" 'Carving a wonderful piece of cherry-blossom, in a panel of cedar.'

" 'Do you remember anything special that you noticed?' he went on.

"I did remember it, and I told him so, how that, as I came into the room, unannounced, he was so absorbed in his work that he neither saw or heard me, and that I was amazed to see him using the palm of his right hand, for a mallet. Again and again I saw it fall unerringly on the head of the gouge-handle with an evident sureness and firmness of touch in its blows that told of skill and long habit.

"'Ah, you remember well, I see,' he replied, 'and I remember, too, how you said you would have thought that the hand would become quite sore by such repeated blows. I told you, you will remember, that when I first began to use my hand for a mallet (because, in extra delicate work, I was more sure of my touch than I could have been using even the lightest mallet) my hand was so tender that I could scarcely open or shut the fingers. But that, presently, the tenderness wore off, and gradually it became calloused over, so that I could take swinging blows, one after the other, upon a big tool-head, and feel nothing.'

"I began to wonder what all this had to do with the case of my poor, sin-stricken soul. He seemed to divine my thought for he turned to me again, as he went on:

"'What I did with my hand and my tools, you have been doing with your soul and Jesus Christ, and it is what He saw those people doing, nearly two thousand years ago. Let me tell you, dear friend, how it seems to me: In His mission of love and salvation Jesus came to Capernaum. There He healed and blessed, with the pardon of his sins, a man who was palsied, while the *most religious* people of the day watched him enviously.

" 'He was found, soon after this, at table with a custom's-house officer, to whom He had spoken in mercy, and many of the greatest sinners in the place gathered to Him, doubtless hoping to get blessed, too. Again the *religious* people watched and grumbled, yet, in their envy, they persisted in following and listening to Jesus.

" 'Presently, Jesus came to the synagogue, and there He healed a man with a withered hand. But still the anger of the *religious* people increased, though, in this case, they were afraid to speak their thoughts. *"But Jesus perceived the hardness of their hearts."*—and the best, Holy scholars of the Greek, Tomassi, say, that the word *"hardness"* would be better rendered *"hardening,"* making it a *process* and not actually an attained state.

" 'Ah, Tomassi, it is thus that souls so often become thoroughly hardened. Just as the constant coming in contact of my palm, with the handle of my tools, wrought a *hardening* of the skin, until the state of callousness was reached, so that I could feel no pain there, so does the constant coming and going of a soul in contact with the Word of God produce a hardening, and presently a real, invulnerable hardness of heart, if the hearer or reader persistently refuses to yield to its power.

" 'Jesus saw how these religious formalists of His day came and went, and refused His love all the time, until their hearts hardened so that they even hated to see Him shed His mercy on the suffering sinners whom He blessed.

" 'And, to-day, looking down from His throne in Heaven, God sees how men and women come and go to religious services, and hear the pleadings of Jesus Christ by His spirit, and yet refuse to yield the heart and life, and thus they become daily more hardened and self-righteous.

" 'Now, Tomassi, dear friend, you have come to that point, where your conscience tells you that it is God who is calling you. You believe God's Word that you are a sinner, that your sin deserves Eternal death, but that Jesus died for your sin, God accepted His death in your place, and now bids you to believe *on* Him, (Jesus) *in* Him. You know your Bible. What is verse twenty-four of John five?'

"Ito waited for me to reply, and I began to repeat the verse: *'Verily, verily I say unto you—.'*

" *'Whom* does He say that to?' Ito interrupted.

"I thought for a moment, then I said, 'To me.'

" 'True, my friend, then put your name in there, and go right through the verse.'

"I began again: *'Verily, verily, I say unto you, Tomassi, if you hear My word, and believe on Him— God—that sent me,* you *have* everlasting life, and shall not come into judgment; but have passed from death unto life!'

" 'Well,' said Ito, 'is that all true?'

" 'Every bit of it,' I said.

" 'Then what is the result of your taking God at His Word?' Ito's face was full of a great light, a Christ-like passion for my soul.

" 'I have Eternal Life!' I replied. And, friends, in the moment of my confession of faith, God came

into my soul, and I have known Him ever since. I
am but a babe, in Christ, but I am daily learning
more and more, how high and holy a calling is
that unto which I had been called, in Christ Jesus."

The train was slowing up again. For the last ten
minutes they had been running through out-lying
London, but none of them had noticed it, the subject
of the talk had been too engrossing for aught else to
intrude.

Just for the night, until they could arrange their
future, the trio put up at the Charing Cross Hotel.

CHAPTER XII.

A HOUSE WARMING.

WITHIN a week of their arrival in London, Jack and Maggie found a delightful, roomy, old-time house out Hampstead way. Three weeks later they were settled in it.

They had been very eager for Tom to live with them, but while tremendously grateful to them, and full of a secret longing to take the offer, he yet refused.

"Young married people," he told himself, "according to the saying of the English, are best left alone, for the first few years of their life, at least."

To Jack and Maggie, he said: "I should be more continually in touch with your great and wonderful London—as I desire to be—if I go back to my old flat, and the Tube, or a Taxi, will always run out to you in double-quick time, and—" this with a little whimsical laugh—"by not seeing me at every meal-time, that deadly 'familiarity which breeds,' etc, etc, will not rob our friendship of its true sweetness."

He had his way—he had a curious knack of getting his own way; very few people could resist him.

Jack and Maggie decided to have a "House-warming," for, among other things, they wanted to lovingly, boldly witness to their Lord, and, in so doing, per-chance to influence some one or more of the invited God-ward.

Nearly all Jack's friends were more or less Artistic; and Bohemian, to a man. He and Maggie, personally, wrote the thirty invitations, carefully underlining this sentence: *"Bohemian! Come as you please!"*

Over twenty wrote in response to say that they would be delighted to come. Three excused themselves, the other seven were out of England, and did not receive their letters in time to reply.

There was not a dress-suit among the whole crowd. They had readily responded to the word: "Come as you please!" Jack, himself, as the host wore his blue-velvet lounge suit.

Tom wore a comfortable looking jacket and vest that was more Oriental than English, and looked remarkably well in it. He was quite tall, for a Jap, with a face that was more Spanish than Japanese.

The other men, guests, wore lounge suits.

Maggie's appearance charmed everyone. She wore a dress of pale blue in some soft, clinging fabric, with a large bunch of white heather, fastened in her corsage, with a handsome silver thistle brooch.

With her fair Scotch face, and wealth of golden hair, and her tall, graceful figure, every man of the guests admired her, and envied Jack the possession of so charming a wife.

The dinner was a very merry meal, Jack and Maggie as merry as any of them.

Coffee was served in the Drawing Room, where every man of the guests had hurried.

A keen observer would have noticed that the same air of curious, wondering expentancy which had characterised the guests on their first arrival, took

hold of them again on their adjournment to the
drawing room.

"May we smoke, Mrs. Quentin?" one of the men
asked.

"Certainly!" she replied.

"Of course, you do not indulge in a cigarette, Mrs.
Quentin?" came from another of the merry crowd—
for they certainly were a merry lot, in spite of their
curiosity as to the new *role* of their old chum Jack,
and their wonder as to what kind of an evening lay
before them.

"No, I do not smoke, Mr. Talbot," Maggie replied.
Her face was soberer than it had been through all
the time, as she added:

"I feel so sorry for our British women and girls
who have suffered themselves to be so drawn into the
swirl of modern things, as to forget their true maid-
enliness and womanliness."

"*You* are not likely to be enrolled among the
'*New* Women' of the twentieth century, Mrs Quentin?" It was the quiet man of the party who fired
off the question.

"No, Mr. Eustace!" she replied. It looked almost
as if she was going to add something else. But another of the men, not noticing this, said laughingly:

"I heard a rattling good description of the New
Woman, the other day. It was given to me as the
utterance of the great Spurgeon, and certainly it has
what one might call the Spurgeonic ring about it.
Someone asked him what he thought of the New
Woman, and he replied, 'She is a creature who has

forgotten how to be a woman, and who will never learn to be a man.'"

"Sweeping!" ejaculated one of the men.

Most of the men had lit pipe or cigarette, but few seemed to be very keen upon the smoke. Tom and Jack had not shown any signs of indulging. One of the men remarked it, and, addressing Jack, said:

"Is the weed taboo to you now, Jack? Don't you smoke, old boy?"

"I did when I was a man," he said, smiling, "but now I am a child, I don't."

The statement was made so whimsically, that everyone laughed softly. The man who had asked the question, returned:

"Which, being interpreted, Jack, means—?"

"That when I was simply a man of the world, I smoked, after the manner of my kind, but now that I am a child of God, I don't."

His face was radiant with a great, a joyful light, as he swept the faces of the interested group with one long, comprehensive glance.

" Oh, believe me, chums, this new life that has entered into me, that I have entered, and which, I know, is puzzling you all so, is a very glorious, a very real, solid, and absolutely joyous, free-and-easy life. A life which, in point of fact, knows no restrictions, for *whom the Son makes free is free indeed.*' I am free to smoke, if I wish, there is no actual prohibition of it, in the New Testament— for one reason because the use of tobacco does not appear to have been known in those days. Yes, I am free to smoke, if I please, for *'all things,'* that are *not sinful, 'are lawful to me, but all things are not expedient.'* When God found me, made me His child, I felt I should honour Him most by never taking intoxicants, and by never smoking, so I discontinued both, and, thank God, I have never known the miss of them,"

"But there's nothing in the Bible definitely against it, as you say, Jack?" remarked one of the interested listeners—there was a query in his statement.

The Jap answered the query, as, laughing merrily, he said:

"Let me tell a curious little thing. I was converted to God during my recent visit to my own dear land, Japan. The man whom God used to lead me into the light, was an old school fellow of mine, a carver, by profession, and also the Salvation Army officer in charge of the corps nearest to my home. After my conversion I said to him: 'Ito, must I give up smoking? Is there any text in the New Testament that prohibits smoking?"

" 'No,' he said, 'none, that *prohibits* it, but there's at least one that sanctions it!'

"I looked at him puzzled, and said, 'One that sanctions it, Ito, where is it? What is it?'

" 'It is in the Book of Revelation,' he said, 'and it is written: *"He that is filthy, let him be filthy still."* ' "

There was a moment's amazed silence, then a roar of laughter, in which the Jap himself joined.

"And I said," he went on, " 'Right, Ito, then I will not deserve the name, so I'll pitch away my smoking.' "

The merriest of the men sighed heavily, and in a lackadaisical tone said: "Poor mere *we!*"

There followed a lot of merry banter over the subject of the weed, but neither Tom nor Jack said anything further.

A few bars of music broke in upon the chat. Maggie was at the piano. There was instant silence for the men all realized the master-touch on those ivory keys.

For twenty minutes Maggie played, and what playing it was. Every one of the men, who heard her for the first time, was amazed, and there was a perfect salvo of hand-clapping when she, presently, swung round on the music stool, to face her friends.

They besought her to play again. Then, when she had given them another quarter of an hour, and there had followed a chorus of thanks, the quiet man of the crowd, asked:

"Do you sing, Mrs. Quentin?"

Jack answered for her. "Yes, George, she does, and sings almost as divinely as she plays. She never, of course, sings anything racy, but just the dear old Irish, English, and Scotch ballads, and many of our old-time sacred pieces. Many of these sacred pieces she sings to sweet old ballad tunes, for, like me, Maggie counts that all music is sacred, though you may degrade music so that it appeals only to the senses."

One or two of the men nodded assent. And again, George Forester, the man who was, as a rule, dubbed *"Quietly,"* because he was usually so silent, spoke.

"How do you mean, Jack," he asked, "that Mrs. Quentin sings so-called sacred pieces to secular tunes?"

"Killarney, Madge!" Jack nodded to his wife as he uttered the two words.

The next moment the exquisite old air rang out on the quieted room, and Maggie's rich, pure voice sang to it:

> "Jesus, lover of my soul,
>   Let me to Thy bosom fly,
> While the nearer waters roll,
>   While the tempest still is high,
> Hide me, O my Saviour, hide,
>   Till the storm of life is past!
> Safe into the haven guide;
>   Oh, receive my soul at last."

Where, in the Irish ballad, "Angels fold their wings and rest," came, Maggie's glorious voice went back to "Hide me, O my Savior, hide."

She sang the grand old hymn through, amid a profound, a reverent silence. Not a pipe or cigarette but what went out. Not a man thought of smoking. There was a quality that was absolutely new to them all, about this singing. They did not understand it, they only knew that it affected them strangely. The quality that was so strange to them, was that rare thing known, in by-gone days, as "Unction."

There was no clapping, no noisy praise, when the final words:

> "Spring Thou up within my heart,
>   Rise to all eternity,"

escaped her lips. But there were deep-toned, hearty thanks, and the request, "Sing us another of your beautifully-married things, please, Mrs. Quentin."

She struck a few preliminary notes that revealed
the air of *"He wipes the tear from every eye,"* and
then her voice broke forth again into song:

"When I survey the Wondrous Cross."

The hush upon the men was even deeper than before.
For a *third* time they begged her to sing, and
she played over "Robin Adair," singing to the sweet
old air,

"God gave His Son for me,
    Oh, wondrous love!
From sin to set me free,
    Oh, wondrous love!

A guilty rebel I,
Doomed and condemned to die,
He did not pass me by,
    Oh, wondrous love!"

There was not a man present but what was conscious of a new, a never-before-felt mood resting
upon him, so that the transition to the next stage
of the evening came as naturally, as the succeeding
courses of a well-arranged dinner. Just *how* it happened no one could ever have told. But each of the
trio was asked, by some one, some question as to
this new life of theirs, and the whole party became
split up into three little camps, each camp clustering
round one of the trio, while each, in response to
requests from their special camp, told the story of
Redeeming Love of Christ Jesus, as they understood it.

It is safe to say, that, when the evening was finally
over, a more profoundly thoughtful lot of guests never
went home from an unique but thoroughly enjoyable
house-warming.

The exchanged comments of two of them might safely be taken as the general opinion:

"If the world was full of people like those three, there'd hardly be room for the much-talked-of coming Millennium."

"You're right, Teddy, old boy. And it's easy to talk of 'fanatics,' out of their presence, but in their company one feels that they are the sane ones, and that it is we who must be the fanatics, for neglecting the *main* chance,' and for frittering life away as some of us do."

CHAPTER XIII.

IN AN ARTIST'S STUDIO.

AFTER the House-warming, both Jack and Tom began to settle down in earnest to their painting. Each was eager to have the picture of his heart ready for next year's May Exhibition.

Ever since his conversion, Jack Quentin's soul had been conjuring up the details of his "Calvary" picture. Yet, somehow, his mind did not get settled to the thing.

The trio were together, one evening, in the new Hampstead home of Jack and Maggie. Tom was spending the evening with them. The "Calvary" subject somehow became the topic of their talk.

"I wish," Maggie suddenly said, "when your picture is painted, and on exhibit, that in some way every one who goes to see it, might be given a copy of 'In an Artist's Studio'"—She looked at them each in turn, as she said: "You know the beautiful story of course."

"Never heard of it, Maggie, mine!" Jack replied. Tom declared the same. Excusing herself for a moment, she presently returned with a dainty little long-shaped booklet in her hand.

"I believe," she said, "the publishers * could be arranged with to supply a hundred copies for two dollars per hundred, and——"

---

* Biola Book Room, Los Angeles.

"Read it to us, Mrs. Quentin, please?" Tom urged.

Maggie was a beautiful reader, and the two men sat entranced with the story, as she read:

Years ago, a painter stood in his studio, his right thumb in the belt of his blouse, and his left hand holding the pipe he had withdrawn from his lips, in honour of his visitor, Father Hugo, the vicar of the rich Church of St. Jerome. The artist had not yet reached middle age. He was famous in Düsseldorf, and some said that his name would some day be known world-wide. When that day came, Stenburg ruefully thought that he would be past the enjoyment of riches which tarried so long. Still, he managed to enjoy life in the present. He loved his art. Now and again he became so absorbed in his work, that he forgot all else than the picture upon his easel.

Still, though good work he had done, he had as yet never satisfied himself, nor reached his own ideal. His was good work, but he desired something more. Thus Stenburg was not a satisfied man. Otherwise, to the world, he appeared a jolly, prosperous man who displayed, on occasion, a shrewd business capacity, and one who knew his own interests well. He was speaking now.

"No, Reverend Father; the sum you offer would but ill repay me for the labor of so large an altarpiece as you honour me by naming. It must have many figures, all carefully studied. The crucifixion is not an easy subject, and it has been so often taken, that it would be difficult to compose a picture different—as I should wish it to be— from others."

"I will not limit you to the price. You are an honest man, Sir Painter, and the Church of St. Jerome will not pay for the altar-piece. It is to be the gift of a penitent."

"So! that makes a difference. Return, Reverend Father, a month from to-day, and studies for the work shall be ready."

So they parted, both well pleased, and during the following weeks Stenburg studied the composition of the altar-piece, and penetrated into the Jewish Strasse for models for his figures.

Father Jerome was satisfied. He desired the central point of the picture to be the Cross of the Redeemer, and left the grouping of the accessories to the artist. From time to time the vicar dropped in to inspect the progress of the work.

With the bursting of the young green leaves, and the upspringing of the first flowers, a hunger had seized upon the artist's soul to leave Düsseldorf, and with his sketch-book wander over the surrounding country. On the borders of the forest he came one day upon a gipsy girl plaiting straw baskets. Her face was beautiful; her coal-black hair fell in waving ripples to her waist; and her poor, tattered red, dress, faded and sunburnt to many hues, added to her picturesque appearance. But her eyes were the feature that caught the artist's regard,—restless, limpid, black eyes, whose expression changed every moment: pain, joy, fun, and roguery were reflected in their depths as swiftly as the cloud shadows chase each other across a lake.

"What a capital picture she would make!" thought
Stenburg; "but then, who would buy a gipsy girl?
No one!"

The gipsies were looked upon in Düsseldorf with
hatred, and even to this day the fact of being a gipsy
is, in the eyes of the law, a punishable offence.

The girl noticed the artist, and, flinging her straw
down, sprang up, raising her hands above her head,
and snapping her fingers to keep time, danced lightly
and gracefully before him, showing her white teeth,
her glance sparkling with merriment.

"Stand!" cried Stenburg, and he rapidly sketched
her. Quickly as he drew, it was a weary position
for the girl to maintain; but she never flinched,
though a sigh of relief, as her arms dropped and she
stood at rest before him, attested to the artist the
strain the attitude had been.

"She is not only beautiful, she is better—a capital
model. I will paint her as a Spanish dancing girl."

So a bargain was struck. Pepita was to come
thrice a week to Stenburg's house to be painted.
Duly at the appointed hour she arrived. She was
full of wonder. Her great eyes roved round the
studio, glancing on the pieces of armour, pottery
and carving. Presently, she began examining the
pictures, and soon the great picture, now nearing its
completion, caught her attention. She gazed at it
intently. In an awed voice, she asked—

"Who is that?" pointing to the most prominent
figure, that of the Redeemer on the Cross.

The Christ," answered Stenburg carelessly.

"What is being done to Him?"

"Being crucified," said the artist.   "Turn a little to the right. There! that will do." Stenburg, with his brush in his fingers, was a man of few words.

"Who are those people about Him—those with the bad faces?"

"Now, look here," said the artist, "I cannot talk to you. You have nothing to do but to stand as I tell you."

The girl dared not speak again, but she continued to gaze, and speculate. Every time she came to the studio the fascination of the picture grew upon her. Sometimes she ventured an inquiry, for her curiosity consumed her.

"Why did they crucify Him? Was He bad, very bad?"

"No; very good."

That was all she learnt at one interview, but she treasured each word, and every sentence was so much more known of the mystery.

"Then, if He was good; why did they do so? Was it for a short time only? Did they let Him go?"

"It was because——" The artist paused with his head on one side, stepped forward, and arranged her sash.

"Because," repeated Pepita breathlessly.

The artist went back to his easel; then looking at her, the eager, questioning face moved his pity.

"Listen. I will tell you once for all, and then ask no further questions;" and he told her the story of the Cross— new to Pepita, though so old to the artist, that it had ceased to touch him. He could

paint that dying agony, and not a nerve of his
quivered; but the thought of it wrung her heart.
Her great black eyes swam in tears, which the fiery
gipsy pride forbade to fall.

The altar-piece and the Spanish dancing girl were
finished simultaneously.   Pepita's last visit to the
studio had come.   She looked upon the beautiful
representation of herself without emotion, but turned
and stood before the altar-piece, unable to leave it.

"Come," said the artist, "here is your money, and
a gold piece over and above, for you have brought
me good luck; the 'Dancing-girl' is already sold. I
shall want you some time perhaps again, but we
must not overstock the market with even your pretty
face."

The girl turned slowly.

"Thanks, Signor!" but her eyes, full of emotion,
were solemn.   "You must love Him *very* much,
Signor, when He has done *all that for you,* do you
not?"

The face into which she looked flushed crimson.
The artist was ashamed. The girl, in her poor faded
dress, passed from his studio, but her plaintive words
rang in his heart.   He tried to forget them, but
impossible. He hastened to send the picture to its
destination; still he could not forget, *"all that for
you."*

At last the pain was not to be borne. He would
face it and conquer it. He went to confession in
vain, to get the peace he longed for, and which can
only be found by faith in Christ alone. A liberal
discount on his picture gave ease of mind for a week

or two. But then up rose the old question, "You must love Him very much, do you not?" and *would* be answered. He grew restless, and could not settle to his work. So, wandering about, he heard of things which had not come under his notice before. One day, he saw a group of persons hastening to a house near the walls, a poor place; and then he noticed others coming in the opposite direction, and they, too, passed into its low doorway. He asked what was happening there; but the man he questioned, either would not or could not satisfy him. This aroused his curiosity. A few days later, he learned that a stranger, one of the "Reformed," lived there—one of those despised men who appealed on every occasion to the Word of God. It was hardly respectable, hardly safe, even to know them. Yet, perhaps, here, he might find that which he sought. The artist had heard how these Reformers risked, and frequently parted with their all, for the truth they held. They might possess the secret of peace. So Stenburg went to observe, perhaps to inquire, certainly not to join them; but a man cannot approach fire and remain cold. He saw a man who might have lived in ease, enduring hardship; one who might have been honoured, despised; who might have been beloved and respected, an outcast; and yet serene, even happy. This Reformed preacher spoke and looked as one who was walking the earth with Christ; yes, one to whom He was all. Stenburg found what he longed for—*a living faith.* His new friend lent him for a time a precious copy of the New Testament; but, hunted from Düsseldorf, after a few weeks, he left, and had to take the book with him; but its essence was left in Stenburg's heart.

Ah! no need to question now.   He felt in his soul the fire of an ardent love. "Did all that for me! How can I ever tell men of that love, that boundless love, which can brighten their lives, as it has mine? It is for them, too, but they do not see it, as I did not.

"How can I preach it? I cannot speak. I am a man of few words. If I were to try, I could never speak it out. It burns in my heart, but I cannot express it—*the love of Christ!*" So thinking, the artist idly drew, with a piece of charcoal in his fingers, a rough sketch of a thorn-crowned head. His eyes grew moist as he did so.   Suddenly the thought flashed through his soul, "I can paint! My brush must proclaim it.   Ah! in that picture His face was all agony. But that was not the truth. Love unutterable, infinite compassion, willing sacrifice!"

The artist fell on his knees, and prayed to paint worthily, and thus speak.

And then he wrought. The fire of genius blazed up—up to the highest fibre of his power; nay, beyond it.   The picture of the Crucifixion was a wonder—almost Divine.

He would not sell it. He gave it, a free-will-offering to his native city.   It was hung in the public gallery, and there the citizens flocked to see it; and voices were hushed, and hearts melted as they stood before it; and the burghers returned to their homes

knowing the love of God, and repeating to themselves the words written so distinctly beneath—

>"All this I did for thee;
>What hast thou done for Me?"

Stenburg, also, used to go there; and, watching,
far back from the corner in the gallery, the people
who gathered about the picture; he prayed God to
bless his painted sermon.   One day he observed,
when the rest of the visitors had left, a poor girl
standing weeping bitterly before it. The artist approached her.

"What grieves thee, child?" he asked.

The girl turned; she was Pepita.   Oh! Signor
if He but loved me so," she said, pointing to the
face of yearning love, bending above them, "I am
only a poor gipsy. For *you* is the love, but not for
such as *I;*" and her despairing tears fell unre-
strained.

"Pepita, *it was also all for thee.*" And then the
artist told her all. Until the late hour at which the
gallery closed, they sat and talked. The painter did
not weary now of answering her questions, for the
subject was the one he loved best.   He told the
girl the story of that wondrous life, magnificent
death and crowning glory of resurrection, and also
explained to her the union that redeeming love
effected. She listened, received, and believed. "All
this I did for thee."

Two years had passed since the picture had been
ordered. Winter had come again.   The cold was
intense, and the wind moaned down the narrow

streets of Düsseldorf, and shook the casements of
the artist's dwelling. His day's work was done, and
by the blazing pine logs he was seated, reading a
copy he had with difficulty obtained, of his beloved
Gospel. A knock sounded at the door, and a man
was admitted. He wore an old sheepskin jacket, on
which the snow had frozen; his hair hung in dark
locks about his face. He glanced ravenously towards
the bread and meat upon the table, even as he gave
his message.

Would the gentleman come with him on urgent
business?

"Where?" said the painter.

That he must not tell, or the agents of the law
might get to know, and drive them out. It had
often so happened before.

" Wherefore do you wish me to come?"

"I cannot say," replied the man; "but one who
is dying wants to see you."

"Eat!" said the artist. "I will accompany you,"
The man murmured his thanks as he devoured the
food.

"You are hungry?"

"Sire, we all are famished with hunger."
Stenburg brought a bag of provisions. "Can you
carry this?"

"Ah! gladly, gladly. But come, there is no time
to lose."

The artist followed. His guide led him quickly
through the streets, and out into the country beyond.
The moon rose, and showed they were nearing the
forest. They passed into it. The branches were

laden with snow, and the great crowded trunks con-
fusing. No path, but the man never hesitated. He
silently and swiftly kept ahead of Stenburg. At last
they came to a glade belted round with trees. Here
a few tents were erected.

"Go in there," said the man, pointing to one of
the tents, and then turned to a group of men,
women, and children, who thronged about him. He
spoke to them in a wild tongue, and lifted his bag
from his shoulder.

The artist, crouching, crept into the tent. A
brilliant ray of moonlight illuminated the poor interior. On a mass of dried leaves, was the form of
a young woman. Her face was pinched and hollow.
"Why, Pepita!"

At the sound of the artist's voice the eyes opened.
Those wonderful dark eyes still were brilliant. A
smile trembled to her lips, and she raised herself on
her elbow.

"Yes," she said, "HE has come for *me!* He
holds out His hands! They are bleeding! 'For
thee.' '*All this I did for thee.*'" And she bade him
farewell.

Long years after both the painter and the gipsy
girl had met in another land, a gay young nobleman drove in his splendid equipage into Düsseldorf;
and while his horses were baited, wandered into that
famous gallery. He was rich, young, intelligent—the
world was bright, and its treasures were within his grasp.
He stood before Stenburg's picture arrested. He
read and re-read the legend on the frame. He could
not tear himself away,—it grew into his heart. The

love of Christ laid its powerful grasp on his soul.
Hours passed; the light faded; the curator touched
the weeping nobleman, and told him it was time
to close the gallery. Night had come,—nay! rather
for that young man, the dawn of Eternal Life. He
was Zinzendorf. He turned to the Inn and re-
entered his carriage, but to turn his back on Paris,
and seek again his home. From that moment he
threw life, fortune, fame, at the feet of Him Who
had whispered in his heart,—

> "All this I did for thee;
> What hast thou done for Me?"

Zinzendorf, the father of the Moravian Missions,
answered that question by his devoted life and his
welcomed death.

Stenburg's picture no longer hangs in the gallery
of Düsseldorf, for when some years ago the gallery
was destroyed by fire, it perished; but it preached,
and God used it to tell of His gift—Calvary's
Substitute— of Whom Paul said, "He loved me and
and gave Himself for me."

CAN YOU, READER, SAY "AND FOR ME"?

Just for one full half-minute no one spoke. The
story, in itself, was touching, arresting, but Maggie's
reading had invested it with a wondrous power.

Jack was first to break the silence. "If God,"
he said, softly, reverently, "would let me paint my
Calvary so that one soul were led to the Christ of
the centre of my three crosses, the Christ of God, I
could fain cry with Simeon, of old, '*Lord, now lettest*

Thou Thy servant depart in peace.' For soul-winning
seems all that one wants their art for, now."

For a few minutes the trio talked on over the
wonderful work of "Stenburg," then Jack dropped a
bomb in their midst.

"Maggie, how would you like to go to Palestine,
to the Holy Land?"

"Why, Jack," she cried, "whatever put such a suggestion as that into your head?"

"Because," he returned, "it is borne in upon me,
that I shall never paint with the surety which I like
to feel, as to detail, unless I make my costume,
facial, and other studies on the spot of my proposed
'Calvary'."

Maggie was delighted beyond measure, at the
prospect.

"Will you come, Tom?" Jack asked.

"No, Jack, I want to study faces, costumes, and
character, etc., in this great London of yours, for I
want my picture to be twentieth century, up-to-date."

A week later Jack and Maggie were gone, eastward.   Tom missed them tremendously, but threw
himself with increased energy into his painting.

He spent most of his time, when he was out of
the house, walking London's thoroughfares, looking
for a face—a woman's—for a model.

One night he had sat reading until half-past ten,
then feeling altogether unlike sleeping, he put on his
hat and coat, and went out for a long walk. This
was a favourite practise of his, at night, for he found
the air, and the exercise, the best of all soporifics
for a wakeful brain. Beside, he was always saying

to himself: "I may find the face I want among the night-birds whom I pass."

It was an hour later, half-past eleven, and just physically tired enough to welcome his bed, he turned to go home. Suddenly he came almost face to face with a woman who entered the thoroughfare he was travelling, from a street that intersected his, on the left.

The woman was tall, fair, with a mass of beautiful hair. Her face was very lovely, but very sad—it was a Madonna face. The stamp of birth and breeding was upon her, in spite of the hideous fact that she reeled slightly, the effect of "drink."

Tom was almost excited enough, over the find of "his face," to speak to her at once. But Prudence caught his eye, and he held his peace, contenting himself with following her, as she moved along with that slight reel and lurch in her gait.

Presently she paused in front of one of the few old-type coffee-houses which, in London, keep open all night. Diving her hand into her pocket, she raked about for a second or two, then appeared to find one coin—the watching Tom thought it was a penny.

She entered the Coffee-House. Tom followed her. The shop appeared to be empty. The woman took her seat in one of the boxes into which the ground floor was divided. Tom passed into the box immediately opposite—there was only an aisle between the two boxes.

A slip-shod girl shuffled along the sanded floor to the table where the woman had seated herself. She was evidently known to the waitress. There was a little whispered confab between the pair, and Tom heard the woman say:

"It's all I've got left to-night, Jenny!"

"All right, my dear, I'll fix yer up all right," the girl replied. Then, turning to Tom, she said:

"What kin I git yer, sur?"

"Oh, a cup of tea," Tom replied. He was not used to such a house, and never supposed it would be possible to consume any viands supplied amid such seemingly malodorous surroundings, yet felt compelled to order something to give him time to study the face of the woman he had followed.

"I kin make yer a fresh pot o' tea all ter yerself, fur freppence, if yer likes, sur!" the girl suggested.

"Do!" he replied. Then, as the girl went away, his eyes travelled across that narrow sanded aisle that separated the two tables; and he tried to sketch, in the book he had taken from his pocket, the face of the woman in the opposite box.

But the light was so poor, and the woman herself kept nodding in a state of semi-drunken slumber, that he was compelled to give up the attempt.

A moment or two later the waitress brought a cup of tea and a plate of thick bread and butter, to the table opposite, and, rousing herself, the woman began to drink thirstily from the thick-lipped cup.

Tom's tray now came. He tendered a two shilling piece. The girl bit it between her teeth, nodded an assurance at him, and was diving for change in the canvas pocket that was suspended round her waist, beneath her apron.

"Keep the change!" he said, quietly.

The girl stared amazingly at him for a moment, then, with a grin that practically cut her face into two halves, she said, with an almost fervent rapture:

"God bless yer, sur, fur a kin'hearted gent, an' may yer never know wot it is to be down on yer luck' or in want o' a two-bob bit yersel!"

"How about that poor soul over there?" he asked, in a whisper, and indicating the woman in the opposite box. "Would she accept a good meal and a pot of tea? Dare I offer it?"

"*I* could git her to take it, sur," the girl replied.

Tom Kavanagh laid half-a-crown down on the edge of the table, as he said:

"Give her the best you have, of that which you know she likes—and keep the change."

"Lor' luv yer, sur! I wish there wur a few mill'ns more like you in Lunding, the poor 'ud love the rich mor'n they does now."

The girl hurried away, and in five minutes was back at the table where the Magdalene-faced woman sat. The tray contained cold ham, pickled onions, a pot of tea, a roll, and a thick slice of cake.

There was another little whispered confab between the woman and the waitress, then the latter left the table, flashing a triumphant look at Tom, as she passed him. Tom had the satisfaction of seeing his neighbour, in the box opposite, enjoying the ham and pickled onions.

He poured out half a cup of tea from his own pot, and ventured to sip it, for appearance's sake. He was surprised to find how palatable it was.

Under cover of reading a very soiled copy of the
Referee, that had been hanging over the high, wooden
back of the seat, he watched the woman until she
had finished her meal.   He heard the sigh of re-
pletion that broke from her lips, as she pushed the
tray aside, and with a much-soiled handkerchief carefully wiped her mouth, and dusted the few crumbs
from the front of her dress-body and lap.

Then, just how it happened he could not quite
tell, their eyes met.   She smiled and made a little
graceful inclination of her head, as though in ac-
knowledgement of something.   Then rising to her
feet, he supposed she was going to leave the shop.
But she crossed to where he sat, and taking a seat
opposite to him, said:

"Permit me to thank you, sir, for your hospitable
thoughts of a stranger, a woman, and one in trouble.
I have enjoyed the meal exceedingly; and the
pickles and tea combined—two articles of food
which either singly or in combination, always have a
distinctly sobering effect upon a person in drink—
have done much to sober me, though my poor
brain never seems wholly clear nowadays; because, I
suppose, I am never really sober, for each waking day
sees me doing what Holy Writ speaks of, when it
says: *'The dog returns to his vomit, the sow to her
wallowing in the mire.'* "

She sighed, and he, wondering much at her voice,
so musically sweet in spite of the roughening effect
which the drink had made upon it, and equally
wondering at the correctness of her speech, and the

frankness of her confession, began to disclaim any
title for thanks.

"Why did you do it, sir?" she asked. "I am a
perfect stranger to you. Is it that you are a Christian, of that all too rare a type, who sees in every
needy person someone upon whose head, metaphori-
cally, you can break a box of spikenard, very costly?
Love, true love to God, and to the needy of the earth,
is more costly than rubies or diamonds, because it is
much more rare."

She lifted her face to his, and, for the first time,
he realised how wondrously beautiful and expressive
were her eyes. Then, while he still marvelled at her
language, she went on:

"You wonder, I see, at this style of talk from
the lips of a woman whose breath, before she ate
those pickled onions, was heavy with the foul odours
of gin and beer. But I knew something of divine
things, years gone by; and the one thing we never
forget—if we really learned it—is the Bible, and the
truths our mothers taught us as children."

He was wearing his hat, for there was a strong
draught through the shop; he doffed it as, with a
bend of the head, as reverent as any gesture of
worship ever made by man, he said, gently:

"I am a Christian, it is only recently that I became converted, but I am not sure that it was
because I am a Christian, that I ventured to send
you that little snack on the tray. I will be perfectly frank and honest with you. Though I did it
out of a kindly fellow-feeling, I should not have

realised your need of the meal, if I had not followed you for another purpose."

She looked sharply towards him, and there was a flash of suspicion in her glance.

"I had no evil intent in following you," he said, quickly, anxious to allay the suspicion of ulterior motives he saw that he had aroused in her.

"I am an artist," he continued, "here is my card—" He laid the card, he had taken from his pocket, down upon the table.

She took it up, and read its superscription, then gave him another searching glance. She uttered no word and he continued:

"I have a picture almost finished, but I am waiting for a face for my canvas, a woman's face, of a certain type of beauty. For weeks I have been searching everywhere for that face, but have come no where near the type I need. To-night, you came up a side-street into the Edgeware Road, just as I was passing along, and in a moment I knew I had found the face I wanted. I followed you, hoping that, somehow, I might get speech with you, and induce you to give me a sitting or two."

"Your picture is not of a Magdalene?" she cried, sharply, adding, with the eagerness of self-justification: "For though I have been foolish enough to give way to drink, my life has been otherwise absolutely pure."

He answered her that she had no need to fear about the character in which he desired to paint her. He treated her, and addressed her with such perfect, gentlemanly deference, that it won her confidence, and they talked long and earnestly.

"Let me help you," he said, "back into a truer life. I *can* help you, if you will help yourself. Let me help you, as a fellow in the great human family to which we both alike belong; let me help you as I would have helped my own sister, had I had one, and if she had got into the same trouble that you have."

A low sob broke from her; she was evidently deeply moved.

To give her time to recover herself, he went on:

"Come and see my picture, to-morrow, and judge for yourself. You need not commit yourself to any promise to sit to me, until you have seen my canvas. I have said come *to-morrow*, but *to-morrow* is to-day, since we are already in the small hours of the morning. Come any time to-day, forenoon, afternoon, or evening; I will not go out until eight o'clock to-night."

Taking a sovereign purse from his pocket, he slipped the slide back, and dropped two of the golden coins into the palm of his other hand, her eyes fixed upon his every movement.

As he replaced the purse in his pocket, and lifted his face, their eyes met. He saw the inquiring wonder in hers, and smiled, as he said:

"Some people might think me a fool, for doing what I am about to do, but I am as certain, as I look into your face, that I can trust you, as I am certain of my own purity of motive in dealing thus with you."

He laid the two sovereigns down before her.

"Take this," he said, "and get all that you need to make yourself as presentable as you yourself may please."

His voice grew grave, as well as eager, as he went on:

"Do *this for your own sake*——"

He paused, an inquiring look was in his eyes. She rightly translated it as an inquiry for her name, and replied:

"Millicent Burn, is my name!"

"Miss or Mrs.?" he asked.

She sighed a little sadly, as she replied:

"We'd better say *Miss*, since I have missed my way in life, somewhat."

Humouring her as to the prefix, though he thought that the more mature of the two titles would have been nearer the truth, he went on:

"Take the money, Miss Burn, and for your own sake, and as a first step in a new career, spend it as you please, only, I need scarcely say, let no part of it go for drink."

For one moment she gazed at him out of her great blue eyes, then, with a sudden burst of tears, she laid her face upon her crooked arm that rested on the table, and wept bitterly.

He watched the heaving of her shoulders as her deep emotion shook her, and his artist's eye noted the shell-like beauty of her ears, the silky texture of her lovely hair, the exquisite lines of her neck. His mind was full of wonder over the whole personality of the woman. She had already proved herself so strange a mixture.

He let her weep without interruption for several minutes. Then, as six or seven noisy market men entered, and she sharply lifted her head, he leant across the table, and whispered:

"Would you rather that I should walk with you, a little way? We could probably talk freer, now that this noisy crowd has come in."

"And you would not be ashamed to be seen walking with me?" she said, in an astonished voice. "Remember, I am known, *by sight*, to all the police!"

"No I am not ashamed to be seen with you, Miss Burn," he replied; and, rising to his feet, he watched her as she placed the two sovereigns in an old purse; then, preceding her, they walked out into the street.

It was getting on for one o'clock, and, in that neighbourhood, it was comparatively quiet.

Tom noticed that, in her gait, his companion showed no signs of the semi-inebriation she had exhibited when he first had met her. The combination of vinegar (pickles) and tea, is notorious for sobering the intoxicated, as she had said, and this had probably sobered her to the degree of steadying her gait.

Tom noticed a policeman stare hard at him, in evident surprise at whom he was companioning with. But Tom only smiled quietly to himself, as he passed on, for there had grown up within him a strong, fixed purpose to, if possible, reclaim this lovely-faced woman from the vice that had gripped her.

"She will tell me, some day," he mused, "how it came about that she became enslaved to this devil—drink. And when she does, I shall find that it was no mere vulgar, sordid story, but something which has in it the pathos of a mighty sorrow."

They came, now, to the corner of a very quiet, retired sort of a street. She turned the corner, and he followed her. A dozen yards down she paused, and turning to him, said:

"I want a moment's quiet with you, sir, before we part, just to say, as solemnly as I know how to speak, that I vow to you by the memory of my dear dead mother, that I will not betray the trust you have shown to me. I will not touch drink, to-day, sir, though the denial of self may mean the suffering of Gehenna's flames within me.

"I am going home, sir, to my miserable, one-room lodging, that I may sleep off the effects of what I had drunk before I met you. Then I will expend the money you have given me, in the best way I know, and I will call and see you and your picture, at three-o'clock this afternoon, sharp; and, before I see your picture, I will promise you a first sitting, to-day, if you wish it."

She paused a moment, and then with a sigh of intense regret, added:

"I hardly know how I dare to take God's sacred Name upon my lips, yet the only language that seems possible to me, is the language of that sweet, old, all-comprehensive prayer: 'God bless you,' sir! Bless you for all your true-hearted gentleness and fellow-feeling as shown to me to-night."

She turned her great blue eyes, shining with tears, full upon him, as with a bow of greatest grace, she said, quietly:

"*Au revoir,* until this afternoon."

He offered her his hand, as he said, "Good-morning," to her.

The gathered drops that hung on her eye-lids fell splashing on the bosom of her dress, as she saw his outstretched hand.

"Perhaps," she said, in grateful tones, "perhaps, *some day,* if ever I feel I am fit to touch your hand, I will take it, but, meanwhile, I thank you for this further proof of your chivalry, of your true gentle-hood, and real charity and sympathy of spirit."

Then, with a sad little smile, and the quietly-uttered words: "Till three this afternoon," she bowed again, and left him.

He walked slowly, thoughtfully homewards, musing as he went:

"I have found the perfect face I wanted. But how about the poor creature that owns it? 'Call me *Miss,*' she said, and the despair in her eyes, at that moment, told how fully she realised all that she had missed by her fall."

His brain was almost too excited to sleep, when he reached his chambers. However, after a time, he did get off. He slept then until eleven in the forenoon. Then he began to wait eagerly, almost impatiently for three o'clock to come.

CHAPTER XIV.

"OH MINE ENEMY."

MILLICENT BURN slept until ten o'clock then awoke with the drink-thirst upon her, and began to dress swiftly, that she might hurry down to the public-house, at the corner of the street.

Suddenly, she paused in her dressing; her mind had recalled, in a flash, all that had passed in the early hours of the morning. With sudden recalling, every incident of her meeting with Tom Itoi, came back to her, every word he had said, and her own vow, taken in association with her mother's name returned to her.

Reaching her shabby dress, she felt for her purse, and opening it, took out the two sovereigns, and held them in the palm of her hand.

"It is like money sent direct from Heaven!" she murmured. Her eyes filled with tears, and lifting the glittering coins to her lips, she kissed them as reverently as the Continental "Catholic" kisses his *"Christus."*

"He did a Christ-like deed," she murmured, "and it would almost seem as though he was bent upon my actual salvation from the awful curse that enslaves me."

She laved her hot, flushed face, her neck, her shoulders, and her beautifully-formed arms, for the drink had inflamed her blood as well as her face.

Then when she had fully dressed, she went out, bent upon making some purchases that should completely transform her outward appearance.

Forty shillings in the hands of a woman who knows her London, will go as far as a ten-pound note would go in the hands of another woman, and Millicent Burn knew *her* London well.

But every step of her way, whichever road she took, was set with traps, baited with bait dug up from hell itself; and her poor, drink-inflamed nature hungered, thirsted, lusted for just one draught of the poison that had cursed her life, of late.

The fighting and battling against the craving was fierce enough to drench her with perspiration. Then, passing a grocer's, the strong, fragrant odour of freshly-ground coffee assailed her sense of smell.

"If only," she began. Then, as her eye took in the fact that the shop next to the grocer's was an eating-house, she hurried into it, and begged them to make her a pint of strong, black coffee.

It came in a few minutes, and, drinking it greedily, she quickly felt the better for it, and went on to make her purchases.

It was half-past one before she returned to her miserable home, then locking herself in her room, she began another fearful battle with the lusting, craving for the drink.

"God help me!" she cried, again and again. And though she knew nothing of saving grace, or of communion with God, He surely heard her cry, for the awful paroxysm passed away, and, spent and breathless with the fierceness of the fight she had passed through, she lifted herself, at last, from her bed, upon which she had flung herself, face downwards, and now began to lay out her purchases, ready for donning.

"Who knows," she murmured, "but what this may be the real beginning of a new life? With this strong, kindly human hand to help me, I may—*may* perhaps have power to overcome the awful habit that has come into my life to curse it."

With an uplifted eye, and with a fervency of utterance that told of her true soul-agony, and of her real longing for deliverance, she cried out once more:

"God help me!"

She grew calmer, she grew hopeful, and an impatience to see her would-be saviour, began to consume her, and she began her preparations for her visit.

A smile filled her face, as she murmured:

"I believe so fully that this is going to be the beginning of a new life to me, that, as far as I can, I'll begin it without a rag of my old clothes."

Full of this purpose she bathed her whole body, then taking some underclothing from one of her drawers (the garments having lain unworn for two years or more, relics of a happier life and day), she began to dress. There was a perfume hanging about the clothes as she unfolded them, that brought crowds of sweetly-sad memories back to her mind.

Before she put on the newly-purchased, good second-hand dress she had brought in with her, she extemporised a dressing-cape, and letting down her glorious wealth of bright golden hair, gave it a long and careful grooming, and arranged it in as simple and striking a style as was possible with such a mass as that which crowned her head.

When she had finally finished her toilette, she sallied out into the streets. That she might escape the sight and *scent* of the public-houses which she must inevitably pass, she took an omnibus to the nearest point to her destination.

CHAPTER XV.

UNDER THE SAME ROOF.

WAKING so late in the forenoon, Tom went out to a neighbouring restaurant, for what little breakfast he cared for. His chambers were the two floors above the offices of an Agency.

Tom, himself, occupied the *first* floor, and a compatriot of his had occupied the floor above him. But his chum and country-man had just returned to Japan, and Tom had both floors on his hands. He had decided not to let the upper floors again, unless he was approached by some very desirable tenant.

A charwoman came in the mornings, to clean up his rooms, and he took his meals at a restaurant. For an hour or two, he was too pre-occupied to realise the fact that the charwoman had not been that morning. Some little domestic trouble, probably, had hindered her, such things had happened before, it mattered little, for Tom was thoroughly domesticated.

The hours moved slowly to him. A curious impatience was upon him. The face of Millicent Burn lived before him, and he wondered what manner of woman she would appear, when sober. Once, for one brief fraction of a second, a flying doubt darted into his mind, as to whether she would come. He acknowledged to himself that the two sovereigns he had given her might prove her overthrow. But it was only for an instant that the doubt had lodg-

ment, the next moment his trust in her asserted itself,
and he smiled confidently.

He worked almost feverishly, trying to kill the
time, and allay his impatience. At two o'clock he
dropped his palette and brushes, and began to think
about luncheon.   Then a new thought occurred to
him. He would wait the arranged hour for her arrival, and have luncheon for *two* sent in. "There's
nothing," he mused, "like a *tete-á-tete* meal together,
for putting two comparative strangers at their ease,
one with another."

It wanted ten minutes to three, when his door-bell
rang, and, excited as a school-boy, he ran down to
answer the summons.

The change in Millicent Burn's appearance almost
startled him.   There was the same wondrous Ma-
donna-like face, and great blue eyes; the same
wealth of golden hair; the same exquisite figure, but
how much more beautiful it all was than when, a few
hours before, he had seen her semi-drunken, and dishevelled.

He was in the act of greeting her, standing in the
open door-way, when a little rabbit of a girl of eleven
thrust herself before him. "Plese, sur," she began,
"muvver kyant kum to clean up your rooms no
more, kos she've got the chronics an' hev been took
to 'orspital, an' my sister, wots fif'een her nex' birth-
d'y 'll kum roun' bum-bye fur the few shillin's wot's
doo muvver, an' wont yer plese ter giv, me a penny fur
meesel' fur comin' roun' ter tell yer?"

Tom laughed at the cuteness of the child's last
remark and request, gave her a few coppers, and

uttered a few words of kindly sympathy, then, as the child raced away, he closed the door, and led Millicent Burn up to his studio.

His eyes, turning upon the model. told all the story of the wonder he was feeling at the change in her appearance. In reply to his wondering astonishment, she said:

"Thanks to your gift of the two sovereigns, the transformation was possible."

"And to your own effort of will, Miss Burn." The smile on his face, as he replied, made his strong, Spanish-featured face look very handsome.

"The power of *a new hope,* is what you ought rather to say," she corrected, "and the hope came from the same source as the sovereigns."

The unuttered thought of his heart was: "How different her speech, even the *tones* of her voice are, compared with last night!"

He excused himself for a moment or two, that he might order the *two* lunches. He did this over the 'phone, in the ante-room.

Returning to the studio, he found her standing before his picture, a look of rapt, delighted admiration in her face.

"It is very wonderful!" she murmured, softly, as he advanced to her side. "Surely," she went on, "it is great, will be greater when it is finished, and should make you famous!"

"I am hoping it may teach, rather than it should make me famous. And now that I have found your face, a belief that almost amounts to a certainty, has taken possession of me, that the picture will sufficiently attract to fulfil the mission it is intended to.

"But I am forgetting my duties both as artist and host," he continued.

He pointed to a door in an angle of the studio as he added: "You will find a little sitting-room there, it is reserved for the use of my models. Will you not take off your hat and jacket, by which time lunch will be on hand."

He caught sight of the surprised protest that was shaping in her face, so he hastened to say:

"There is nothing like a *tete-á-tete* meal to help people to know each other, besides which it always seems such a saving of time, since you kill two birds with one stone—you take your necessary meal, and you talk over the business in hand, at the same time."

Millicent looked at him, and sighed softly, as she thought: "There's no resisting this man!"

She passed on into the sitting-room he had indicated. Returning, a few minutes later, she amazed him still more, for, without her hat and jacket, her beauty and grace were enhanced ten-fold.

The meal which followed, soon began to be a very pleasant one, for both of them. *He* was delighted to note how perfectly well-bred all her table-habits were. And *she* felt all the pleasure that comes to a well-bred person who, after long separation from the nicer refinements of life, is suddenly brought once more in touch with them.

During the meal, some chance allusion to their first meeting, led her to say—and her cheeks filled with colour, as she spoke:

"I fear that there must have been much that was bold and unladylike in my speech and manner then, for strong drink is a fearful degrader."

Her eyes filled with tears. "God help me!" she continued. "For I am as weak as water whenever the odour of the drink assails me. I can never explain to you all I have suffered since I awoke at ten o'clock this morning. I wanted a drink then, but I recalled my promise to you, and with a desperate fight overcame the desire. I went out to make some purchases, and at every yard or so a public-house, with its hideous fumes, greeted my senses, and, oh, the fight was awful. I went back to my room, locked my door and there began an awful fight with the fearful desire.

"Men, preachers and others, and writers upon the subject, scout the idea of there being anything akin to demon-possession in these materialistic days. Let such pass through the experience I did this morning, they will change their key.

"I called upon God, again and again, and surely He must have helped me, for, at last, I overcame."

The look in her eyes, as she turned them up to his face was so intensely pathetic, that it moved the heart of Tom Itoi, as not even tears would have done.

"If I am really to overcome this hideous besetment," she went on, "I must change my lodgings; I must find a neighbourhood— if that be possible, in

this city of temptations—where one may walk at least
a few hundred yards, without the sight and smell
of those awful drink-hells."

Tom's mind worked swiftly at all times, and while
she had been talking, he had been. rapidly maturing
a plan of help to her, and of some assistance to
himself.

"Miss Burn," he said, as she finished, "it has occurred to me, as you were speaking, that we might
be of mutual assistance to each other, if you could
see your way clear to drop into line with a plan I
have thought of."

She looked up eagerly, questioningly, at him, as
he spoke.

"Above this floor, where we are now sitting," he went
on, "is a suite of three rooms. I rent them. They
were occupied by a lady journalist, before I came;
and, since I came, they have been occupied by a
young country-man of mine, who has now returned
to his own land. They are comfortably furnished, and
only need the feminine touch to make them cosy as
cosy."

He noticed how her eyes flashed around the room
where they were sitting, as he spoke of the "feminine touch." He laughed, in acknowledgment of the
look, as he said:

"Your glance is a true one, Miss Burn. This room
too, needs the 'feminine touch'."

She smiled—how a smile transfigured her beautiful
face—but let him continue his proposition.

"Now, this is what I propose. Occupy those rooms
upstairs, come in as soon as you please, to-day, even,

if you like. You will be as cut off from the other
part of the house as though you had a detached
cottage to yourself. Sit to me for my picture, and
not for this one only, but for others, I hope. I
will pay you a certain sum in advance; this will en-
able you to make any additions or embellishments to
your rooms, and also to start your housekeeping. All
this will give you an entire change of surroundings
—this, in itself, will be a help in the fight you have
already put your hand to—you will be living, too, in
a healthy neighbourhood, where you can walk freely,
by taking certain routes, without fear of coming
across those houses so full of snares to you. This
plan will mean, too, helping me in my work, while it
will, I believe be a real bulwark of strength to you.
What do you say, Miss Burn?"

"Say?" her voice choked as she essayed to answer
him. "What can I say, except that your proposition
is of a piece with all that you have said and done
to and for me, ever since I set eyes upon you, twelve
hours or more ago."

She caught her breath in a quick little sob, then, re-
covering herself, she said: "I must however make
one stipulation, that is that you permit me to take
charge of your rooms. I, of course, overheard all
that that child said about her mother's inability to
come to do your rooms any more. Now I am strong,
thoroughly domesticated, and shall not only delight
in doing all that that poor woman did, but could
easily cook for you, to a large extent, certainly your
breakfast and supper, and your lunch and dinner if
you will let me. But these other matters   we can

settle as the days go by, but unless you allow me to clean your rooms, and care for them generally, I will not fall in with your plan at all."

She had her way. Tom saw that her suggestion would in many ways, breed within her, among other things, that sense of responsibility, and general interest in things, that would make for a healthy mind.

Forty-eight hours later saw the whole plan an accomplished fact, and Millicent Burn, with strong womanly purpose, and with fresh hope burning within her, made an accomplished housekeeper.

The very morning after she had settled into the rooms, the sittings for the picture began. His long-deferred hope of finding the model he wanted, being now so fully fulfilled, he worked with an almost feverish rapidity, and with a sense of real inspiration.

The days moved swiftly on, every hour proving how fully Millicent Burn was worthy of the redemption upon which Tom had set his heart. While, at the same time, to the woman herself, the new life of hope that had come to her, had transformed her, daily, into a more wondrously beautiful creature, for her soul, save for its declension through the snare of the drink, was naturally chaste and refined, and now more and more, day by day, began to shine out through the glorious lustre of her exquisite face and eyes.

When Tom had put the last stroke to his picture, and he looked at it, he knew that he had completed a great work, which he did not think Fame, with all her proverbial fickleness, prejudice, and coquetry, could fail to smile upon.

Millicent, who was in the room, and who had learned the meaning of every changing expression of his face, read all the great hope that now filled his soul.

"It is *great!*" she said. "Great enough, I believe, to compel the Critics (who, after all, are Fame's mouth-pieces) to acknowledge the genius in the picture."

"I believe it, Millicent. Yet I feel so intensely desirous that my picture should preach, should fulfil its mission, that I could welcome the banning of my work by the critics, if only its message might reach, and teach souls."

He had uttered her Christian name all unconsciously, and for the first time. And, turning his eyes back again to his picture, he missed the almost rapturous light that filled her eyes, and the hot, swift colour that flushed her cheeks, at his use of the "Millicent."

"Yes, I do believe, Millicent," he went on, "that the picture will be a success. And when the success comes I shall have to acknowledge, as I do now, that a large share of it belongs to you; since, without the inspiration of your really marvellous face, I could never have crowned my picture, as, through you, I have done."

She made no reply. She could not trust herself to speak.

He celebrated the completion of his picture by an evening that became quite a festive time.

The life the pair were living was a strange one, if judged by the ordinary conventionalities of life. But it seemed perfectly natural to them both, for it had almost seemed as though influences, outside themselves, had shaped the unconventional arrangement.

Had Jack and Maggie been at home, it would probably have been all very different, for they—Maggie, at least—would have urged the conventionalities.

Tom had told the pair, in his letter, that he had found his long-desired model, but that letter had been written in the forenoon after he had met Millicent. The momentous meeting, of the afternoon, had not then taken place. Tom was not great at letter-writing, disliked it exceedingly, and had not written his two friends, since.

To Millicent Burn the days became as days of Heaven upon earth, her life was an Eden, where no serpent-voice of her special temptation ever came near to her. While, to Tom, the exercise of her womanly influence upon all his life, and upon everything that made up his surroundings, was very pleasant.

His delight in her evident reclamation from the drink was unbounded; while the effect of her wonder·ful personality upon him was, already, much more powerful than he actually realised.

Dropping, at first, unconsciously, into the utterance of her first name, Millicent, he now never called her anything else, and she had grown quite used to it.

She had done the hundred and one little things in his rooms that a man's bachelor apartments would suggest, to a woman, the need of being done— to a woman, we mean, who, with a love for home, has the taste and ingenuity for the true adornment. And Tom *felt,* as well as saw, the improvement in his surroundings.

Two factors which helped to bring about more fully the close, pleasant relations into which the pair had so imperceptibly, to themselves, glided, were the facts, *first*, of her dwelling under the same roof with him, thus bringing them within constant touch of each other, and *second*, the equally powerful factor in the case—the absence from town of almost everyone of his visiting acquaintance.

And now a new feature to their companionship began to be added to all that had gone before. They gradually got into the habit of spending their evenings together. He would read to her, while she worked at some needlework. They discussed together the books they read, and often he would contrive to turn the conversation into spiritual channels, for he had a deep anxiety for her soul's salvation.

Up to the present, Millicent's soul had seemed to grasp very little of divine things. But Tom sowed in hope, remembering that "God giveth the increase."

They had spent a fortnight of these associated evenings when something happened that accelerated matters between them.

CHAPTER XVI.

FACING FACTS.

TOM had to decide the most crucial question he had ever been called upon to decide, save when he decided for God. And, to do this, he wanted to be alone.

"I am going out, Millicent," he said, on the day in question. "I do not expect to be more than a couple of hours. Sit here, if you prefer this room to your own."

She answered him very quietly: "Thank you, I will." He passed out of the room, little dreaming how she was feeling.

"Prefer this room to my own?" In her excitement, she could almost have screamed the words. "As though, compared to my own apartment, every nook of these rooms was not as heaven to me. Everything I look upon here, everything I touch, is all associated with him."

When she was quite sure that he had left the house, that she was quite alone, and that she dare give vent to her feelings, she went to where a cabinet photograph of Tom stood on a miniature easel. Long, and ardently, she gazed at the pictured face, two great tears splashing down as she returned the card to the easel.

Returning slowly to her seat, she dropped wearily into it, tears falling from her eyes as she sobbed:

"My darling! You must never know what, all unwittingly, I have dared to do! How that all my heart has gone out in deepest love to you!"

She lifted her head, suddenly, with a startled look in her eyes, for, swift as thought can be, there had flashed upon her the temptation to fly away, to somewhere where she would neither see or hear him.

Then she laughed, low and painfully, as she murmured:

"But I could not, I could not! Perhaps my love has made a coward of me, but I could not live now, I think, without seeing him, for he is dearer to me than life. And yet—yet—."

A shiver went over her, as she added:

"And yet of course, I can never hope to be loved by him, even if I stay. He is kind, he is brotherly, he *has* done, and *is* ever doing, all and more than any brother would do for me, but he can never love me, of course."

She shivered again, for the full memory of all her past swept over her, and, with a thick sob, she cried:

"Our lives must ever be sundered as far as the poles. He so strong and pure, a very Bayard, and I, so lost and drink-cursed until his eye pitied me, and his strong arm dived down into my special gutter, and lifted me up."

She lifted her eyes heavenwards, as she cried:

"God bless and reward him, and give me strength to bear my load, in silence."

With a cry of passionate pain, she spread her hands abroad, as though in entreaty, as she cried, piteously:

"Oh, my love, my love! You must never know. I will suffer in silence, and yet it will not be all suffering, since the sweetness of seeing you, of hearing your voice, of being able to serve you, will be mingled with the bitterness.   Oh, Tom, Tom! My love, my love!"

With a heart-breaking sob, she dropped upon her knees, and buried her face in her hands, on a cushion of the couch.

       *   *   *   *   *

Alone, in a retired path of the Park, Tom was facing the question which had forced him out from his rooms.

While Millicent Burn had been supposing that all his *special* kindness, of late, had been born of a great brotherliness, he knew that it had been the outcome of a feeling infinitely warmer, and the questions had forced themselves upon him: "How is all this to end?   What are my exact feelings towards this lovely woman?

"Is it *love* that I *feel* towards her?" was a question which insisted upon being answered.

"Is it possible," he mused, "that the love of my manhood's love is given, at last, to a woman?"

And every throb of pulse, and beat of heart, and thought of his brain, answered his question in the affirmative, and he knew that he loved his *protégée;* while, deep within his soul, there spoke the conviction, that, though, as yet, he had not heard the story of

her past, save for her lapse into the drink-habit, she
was wholly worthy of his love.

So powerfully was he impressed with the double
conviction, first, that he could not live—to be happy—
without her love and life companionship, and next,
that she was wholly, utterly worthy of him, that,
with the eagerness of a boy, almost, he hurried from
the park, and sped straight home, saying, to himself:

"I must settle this matter, at once."

He had told her, before he left the house, that he
would not be more than *two* hours. It was actually
under the *one* hour when he reached home. He let
himself in with his own key.   He passed up the
stairs, thinking:

"I wonder what she is doing in my absence?
something useful, I'll be bound."

The desire to see her before she saw him, to look
upon her through the eyes of his newly-acknow-
ledged regard for her, was upon him, and he made
his way quickly up the carpeted stairs.

Before the door of the room, where he had left
her, there hung a light curtain, that, gently waved
by the light air that moved through the house,
acted as a kind of punkah to the room, the door
itself being set wide back on account of the close-
ness of the weather.

He had left the door wide open. It was so now.
There was nothing between him and the woman he
loved, save that light fluttering curtain.

He paused a moment on the mat outside, amazed
to hear the sounds of sobs within. Silently he lifted

the curtain aside, and stood in the door-way, where
he could command a sight of the whole room.

Through one of the windows that faced the west,
the glory of the sunset streamed, and in the centre
of that glowing warmth of light, stood the woman
of his heart.   Every thread of her robing, every
line of her face, every golden thread of her lovely
hair, was steeped, was bathed in the glorious light.
It etherealised her; it transformed her wondrous
beauty into something beyond the human.

Yet, upon her face, and in her great blue eyes,
there was an expression of agony great enough tc
move the heart of a stoic.

He heard the mighty sob that broke from her, he
saw how it shook her whole frame, and her every
word reached him, as she cried:

"Our lives must ever be sundered as the poles. He
so strong and pure, a very Bayard; and I, so lost,
and drink-cursed."

He saw her as she lifted her eyes heavenwards, to
where God's glorious ambassador-sun made glad and
warm all the western heavens. He heard her cry of
passionate pain, saw her stretch her arms abroad, and
spread her beautiful hands in a gesture of half-a-
bandonment and half-entreaty, and her tones of agony
wrung his soul, as she cried, piteously:

"Oh, my love, my love! you must never know. I
will suffer in silence! And yet it will not be all suffering, since the sweetness of seeing you, of hearing your
voice, of being able to serve you, will be mingled
with the bitterness. Tom, Tom, my love, my love!"

With another heart-breaking sob she dropped upon her knees by the couch and buried her face in its cushion.

The sunset light, warmer and deeper, flooded all her bowed figure, every line of the pose of which told of her sorrow.

If Tom had never loved her before, his pity for her, at that moment, would have turned to love. With a swift run he cleared the space that parted them, and bending over her, lifted her to her feet crying: "Millicent! dear love! nothing shall ever part us. I love you, as you love me!"

She gazed at him in a kind of dazed, fearsome wonder. The shock of joy almost robbed her of her powers of comprehension.

His eyes searched hers, and he laid his lips upon hers.

His kiss recalled her to full consciousness. Her cheeks flamed like a rose. Her heart, where it lay against his, throbbed so that she could scarcely breathe. Her eyes gazed rapturously into his.

"I went out this evening, Milly," he whispered, only that I might be alone to think out whether I dare ask you to be mine, whether I dare tell you all my love. For you are so wondrously fair, my love, that to possess you, to possess your love, seemed almost more than I dare hope, or expect."

"And yet," she cried, obliged to find her voice, "all that I am to-day is what you, what your love has made me."

She broke into a torrent of grateful, loving explanation of all that he had been to her, and all the life of love he still was to her.

He listened in wondering silence as he realised the marvellous gift of speech that love had suddenly given her.

In this moment of her great bliss, the very sense of the greatness of his love, helped her to remember to be wholly righteous to him, and she said:

"But, my darling, you have not heard my story. You do not know who I am, where I came from, or what my past has been. You found me wandering half-drunken in the streets of London, at an hour when all respectable women would have been in bed. You offer *me—me* your love; you put your whole future happiness into my keeping when you ask me to be your wife. But, oh! my darling! let me tell you, that though to lose your love, or to be driven from your presence would, it seems to me, be the death of me, yet I dare not promise to marry you until you have heard my story."

For answer, he drew her into a closer sweep of his arms, and as he kissed her, he cried, between his caresses:

"You shall tell me your story, Milly, but nothing that you can say will alter my love for you, or change my purpose to make you mine!"

Her gaze met his. Love such as this would have been beyond her powers of belief, only that the *trust* of a love like hers is equal to every strain put upon it.

He drew her towards a wide arm-chair. He would have seated her in it, but, with an adroit movement, she contrived to seat him in it, while she dropped down upon a footstool at his feet.

Just for one moment the pair were silent. Then, as he let his hand rest lightly upon her gathered-up golden hair, he said softly, tenderly:

"Tell me your story, Milly, but believe me. dear, I do not ask you for it; I do not need you to tell me one word; and I would rather that you were for ever silent, if the telling is to pain you."

"Were the pain to be greater than was ever given to any mortal to bear," she replied, "I would yet persist in telling you, dearest, for it is due to you, and it is equally due to myself."

He bent down over her, and they exchanged caresses, and she began her story:

CHAPTER XVII.

"A TALE HAVE I TO TELL."

"MY earliest recollections," she began, "are of a
beautiful villa home in Italy, in a suburb
of Rome. My father was an Austrian, a reputed
wealthy man. My mother was Scotch, very fair,
very beautiful, and very, very gay until I was seven
years old. Then, when travelling alone, with a maid
and myself, in Austria, she met in a hotel, where
we were staying, a countrywoman of her own, whose
influence led my mother to face the great question
of God's claim upon her, with the result that she
gave herself wholly up to living the divine life.

"For two years she lived on, ever growing into a
life of sanctity, such as it seems to me now, as I
look back, none ever lived more fully before, and
certainly I have never met anyone since who lived
half so holily.

"Then there came a day, when, climbing one of
the lesser Hungarian Alps, she slipped and hurt her
spine. She was borne home, by slow stages, to Italy,
a helpless invalid!

"Two years and-a-half after this, she died. After
mother's death I grew up lonely and unloved, for my
father never showed me one atom of affection. I
soon shewed signs of developing into a beautiful
woman—there is no vanity in my saying this, seeing
that everyone told me the fact. When I was fifteen
and a half, my father introduced an Italian gentleman

to me, a Count Paulina, who, from the first night of his introduction, began to make love to me.

"I disliked him very much, had a strange *physical* shrinking from him, so that I used to feel myself shudder whenever he came near to me. Then, one night, he told me he had my father's consent to marry me, and wanted to know how soon I would wed him.

"I was horrified. Remember, dear, I was not sixteen years old—."

She paused, and a little shiver passed over her; she lifted her eyes piteously to Tom's face, as she cried:

"I need not detail all the horrors of those days. It must suffice to say that there was repeated in my life, an old, old story of a child terrorised into doing her father's will, and I was married before my sixteenth birthday.

"If ever my husband had had any real affection for me, it soon died, and certainly he never showed it. One night, seven months after we were married, when he was the worse for drink—for he was a hard drinker, I found—he dragged me from my bed and flogged me unmercifully, flogged me until I swooned.

"I was ill, scarcely ever conscious for two months, the unconsciousness caused, I believe, by being drenched with powerful French Brandy every two hours. When, therefore, I did slowly return to life, I was always in a semi-dazed condition. I knew, afterwards, that I was purposely kept in a semi-intoxicated condition, by my husband's orders. Just his reason for this, I cannot tell, unless it was to kill me off, without putting himself within reach of the law, he believing that the little legacy of my mother's property, which had come to me, was much larger than it really was.

"In the midst of this hideous plot, my husband committed suicide, to save himself from the law. Taking advantage of the unknown whereabouts of the real Count Paulina, he had cleverly personated the absentee, and had succeeded in entering into possession of the estates. But the rightful heir suddenly turning up, a warrant was issued for my husband's arrest, he fled, was run to earth, and poisoned himself rather than be taken.

"I managed to reach England—for my father had died when I had been married a month—I travelled to Scotland to some relatives of my dear mother's. But we did not get on together. They had lived close, cramped lives, they were hard sour folks, who made life, for me, a burden.

"Through that hideous drenching of my system with brandy, I had imbibed a love of drinking,. I drank secretly; was discovered by these people, cast adrift, and—well, since then, I have lived the life of a more or less drinking woman, until, you, my darling, found me, and brought into my life the one thing necessary for my salvation—kindness and love.

"I lived on the thirty shillings a week derived from the little estate left me by my mother. I lived, I say; that is I found means, out of it, to keep a roof over my head, food just sufficient for me, the rest I spent in drink.

"Men on the streets troubled me, at first, because of my looks, but I soon learned to take care of my-

self, and the men learned that it was unwise to
meddle with me. It is all a very sordid story, dear;
but I dared not keep anything back from you. Now
you know who and what I am, now—."

It was his voice that finished the sentence she
had begun.

"Now!" he cried, and there was a sob in his
throat, as he spoke. He bent over her, lifted her
bodily in his arms, and cradling her thus, kissed her
again and again, the pitying tears that fell from his
eyes bedewing all her lovely face.

"*Now!* you are mine, dear love," he cried, "and
life will be all too short for me to give you peace
and joy and love, for all the past that you have
suffered."

He held her close to him in silence a moment,
then gently added:

"I knew, my soul assured me that you had been
more sinned against than sinning. My poor darling!
How you have suffered!"

Half-an-hour later, he said suddenly: "Milly, dear
heart! When will you marry me? It must not be
long, dear!"

"When you will, Tom!" she said, softly.

"This day week, then, Milly!"

She lifted herself in his arms, so that she could
really see his face. Then, as she saw how serious he
really was in his proposition, she gave a little gasp
of astonishment, as she said:

"I thought you were joking, dear, to talk about it
being in a *week*. I thought you would have said
six months!"

"*Six months!*" he gasped. "No, no, Milly! It must not be more than a month, at the outside."

It was finally settled so.

When they had parted for the night, he sat for a long time silent, immoveable, wrapped in a deep thought. He sighed, at last, as he murmured:

"Not twenty-three yet! Yet, oh how she has suffered! What she has gone through!"

As he sat on in the semi-darkness—the only light that came into the room, was from a street lamp outside; they had not troubled to light the gas in the room—his mind was busy with many thoughts. The chief of these thoughts was as to her soul. He longed to see, to know that God's claims had fully gripped her, that she was truly saved, and surrendered to God.

It was curious that neither of them appeared once to have thought of the matter of "mixed marriage." It was equally strange that to Tom, with his deep love for the precepts of the Pauline epistles, there had not, as yet, appeared to have come the memory of the command: "Be ye not unequally yoked with unbelievers." One can only suppose that in these first days of excitement of love, he lost the fine edge of communion with his Lord.

CHAPTER XVIII.

CAN THERE BE CURSE IN A KISS?

THREE weeks of the month had passed, and as the day drew near for their wedding, the hearts of the pair grew very buoyant. Both of them were very busy, but there was a constant mirth in their hearts, and a song often on their lips, when they were at work alone.

To-day, Millicent had been out most of the day, shopping; she was thus spared the pain of witnessing the physical agony of her lover, as he writhed in the throes of an attack of some kind of colic.

Tom was glad, in a sense, that he was alone, for he could ill have borne to see the distress which his pain would have caused his *fiancée*.

There had been a period in his life when these attacks had been somewhat frequent, but he had not had one now for a couple of years.

He had been accustomed, in the attacks, to take a dose of a very powerful mixture, which he kept in a stoppered bottle in a small cabinet in his studio, and now, when the paroxysm was at its worst, he remembered the mixture, and staggered to the cabinet to get it.

He found the bottle, but it was empty; and now the agony grew unbearable. He had a decanter of brandy, locked in his cellarette. Crawling to the polished oak case, he unlocked the door of it, and in a moment he had drunk a deep draught of the raw spirit from the neck of the bottle.

Very rapidly he grew easier, and presently the attack passed off, and he decided to take a turn in the Park, since the fresh air would help to restore him, now that the paroxysm had passed.

Bathing his head and face, and changing his coat, he prepared to start, leaving a note upon the small table, in the corridor outside the chambers, addressed to his fiancée, saying that he had gone out for an hour, but that he would be back by that time.

His note written, he went to the sideboard, where he had stood the brandy decanter, and, pouring out a very small wine-glass full, he drank it off, as an additional ward-off against another attack.

He had got as far as the outer door of the corridor, when Millicent appeared, having just come up the stairs. He explained how fearfully ill he had been, how he had just taken some brandy, and was now going out for an hour.

"I won't be longer, my darling," he added, as, taking her in his arms he kissed her good-bye, his lips lingering long and caressingly upon hers.

A moment later he was gone.

Millicent stood just where he had left her. Rigid and silent and tense, she might have been cast in bronze, so still was she. Only in her eyes was there any sign of anything unusual about her. A sudden, fearful lust had leaped to birth in her. Desire, passionate desire, filled all her face; an eager yet frightened look was in her eyes.

She drew her breath in sharply, and the spirit of the fiery draught her lover had taken, rushed hot and poisonous through her frame.

Standing there, with all her being trembling with an awful excitement, her fingers clasped and unclasped themselves in a quick, nervous way. The movement of the fingers grew fiercer, quicker. The blood coursed madly, hotly, through all her veins; and in her eyes there crept the stealthy look of some panther who scents its prey.

She was beside herself. The fiery breath of the spirit-odour she had drawn into her system with that long, lingering kiss from her lover's lips, had stirred the slumbering devil of drink within her, and she lusted for brandy, as the fabled vampire lusts for blood.

All thought of everything else, for the time, was lost to her. Not a memory of aught save the hunger for drink was left to her in that awful moment.

She glanced around the room her lover had just left, and her eyes lighted on the decanter and glass, just where he had unthinkingly left them.

An unholy light flashed into her eyes. She almost leaped across the room, the decanter was in her hand —then she remembered the past, and, with a shuddering cry she put it down again.

Why did not some warning impulse prompt her to smash the thing, and let the deadly, tempting fluid run away! Because, even when she had put the bottle down, she knew it was there. One outstretch of her arm would reach it. And all the time there was a fiery lusting burning through all her veins—this she could *not* destroy.

Millicent, Millicent Burn! Poor tried, tempted soul! Why did you not hurl that bottle from the window, into the yard below, then cast yourself upon your knees, and your poor tempted soul upon God?

It is so easy, in cold-blooded safety, for us to pen these questions! It is easy for the reader, especially the dogmatic reader, the pharisaical reader, to ask the same questions, and to burn and blister the character of the poor tried soul with self-righteous blame. But it is quite another thing to feel the flames of a very hell of lust in your veins, driving you on whither you would not, when the fire of desire eats up all caution, saps all wisdom, swamps all thought, save the thought of delight which the one draught of the Forbidden thing will bring!

In the abject misery of mind, in that one moment of recalling, she cried:

"I will put the decanter away. I will lock it up. Then I will go to my own room and lock myself in."

She seized the decanter, knelt before the cellarette, the door, which was ajar, telling from whence the spirit had been taken. She had got the cut-glass thing half-way through the door, she was trembling in every limb with the excitement of her fierce desire. In her haste, unnoticed by her, the diamond fringe work of her silk neck scarf, hitched underneath the stopper of the decanter, and hauled it out.

The fumes of the fiery spirit floated upwards to her nostrils; it drew the water of fierce desire from the corners of her mouth; she——

Death is said to be cruel, though it is often merciful; but the drink-demon is hellish in its cruelties. The demon got a hold upon all Millicent Burn, at that moment, and gripped her every sense. He laid his hellish hand to the axe, and the axe to the root of the tree of all her new-found life and joy—and struck it all.

It was all done in a moment. She took her first draught, then——

*   *   *   *   *

Tom had felt weak and shaky after two hours of such physical agony as he had suffered. The hour in the open air, however, had done him a world of good, though his head felt a little dizzy from the effects of the brandy he had taken; for he was a most temperate man, and never used intoxicants of any kind, save for medicine, when unable to lay his hands on a medical remedy.

As he drew near home he looked at his watch, and smiled in anticipation, as he murmured:

"I shall be home by the time I said I would, and Milly will have got the coffee-water boiling. A strong cup of coffee will help to put me right from the effects of that beastly brandy."

He gave a sudden start, as he asked himself:

"What did I do with that decanter? Did I put it back in the cellarette, or did I——?"

He uttered an exclamation of regret and annoyance, as he added, a distinct note of alarm in his voice:

"What a careless fellow I am! I left that brandy out on the sideboard! Who knows, who can tell

how the sight, the smell of it, may have tempted
poor Milly!"

He quickened his pace. "God grant——."

The prayer was never finished, as regards the
words. He reached the door; let himself in; and
with a sense of fear and foreboding upon him, he
raced upstairs.

His first glance into the room filled him with
horror. Millicent was lying upon the floor; her face
was drink-flushed; her wealth of golden hair loosened
and dishevelled; her dress disarranged, her beautiful form asprawl.

"Oh, God! Forgive me!" His cry rang through
the room with all the horror of a death-wail.

In that moment, when all his hopes seemed shat-
tered at one blow, he took all the blame upon himself; he could find no thought of blame of her.
The tears of a strong man's mighty grief filled his
eyes, and fell splashing upon her dress, as stooping,
he lifted her in his arms, and bore her to the wide,
comfortable couch.

With the tender touch of a mother laying her
little one to rest in its cot, he made her as comfortable as he knew how, with the pillows and cushions.

But the movement had partly aroused her; and
opening her eyes, she muttered, in maudlin tones:

"Itsh no use to try—didn'tsh meansh to do itch—
his faultsh—he kiss-h me witsh hish brandy breathsh
—thatsh woke the sleepinsh devil-sh in me — he
leftsh his brandysh outsh—triedsh to putsh it away
—stoppersh fell outsh—an I fell in—I thinkshs, an'—

The line of a Music-Hall song evidently came to her poor brain, and she gurgled, out of tune:

> "Oh, it wash beautifulsh!
> Absolutely beautifulsh! (hic)
> I never feltsh so swhimmy in my lifesh—
> It wash—wash—(hic)—."

The doggerel was never finished; she passed again into a slumberous, drunken doze.

Tom sat beside her, horror-stricken, conscience-stricken. He gazed on the face he loved, and as he saw how different it was now from what it had been, months before, when he first found her, he murmured, brokenly:

"Mine was the hand that wittingly, designedly, set about her salvation, and mine also was the hand which, all unwittingly, has cast her down into the slough of her old habit."

The anguish of his soul in that moment was truly awful.

"Dear heart! My Millicent! My love!" he cried, sorrowfully. "Even in your unconscious babblings you have given me the key of your fall, so that I know that what was meant for a love-caress proved after all, a curse to you. God forgive me for my blundering!"

For a time he sat, silent, dealing with God, and letting God deal with him. After a time, his eyes travelled to the face of his sleeping *fiancée*, and he softly prayed:

"And when my overtried loved one wakes, dear Lord, let not shame and discouragement hurl her back into despair. Oh, give to me the power of a

love so great that she shall lift up her head again!
And above all let her learn to trust herself wholly
to Thee. Teach us each to make Thee, and Thee
only, our trust."

Her lips moved as she mumbled something. He
lifted his eyes to her face, but could not catch any
meaning to her mumble.

She rolled partly over, and was then lying in what
he knew must prove a cramping, uncomfortable posture. With all the tenderness of some mother with
a sick child, he lifted her into a more comfortable
position.

For another quarter-of-an-hour he sat by her side.
Her breathing was heavy and stertorous, her sleep
grew deeper. Thought was very busy with him, and
his self-blame was very bitter. At last he rose to
his feet, his face full of a stern resolve.

"Cost me what it may, *socially*," he muttered, "I
will never again touch the thing that can do this
deadliness to one so lovely, so otherwise pure. *Personally*, it will not inconvenience me to forswear the
damnable stuff; *socially*, it may, in some measure.
But the souls of men and women are worth more
than conventionalities, more than personal or social con-
veniences."

He gave one more glance at his sleeping *fiancée*,
then, with a stern, set, pale face, he picked up the
decanter from which she had drunk, and, carrying it
away to a sink where he washed his brushes, etc.,
he poured the brandy that was left, down the sink,
rinsed the decanter, and turned it upside down to
drain. While it was draining he fetched another

decanter, and sundry bottles from the cellarette—
liquors, liqueurs, etc., and drained them away also.

As the various fiery liquds ran away, the memory
of a picture he once saw, crossed his mind. The
subject of the picture was "Searching the Leaven,"
and represented a Jewish family at Passover time,
with the head of the house searching every cup-
board and shelf, every nook and corner, for even a
crumb of bread, cake, biscuit, etc., containing leaven.

The same spirit which actuates the pious Jew at
Passover, in his search, filled the young Japanese,
now, in his search for, and clearance of every drop
of alcohol. Only 'when he was assured that there was
not one drop left in the place, did he desist from his
work.

Returning to the side of his *fiancée's* couch, he was
startled by the powerful, spirituous odour that filled
all the place.

"This is awful!" he cried. Why, if the smell of
my breath was sufficient to arouse the slumbering
taste in my darling, what would the atmosphere of
this place be like to her, if she woke now?"

As though to emphasise his fear, Millicent roused
herself at that moment, and, sitting upright for a
single second, she then staggered to her feet, before
he could check her.

Some half-recognition of him came to her, and, in
a maudlin way, she tried to embrace him, as she
said:

"Wantsh some brandish! Can't live w'out the
brandish!"

Too unsteady upon her feet, at first, to do as she would have done—embrace him—she made a false grab, caught only at the air, and plumped down in a sitting posture on the floor.

Lifting her to her feet, he tried to lead her to the couch again.

She did not seem to notice him, her sense of sight, all her senses, in fact, seemed suddenly to be absorbed in the one—the sense of smell. She sniffed the heavily-charged, spirituous atmosphere of the place, as a desert beast will sniff the coming rain-storm, or the bush stock-horse will scent a far distant water-hole.

No other sense was present to her, save the strong lusting for a drink of the damning curse that had got her once more in its temporary, but horrible grip.

"Millicent, Milly, my darling!" With his arms about her, he tried to induce her to lie down again upon the couch. "Try and sleep, dear, you are not well, and sleep will serve you best, now."

But breathing-in the alcohol-charged atmosphere of the place, her whole being was animalised, demonised, and she struggled to get free of his arms.

She made no noise, she did not yell, or shriek, but she fought for her liberty; raging physically, and ravening with foaming mouth.

A fearful battle began. Tom had heard and read that epilepsy and drink-madness alike gave supernatural strength to their victims. Now he proved it; for, strong man that he was, the raging, struggling woman *almost* overcame him several times.

For nearly twenty minutes the battle lasted. Then, with a sudden burst of tears, Millicent's strength succumbed, and panting, and flushed, with torn disordered clothes, and her long, beautiful hair loosened and flying, she suffered herself to be lifted on to the couch.

In her gasping, breathless, hiccoughing speech, she pleaded that he would hold her in his arms.

With his eyes full of tears of pity, he held her, until she finally fell into a deep sleep.

For a full hour he held her thus, then when he could bear the cramp of his position no longer, seeing how deep her slumber was, he gently released his clasp of her.

CHAPTER XIX.

A BITTER AWAKENING.

NIGHT had closed in! London's roar grew fainter, and, silent and sad, Tom sat beside the couch, watching, by the light of the lamp he had lit, the beautiful, but drink-flushed face of his *fiancée*, his mind, the while, full of thoughts of many things.

As the night advanced, he lit the spirit stove, and placed a kettle of water over it, then laid the table for a meal.

"Strong coffee will help her most when she wakes," he told himself.

It was four in the morning when the awakening came. Even London, in some parts, at least, can be beautiful at dawn. And now birds sang; the earth glowed with light; and all the trees of the park clapped their hands to greet the coming of the new day. The clock of the universe had struck the day-hour, and the new day, catching its cue, sprang to the horizon-stage, and, led by the sunlight, to the liquid music of a feather-throated orchestra, it made a pageant all its own, as it marched across the wide earth, the pageant growing stronger and brighter each step it travelled.

"A new dawn! A new day!" the watching Jap murmured. "God grant that the parable may extend to my darling's life."

There came a movement from the couch, followed by a deep sigh, and, in a moment, he was kneeling by the side of his awakened *fiancée*.

"What is it, Tom? Where——?"

Her eyes wandered round the room, and she recognized where she was.

"What has happened?" she asked.

Then sudden, awful realisation came to her, and with a fierce shudder that shook all her frame, she gave a low, agonised cry.

"You have been ill, my darling," he said, and his voice was very tender. "You will be better now. I want you to have a cup of coffee with me, at once. Excuse me one moment while I make it."

She had covered her face with her hands, and did not see him go from her side. But, a moment later, the smell of the fragrant coffee pierced her senses, and with the raging thirst that filled her, she dropped her hands from her face, just as he returned to her side.

The flush of a great shame filled all her face, as her eyes met his. There was nothing but tenderness and love in his glance, and it filled her with a wonder that was almost great enough to thrust a little farther back the shame that was overwhelming her.

"Come and drink a cup of coffee, Milly!" He put his arms about her and lifted her to her feet as he spoke.

Just for one instant her gaze was fixed upon his face. Then, with another shuddering cry, she dropped her face upon his breast, and wept heart-brokenly.

He let her weep, assured that it would do her good.   Presently he bent his head and kissed her brow, and whispered:

"Forgive me, Milly, my darling, for the awful injury I, all unwittingly, did you!"

She lifted her tear-bedewed face to gaze wonderingly at him.

"*You* ask *me* to forgive you, dear Tom? What can you mean? Surely it is I who should ask forgiveness, then crawl away out of sight of your face, and die out of the way of all temptation."

For answer he wrapped her in the tenderest of embraces, and kissing her hot, trembling lips, said:

"It was my unguarded folly and thoughtlessness, Milly, that brought all this trouble and suffering upon you."

She began to protest, but as he had proved himself stronger in that physical battle—which, fortunately, she had evidently completely forgotten—so his mighty love for her, and his deep, sorrowful realisation of his own share in her fall, made him strong enough to overcome all her objections now.

When, with a sigh, and with eyes streaming with penitent and grateful tears, she was at last forced to give in, he persuaded her to drink one cup of coffee before going to her room to have a refreshing wash.

"Then, when you have bathed your face, dear," he added, "come back here, and we will have an early breakfast, and then we can talk."

As she left him, to do his bidding, he took her for a moment into his arms, and kissing her tenderly, he said:

"Don't stay away from me long, Milly!"

In twenty minutes she returned. The change in her appearance was marvellous, though there was a shamed, drooping look about her, all unlike her usual self.

Tom recognised this, and set himself to work to remove the last trace of it, even though his heart quickened with pleasure as he saw how deeply her slip had affected her.

"If she were not a true girl at heart," he told himself, "she would not so fully feel her position."

Neither of them ate very much at their early meal, but both drank several cups of the strong coffee.

When they had finished, he arose from his seat, and walking across to her, slipped his arm through hers, saying:

"Let's go into the studio, Milly, and have our chat."

She went quietly with him, and as he sat with his arm about her, he began to urge that he should get a license, at once, and instead of waiting until the end of the week, as at first arranged, that they should be married on the morrow.

"But, Tom," she cried, "I am not worthy! I have surely proved that to you, already, by this awful, disgraceful fall. You would always mistrust me."

He smiled tenderly down into her face, as he replied:

"Once you are mine, dear, I shall have no mistrust of you. I have no real mistrust of you now, for I have learned some lessons during the night that has just passed, that have taught me many things, about myself, as well as what temptation means, things which have proved as startling as they were new to me. And I say this reverently, and with shame for my careless folly, Milly, my darling, that I consider myself wholly responsible for the trouble which came upon you."

He bent over her, and kissed her again as he went on:

"Now, not another word, dear one. You will let me have my way about the immediate marriage, will you not?"

She had been gazing with tear-filled eyes up into his face, and now as he waited for her reply, she suddenly wreathed her arms about his neck, crying:

"Do as you will, dear! I have neither the right nor strength to resist you. I am yours—and——"

A low sob choked her, for a moment. When next she spoke, she said:

"I *must* know God, and *His* power to keep. You have tried to make me seek Him fully, dear Tom, but I have been too satisfied with my reformation and too absorbed by my great love for you, and yours for me. Perhaps, dear, God has suffered me to fall, that I might the quicker realize my own weakness and helplessness."

Some mutual impulse drew them to their knees.
All that passed during the next hour is almost too
sacred to be spied upon. But when the full hour
had passed, Milly, very humbly, whispered, more to
God and to herself:

> "I am my Beloved's,
>   And my Beloved's mine,
> He brings a poor vile sinner,
>   Into His house of wine;
> I stand upon His merit,
>   I know no other stand,
> Not e'en where glory dwelleth
>   In Immanuel's land."

For awhile longer their talk was of divine things.
Then, after a time, Tom said:

"Where shall we go for our honeymoon, Milly?
We *had*, you know, thought of Cumberland and the
lakes. But I hear it is always wet there, this month.
I somehow yearn for Venice. In spite of your Italian
travel, you have never been to Venice. I should like
you to see the Piazza S. Marco, 'the *al fresco* drawing
room of the world,' someone has fancifully called it,
and certainly the people of Venice know how to
enjoy this drawing-room. Nowhere in all the world,
Milly, I suppose, are there such nights as at Venice.
The Lagoon, like some blue mirror, is studded with
the unruffled reflection of the myriad stars over head.
The songs of the gondoliers; the echoes among the
arches and arcades; the music of lute and guitar;
the delicious stillness, from the absence of all vehicular
traffic; the quiet gliding of the gondolas; the wondrous effects of light and shade, and a myriad other
things to be found there, that are found nowhere

else in the world, all help to make Venice unique for the most travelled person; while it is a perfect Eden for honeymooners."

With talk like this, and with every expression of tenderness that his love-filled soul could suggest, Tom had the joy of seeing something like her old smile of peace creep back into his fiancée's face.

CHAPTER XX.

"TO-MORROW!"

TOM had secured the license, and at nine o'clock in the morning of the next day, Millicent and he were to wed. All was ready for their immediate departure, *after* the ceremony, by train, from Victoria, to catch the tidal boat for the Continent.

This last day of separate life had been a busy, but a very happy one. Whenever business had taken Tom out, he had taken Millicent with him, and had been, (as he laughingly said) "ante-dating the days to come."

Now the time came for the pair to part for the night. "To-morrow, my darling, we shall be one," Tom said, "never to part again, I trust, while life shall last."

He smoothed her beautiful hair, caressingly, as he continued:

"My joy, my happiness, Milly, seems almost more than I can bear!"

"Then think what mine must be, dearest," she answered, as she gave him back caress for caress.

A tender, lingering "Good-night," followed, then they parted.

    *   *   *   *   *

Tom could not sleep, he knew he could not, and did not, therefore, undress. Within five minutes of parting with Millicent, he had quietly left the house,

bent upon getting some fresh air and exercise before
going to bed.

It was an hour later, about a quarter after eleven,
he was nearing his rooms, and barely realising the
way he was taking, he came up a side street that
he suddenly remembered traversing on the night of
his first meeting with his *fiancée*. Just for a moment
he stood, thinking of all that had happened since;
of the transformed life of his *fiancée;* of his own
great joy in her love; and of the consummation of
that love and joy which was to come to them both
in the morning.

In the silence of his soul he cried: "My God, I
thank Thee for all Thy grace and gifts!"

If he had not been so absorbed with his own
thoughts, he would have noticed the ever-deepening
hum of a crowd of voices nearing him.

*   *   *   *   *

Millicent Burn could not sleep, and made no attempt to go to bed. The night was sultry, and she
was too excited to sleep.

"Oh! for a wild, wide moor!" she mused, "or
miles of a firm sandy beach, where the waves lap
the rim of the sand, and every tiny grain is an echo of
the voice of Him who strewed the coasts with His
great sand barrier, and said to the encroaching ocean,
'Thus far shalt thou come, and no farther.' 'Oh!
for a stretch of grassy Downs, or league upon league
of silent country, where I could be alone, and walk,
and talk to God out of my overflowing heart."

But none of these things was possible to Millicent
Burn, since she was in London, so she must needs

make the best of the by street, and quiet squares of that part of the great city where she was now dwelling.

She began to don her walking things, her heart busy all the time with her own thoughts of the past, of the present, and of the future. Like some strange life-like panorama, all that strangely chequered past swept before her mind.

"And to-morrow morning we shall be married!" she mused, "and he, my loved one, the man who rescued me from the slough of sin into which I had fallen, is to be my husband. I shall bear his name——"

She brushed two great glittering drops from her eyes, then, with both arms uplifted, she stretched her veil across her face.

"And we shall never, never part again," she went on, tying the veil behind her beautiful head, as she spoke.

When, at last, she was ready for walking, she stood, with clasped hands, for a moment, in the centre of the room, her eyes uplifted, as she whispered out softly on the silence:

"God bless me! Be ever near me, and keep me from ever falling into the sin of my past life."

With a low, pathetic cry, she went on:

"Better, far better, that I die, my God, than that I fall into sin again!"

With this prayer upon her lips, she opened the door of her room, passed quietly down the stairs, and into the street, not knowing that her *fiancée* had preceded her by a few minutes only.

Not six minutes' walk from her home, there were
three of the quietest squares to be found in all the
London district, and there, at that hour, she knew
that she would find as much of the solitude and
quiet she sought, as was to be found for many a
mile.

She had just entered the first of the quiet squares
when a door of one of the houses opened, and a
child, robed only in a night-dress, bare-footed, and
with her hair all astream, came flying down the
steps of the house, screaming: "Oh, my mother, my
mother!"

How did it all happen? How do these things
happen? How impossible to describe, in detail, for
certain!

A frightened, screaming child; a motor rushing
round a corner; a woman on the pavement sees
what the panic-stricken child does not; the rush
of the woman to save   the child—then, oh, the
pathos of it all—a crowd, an ambulance-stretcher, a
procession to the hospital.

It was the hum of the voices of the crowd which
followed that ambulance-stretcher, that broke upon
the ear of Tom. He paused to watch the passing of
the procession.

A moment later the stretcher was abreast of him.
For one flashing instant he got a glimpse of the
face of the woman who lay upon the stretcher, for
the full glare of the street lamp, by which he stood,
shone upon it.

With the startled, agonised cry of "Millicent! Milly! What has happened?" he forced his way to the side of the injured one.

The police — four of them were carrying the stretcher—paused. One of them, a sergeant, asked:

"Do you know the lady, sir? Just run over by a motor-car, she was saving a child!"

Tom was on his knees upon the pavement, his arms about the silent form, his sobbing lips, crying:

"Milly, Milly, dear love! Can you hear me? It is Tom!"

The crowd was awed and silent. Many of the women were weeping, and strong men brushed their eyes with the cuffs of their coats.

It was a wonderful sight for a London pavement. The helmeted police; the stretcher; the lovely-faced, golden-haired woman lying prone, still, dying; the kneeling, broken-hearted lover or husband, whichever it might be—for no one of the crowd knew.

"It's like a *hact* in a dramer at the 'Drury'," a girl softly sobbed.

At the sound of her lover's voice, the injured Millicent opened her eyes, and gazed at him with all the mighty love of her heart shining in her face, a little smile wreathing her lips.

"Take me home, Tom; not hospital," she murmured.

One of the police caught the words, and asked:

"How far is her home, sir, and would you prefer her being taken there?"

Tom gave the directions, and the procession re-
started, his hand clasping his *fianceé's*, as the caval-
cade moved through the streets.

*   *   *   *   *

Millicent Burn was dying; nothing could save her.
The doctors had told Tom so, in the first moment
of their examination.   She had known it herself in
the moment of her recovery to consciousness.

"Tom, dear love," she murmured.   "It is best so,
you may be sure! God permits it, and He can
make no mistakes either in His permissions or in
His willings."

He dashed the falling drops from his eyes, glad
that, for one moment, she had closed hers, so that
she could not see his tears.

"It is strange," she went on, "that before I came
out—(I could not sleep, so I came out for fresh air)
—I cried out to God in the excess of my joy at the
thought of all that the morning would bring, and
asked Him, if it were best, lest I might ever fall
again, and spoil your life or happiness, to let me
rather die."

A sob shook Tom's frame, though he succeeded in
stifling the sound.

She opened her eyes at that instant, and saw the
quivering of his frame, and understood.

"Don't my darling!" she breathed out, brokenly.

He gazed at her hopelessly, as he cried:

"But to lose you, Milly, my love, my love!"

"Not *lose* me, dear," she whispered.   "*Miss* me for
a little while.   I have sinned grievously in the past,
but God has forgiven me, and is taking me from

the evil to come, my dear one. You must let Him comfort you, dear Tom. Then there is the glorious resurrection of the dead, to help you to know that we shall meet again."

He kept silence before her. How could he tell her that he was thinking hard things of God, in that moment of his great grief?

She grew rapidly weaker. Tom had had her laid upon his own bed, as nearer for her to be carried than to her own room.

"Come closer, dear," she gasped, after a long silence of exhaustion.

He leant over the bed.

"Take me in your arms, dear one," she pleaded.

He put his arms about her, and seating himself on the edge of the bed, cradled her head upon his breast.

Her eyes gazed into his, full of an adoring love. "Shall — not — be — long — here — now!" she gasped. "Don't—interrupt me—listen, and—remember, you—are—young—yet—Tom. Some day—you get—over my—death—not quickly—I know—but *some*—day. God—may—will give you—someone else—remember —if I—can see—shall be—pleased."

Her voice choked, for her life's blood was crowding into her throat. Tom laid her gently back, but kept his arm beneath her neck.

She was past all speech now, save when once she murmured: "Where *sin abounded*, grace doth *much more* abound!"

The end was very near. Like a broken sigh there escaped her lips the two words: "Kiss me!"

With his eyes streaming with tears (in spite of the almost stern stoicism of his race) he laid his lips upon hers.

She was at the last remnant of her strength, but she managed to make her own caress felt.

He felt a quiver pass through her; her eyes gazed up into his; a light like unto a stone most precious flashed into her dying face. Then as the softly fluttering pulse became suddenly stilled, he knew that she was not, for God had taken her.

CHAPTER XXI.

SCARLET AND PURPLE.

IT was noon of the day in the early morning of which Millicent Burn had gone home to her God. A wire came for Tom. Breaking open the terra-cotta envelope, he read the message, dated from Dover: "Shall be with you, on the way home, this afternoon."

"They had hurried home for the wedding," he sighed. "They will be in time for the funeral!"

Tom had, at last, written Jack and Maggie, telling them the whole story of his meeting with Millicent, and all that had followed, with the date of the wedding—before the change to the sudden and earlier date had been made.

It was good for Tom that his friends came thus upon the scene, just when his heart was so sore. And he felt it to be good that they had come.

After the funeral they easily persuaded him to come and stay with them for a time. There were *two* ideal studios in the Hampstead house, both having a good north light, and Tom settled down to hard work as a panacea for undue grief.

Jack, too, was tremendously busy with his picture. He had rightly divined that on the actual spots associated with our Lord's life and death, he would catch the inspiration for his subject.

May found his picture "well-hung" in the chief gallery, as were both of Tom's pictures. Tom had two instead of one, because, after Millicent's death he felt that he could not have her included in his Allegorical

subject, and therefore completed the full-length
portrait he had made of her, exhibiting this as his
second picture.

This portrait was wonderful. There was a quality
about it that puzzled everyone, artists most of all. It
was difficult to conceive that it was not an actual,
living, breathing woman. Perhaps the *real* secret,
above and beyond the curious, almost uncanny painting power which the young Jap possessed, was, that
love, a mighty love, had limned every line. Certain
it was that no such portrait had ever before been
hung on the historic walls of London's chief Academy.

His allegorical picture was equally remarkable, only
in another way. Its title was "Scarlet and Purple," and,
for sub-title, "A 20th Century Allegory." By way of
explanation there appeared on a wide, flat, gilded
name plate, on the lower edge of the wide frame,
this wording:

"Rev XVII. 4. "*Scarlet is the emblem of human and
earthly dignity; purple, the combination of scarlet and
blue, is emblematic of authority which unites the heavenly
and spiritual with that which is earthly and carnal.
False doctrine is, for the most part, a corruption of
Divine truth—error overlaid with a thin layer of truth,
like base metal gilded. The 'precious stones and pearls'
are emblematic of spiritual truths, and of those wondrous
revelations of the church's position and prospects made
known in the sacred Scriptures, but* CORRUPTED BY THE
WOMAN."

The picture represented the interior of a splendid
church—there was nothing to denote the denomination,
since the message of the picture was to all sections

of the professing Christian church. On the south side of the building, the morning sunlight streamed through the gorgeously coloured stained windows.

The church was filled with "worshippers"(?) The rostrum was an exceedingly handsome one, massive, too, and large. Behind the rostrum were the rising choir seats. Fashion had run mad in the toilettes of the women in the choir.

On the wall on one side of the rostrum was a large Hymn-board, with the numbers of five hymns let into the grooves. On a similar board on the wall on the other side of the rostrum was a "Course of Subjects," and beneath the following list of the Subjects:

The Virgin Birth of Christ—A Myth."

"The Resurrection of Christ—A Fallacy."

"Science Demonstrates Miracles Impossible."

"Man Evolved, not created."

"Immortality—Speculative, unproven."

"Doctrine of sin, a misnomer."

"No Eternal Punishment, since no immortality."

"Man must make his own Millennium."

"Idea of a personal Devil—A Fable."

"The Bible not divinely Inspired."

Standing at the book-rest, in the centre of the rostrum was the preacher. Tall, olive of skin, black-browed, wearing a black pointed beard and moustache, his head crowned with a mane of black hair. He wore a deep purple-black gown with voluminous sleeves.

The large stained glass window, nearest the rostrum, through which the brilliant sunlight poured, represented. the "Temptation in the Wilderness." Satan, in the glass, was a huge figure. A freak of light had thrown a reflection of the Satanic form, slightly above, and immediately behind the preacher, so that, in the picture, the grinning Devil overshadowed the Mephistophelian preacher, and was made to appear to be actually prompting, energizing him.

A figure of the Christ, in His seamless Robe, of white, was pictured leaving the rostrum—the figure was at the foot of the stairs—, His face bowed in grief. A glory of light surrounded his form, and only a shade darker than the glorious haze, and floating in the haze, were the shadowed words: *"When the Son of Man cometh shall He find* THE FAITH *on the earth?"* "BEHOLD, I COME QUICKLY."

In the picture, no one of the congregation seemed conscious of the departing presence of the Christ. Like human sponges they were absorbing the flood of Hell that was pouring from the Devil-inspired preacher.

It was not to be expected that the avowed message of such a picture would pass unchallenged, or unattacked. Almost every leading London paper had a special leaderette about "Scarlet and Purple." More than one leading journal asked in one form or another, the question: "What will the Christian papers, and denominational organs, have in reply to the avowed teaching of this picture? For, to our way of thinking, the picture is a challenge to the churches. That there are notable, and glorious exceptions to this *pictured* church, we are eager to admit. And that the artist has given us an exceptionally gross case of spiritual defection in the teaching of the churches, we equally admit.   Yet, in spite of this, if we know anything of the trend of modern religious services, we are bound to confess that, in the main, the principle of the painted indictment is glaringly apparent to the outsider, who, as 'a chiel takin' notes,' goes in and out many of our British churches."

Jack Quentin's "Calvary," had met with almost unqualified approval from all the art critics, while the "People" high and low, educated and uneducated alike, thronged about the great canvas, so that, as in the case of Tom's "Scarlet and Purple," the authorities were compelled to erect barriers in front of it.

Maggie and Jack had succeeded in carrying out their suggestion as to "The Artist's Studio."   The little booklet had been produced in a dainty and taking style, and every person entering the exhibition received a copy, gratis.   Behind the gift, there were daily prayers for blessing on the teaching of the book.

So great was the newspaper discussion over Tom's Allegorical picture, and so many were the questions hurled at him through the press, as well as privately, by letter, that he announced, through the press, that he would deliver an address—or several, if the length of the subject demanded it—on the many animadverted matters in his picture.

*   *   *   *   *

The West End Hall was crowded. The place
was seated for two thousand, but there must have
been nearer three than two thousand people packed
in. The platform was a remarkable one, for the Jap
was supported by clergymen and ministers of every
Evangelical Church, doctors, lawyers, military officers,
representative leaders of the Salvation Army, and of
many other Evangelistic Missions. Jack Quentin and
Maggie were there, of course, sitting immediately
next to Tom, on his right.

Many things had conduced to gather so large and
representative an audience, and platform. There was
the unique fact that the painter of the controversial
picture was a Japanese, a recent heathen, and the
well-known fact that he had approached his subject
from a standpoint that was absolutely unaffected by
preconceived views, religious traditions, or religious
prejudices. He had approached Christian teaching, in
the first place, from the standpoint of the nominal
heathen. Christianity, according to the teaching of
the Missionaries who had worked in his country, was
a living-out of the revealed will of God, as given in
the Bible. And every day, and every hour of his
long residence in England had revealed to him that
the people of professed Christian England, even the
members of the professed Christian Chuches, neither
lived the life commanded in their Bible, nor *attempted*
to live it.

Then, too, another source of keen interest on the
part of many of the people gathered that night, was
the fact that Japanese as the artist was, he had

painted two pictures that were acknowledged, by all the art critics, to be superfine.

The controversial side of the gathering, too, helped to electrically charge the air of the meeting.

A well-known military officer, a writer on prophecy, was in the chair. Hymn leaflets had been distributed, and the meeting began by singing:

"Author of faith, Eternal Word,
    Whose spirit breathes the active flame;
Faith, like its Finisher and Lord,
    To-day as yesterday the same;

To Thee our humble hearts aspire,
    And ask the gift unspeakable;
Increase in us the kindled fire,
    In us the work of faith fulfil.

By faith we know Thee strong to save;
    (Save us, a present Saviour Thou!)
Whate'er we hope, by faith we have,
    Future and past subsisting now.

To him that in Thy name believes
    Eternal life with Thee is given;
Into himself he all receives,
    Pardon, and holiness, and heaven.

The things unknown to feeble sense,
    Unseen by reason's glimmering ray,
With strong commanding evidence,
    Their Heavenly origin display.

Faith lends its realizing light,
    The clouds disperse, the shadows fly;
The invisible appears in sight,
    And God is seen by mortal eye."

A well-known, West-end Christian doctor led in prayer. Then the chairman spoke a three-minute introductory word, and then called upon Tom, to speak.

He was received with hearty applause, this he sharply checked with a gesture of his shapely hand, saying, when his voice could be heard: "The theme of our evening, dear friends, is, to me, too infinitely sacred to allow room for the ordinary clapping of the public meeting, music hall, or concert."

His expressive face lit up with a brilliant smile, as he added: Don't misunderstand me, friends, I am truly grateful to you for your kind greeting and reception.

"I come before you, to-night, to answer the many questions that have been fired at me from that multi-chambered weapon, the daily press of our land —you see, I identify myself with you, Japanese though I am, for I love your land, and its people, from whom I have received nothing but kindness. And will you, please, remember, as I speak to-night, that I speak as one of another race, who, coming into your midst expecting to find certain things, and failing to find them, have but used my brush 'to point a moral,' and to paint my disappointment, and in doing this have raised the controversial points which have gathered us together to-night. Will you too, if you please, remember that as a foreigner, and an Oriental, I may not always be able to present all I fain would in the clear, lucid way that the accustomed English speaker would do—for this is my first attempt at public speaking."

The audience forgot his words about clapping, and treated him to a storm of it.   The chairman whispered:

"Let them have their own way!"

There seemed nothing else to do, so Tom made no further protest, but continued with his speech:

"The thoughts which I have expressed in my picture, were the thoughts of my heart, even before I was actually a Christian, actually converted to my God. The actual idea of my picture came to me, I think, through reading a small, but very valuable book called 'HOW CHRIST CAME TO CHURCH! *The Pastor's Dream*,' It is called: 'A *Spiritual autobiography*, by A. J. Gordon. *With a Life-story and the dream as Interpreting the man*, by Dr. A. T. Pierson.' The title-page bears the publisher's imprint as '*The Baptist Tract and Book Society*, 16, *Gray's Inn Road, Holborn, London*,' and it is dated 1896. I announce all this so fully, for two reasons, first, because I would fain incite every one of you to purchase a copy of the book, at once, and second, in the hope that the publishers will hear of my mention of it, to-night, and accept and act upon the suggestion which I venture openly to make to them, that they rush out a cheap edition, paper covers (it could easily be produced at two-pence, and like the recent penny 'Finney,' would probably sell by tens, perhaps hundreds of thousands).

"The little book records an actual dream which that wonderful American Pastor, Dr. Gordon, had. He dreamed that he was in his pulpit, facing a very full congregation. He was preparing to begin his sermon, when a stranger entered and passed slowly up the left aisle of the church, looking first at the one side and then to the other as though silently asking, with his eyes, that some one would give him a seat. He had proceeded nearly half-way up the aisle when a gentleman stepped out and

offered him a place in his pew, which was quietly
accepted.

"All through the sermon the dreaming preacher
found his eyes travelling to the stranger's face, and
continually saying to himself: 'Who can he be?'
Mentally resolving to find out, by going to him, at
the conclusion of the service.   This he did, in his
dream, but before he could reach the pew, the stranger
had departed. The gentleman who had offered him
a seat had remained behind, and to him the Pastor
said: 'Can you tell me who that stranger was who
sat in your pew this morning?'

"In the most matter-of-course way, he replied:

"'Why, do you not know that man?   It was
Jesus of Nazareth.'

"With a sense of keenest disappointment, the
preacher, in his dream, became next conscious of a
certain unrest.   'To think that the Lord Himself,
whose I am, and whom I serve, had been listening
that day!' How was he preaching? What was he
saying? Was he preaching 'Christ crucified' in a
crucified style? Or had he, while professedly preaching the crucified One, magnified himself, and *his sermon?* Other questions came to him, 'What did he
think of the sanctuary, its gothic arches, its stained
windows, its costly and powerful organ? How was
He impressed with the music and the order of
worship?'

"In the midst of great perturbation of mind he
awoke, with the words on his lips: *'He has been here
to-day, and will no doubt come again.'*

"'There are many wonderful, but natural reflections following. How the sight of Christ in a congregation would affect the worship! How would the minister preach? How would the people worship? How the minister would urge the immediate—though unseen—presence of Christ, '*Wheresoever two or three of you are gathered in My name, there* AM *I in the midst.*'

"How the fact of His coming again soon to catch away to himself, all His own true people, would be urged upon the congregation by the minister.

"Dr. Pierson says, concerning Adoniram Judson Gordon, the Pastor who dreamed that Christ came to his church: 'You that know Dr. Gordon, need not to be told that such a dream is not a mere, incoherent and senseless vagary of the mind, for it invests with poetic and allegorical form the ruling ideas and ideals of his whole later life, which may be classified somewhat as follows:

1. Loyalty to the *Person* of Christ as Son of God, and his own Saviour.
2. The blessed hope of His personal coming as an imminent event.
3. The high vocation of the preacher as Christ's herald, witness, and ambassador.
4. The purity of worship as the exaltation of God alone in His sanctuary.
5. The supreme authority of the inspired and infallible Word of God.
6. The conformity of entire church-life to a Biblical pattern.
7. The invisible presence and power of the Holy Spirit in the Church as His temple and seat of administration.' "

There was a great hush upon the immense audience,
as the gifted, godly young Jap enumerated these
ruling ideas of Dr. Gordon's ministry.   The hush
deepened, as his clear, rich voice rang out in the
question:

"Will anyone here, or in all London, attempt to say
that these ideas are those of the average church of
to-day? They are not even set up as the ideals. What
would Christ say if He came to Church to-day?
Would He, as I have pictured in my Academy
Allegory, bow His head in sorrow and shame, and
departing from the building, cry *When the Son of
Man cometh shall He find* THE FAITH *on the earth?'*

"Go over in your minds, friends, all the teaching
in the churches with which you are familar, and can
you say that they ever attempt to uphold the
whole of the Pauline teaching? Take one point only:
We have gathered here, to-night, in our thousands, we
have come from every section of the 'Christian'
church. One of the *chief fundamentals* of the 'church'
teaching in the Epistles, is that we are to look for the
second coming of Jesus Christ, and *not* for death.
How many of us present here, to-night, *believe* this
fundamental? How many of us live hourly, daily, in
expectancy of His coming? Yet, as *professed* Christians,
as believers in the Church Epistles, and in the whole
of the New Testament, we should see the imminence
of the Second Advent, we should see it in every sign
around us—In the Political realm; the Social realm;
the Industrial realm; the Commercial realm; the
Religious realm; the Jewish realm. It is not only
that we *should* see the signs of our Lord's near

return, but that *if* we knew our God, and knew His word, as we should do, as professing Christians, *we could not miss seeing* the signs.

"But while the preaching from a huge number of our platforms and pulpits, contains one or more, or many of the open blasphemies which I have depicted upon the Notice Board in my picture, we can never expect that the worshippers—so called —will attempt to live up to the Church idea promulgated by the Holy Ghost, through the Apostle Paul.

"It matters not what religious creed you may hold, or whether you hold no such creed, I am sure I am not mistaken in saying, that you believe in preachers and people alike being honest, and, given this, I ask you, is it honest to call ourselves Christian, and then by thought, speech, and action, repudiate practically all that God specifies as Christian?

"Men who preach (paid to preach Christianity) and men and woman who listen (who pay their preachers, professedly, to preach a Crucified Christ) are learning more and more to love—not *a* lie, but —THE LIE. Modern 'Christianity' denies Christ, and declares the distinctive teaching of Himself and His apostles, to be absolutely obsolete.

A leading member in the greatest Evangelical body of Christians, in this land, speaking of the rank heresy preached in their pulpits in these days, said: 'As——ists we are perfectly powerless.' 'Yes, perfectly *powerless,* in more senses than one because the dry-rot is in your whole organization,' was the reply of the friend with whom he conversed. 'But,' continued this

friend, 'there is one thing you can, and ought to
do, that is, to act upon the injunction of Proverbs,
19th, twenty-seventh: *"Cease, my son, to hear the instruction that causeth to err from the words of knowledge."*'

"In the same denomination, a meeting of their
ministers was held, a year or two back, in London,
to listen to an 'Important and interesting paper on
"Inspiration and Biblical Criticism" to be read by
one of the Professors of one of the colleges for train-
ing their Divinity students.' The chair was taken by
one of their leading divines and theologians. *The
lecturer held that it was possible with a perfect con-
sistency, to unite an acceptance of the Bible *as a
guide of conduct* with a willingness to recognize the
results of free textual criticism. . . . In a brief
speech at the close of the paper, Dr.—— (the chairman, endorsed the views of the lecturer, and several
other speakers recorded in the highest terms their
appreciation of the Professor's paper, and their
sympathy with the main position which he had
taken up.

"There must be thousands of true-souled men and
women, in that great denomination, who recoil from
such veiled blasphemy against God and His Word,
but there is an even greater horror than this. For
when a godly layman challenged the statements,
and the whole position of the Professor, a special
sub-committee of the denominational Theological
Institute was called, composed of the leading men—
Drs., Professors, Revs.,—this committee endorsed the

---

*The "Times" (London) report.

professor's views, so that as a notably sound and
safe Christian journal remarked:* 'They have not
only justified Professor ———, but they have gone
even further, and sympathized with him as the victim
of unjust suspicions and uncalled-for condemnation.
The denomination has now accepted the new views of
the Bible.———Students are to be taught, and ———
preachers are to teach, with the full approval of
General assembly of that august body, that Genesis
is a collection of myth and fable * * * that the
Law did not come by Moses, but was manufactured
by men of the Exile, who did not scruple to put
their own words into the lips of Moses and of God
Himself; that our Lord and His Apostles shared
the ignorance of their times; and that they taught
us in error that laws were given by Moses, and that
Psalms were written by David, which did not come
into existence till centuries after these writers had
passed away.'

"I said just now, friends, that, to-day, the people
in many of our churches are being taught, not so
much A *lie*, but 'THE *Lie*.' *The* Lie spoken of in
two Thessalonians two eleven. Every month, every
day, now, that this world goes on, the power of *The*
Lie increases. It began with one veiled utterance in
Eden—the Devil, the 'Father of Lies,' beyond it, and
he has been infecting the human race more and
more, with his lie, all down through the ages. Of
late years he has learned how rapidly his time is
shortening, and, by an infernal process, he has begun
to inoculate all of the human race he can possibly

—————————————————
*Word and Work.

reach with his damnable lie, that the world may presently be in the ripe condition for receiving the MAN, himself, and the sway of the Man, whom he will foist upon the earth—'*The Man of Sin,*' '*Antichrist.*'

"In this later development of his hellish scheme to frustrate Christ, and Christ's purposes, he has got hold of the ministers and teachers—'Down-Gradeism,' it was called at first, then the 'Higher Criticism,' and now the 'New Theology.' He inoculated the writers of Theological works; these the Theological professors absorbed; then the Professors taught *The* Lie to their students; the students became ministers and taught it to their peoples. A few of the elder, unstable, unsaved members accepted the lie, a large part of the younger ones accepted it, and now their children, the youth, and young manhood and young womanhood of the present day, tell you flatly, that the Bible is exploded, it is a trick of priests of bygone days, to keep the people's souls in bondage. That there is no here-after, that this life is all there is, and that they are bound to have as good a time as they can while they are here.

"Some good people are continually expressing their amaze at the religious attitude—perhaps I ought to say *non*-religious attitude—of the young generation, the generation of to-day. For myself, knowing all I do—from reliable journals and books—what has been happening in your colleges, your pulpits, your Sunday-school classes during the past thirty or forty years, I should be amazed if your newer generations were Christian. The whole non-Christian position in England, today, is a matter of 'cause and effect.'

"Those responsible for teaching Christ, from God's Word, began years ago, by sowing *doubt*, the next generation of teachers sowed *denial*, and the crop of an atheism worse than Voltaire's or Tom Paine's, or Bradlaugh's, is the reaping of to-day.

"When Antichrist, *'The Man of Sin,'* appears, Christendom will be ready to receive him, to receive the *fulness* of the colossal 'LIE,' which, already has begun to work. His coming is to be *'after the working of Satan, with all power and signs and lying wonders, and with all deceivableness of unrighteousness in them at that period; because they received not the love of the truth, that they might be saved—'* and because the people will not receive *The Truth,*—Christ Jesus, when the Incarnate Lie—Antichrist, shall come they will be wholly, absolutely duped by him, and be damned in their duping.

"Take the conditions of thousands of our churches, to-day, friends, and you will have no difficulty in seeing how the work of preparation for Antichrist's coming, is going forward. Romanism boldly declares its aim to win, or coerce England back into her harlot fold, and the mothers and fathers of England, beguiled by the specious offers of *cheap* education for their girls, are helping forward the plans of the great Harlot. Another section of the Church—the State Church, is so honey-combed with Ritualism, and Rationalism, as to become, really, an ally of the Harlot. The Nonconformist bodies are filled with infidelity, materialism, and worldliness. Thousands, in all our churches, are having illicit intercourse with demons, by the aid of that cult of hell, Spiritualism.* And like a swarm of foul, slimy things, there is covering this beautiful Britain of yours, such vile spawn as Millennial-Dawnism, Mormonism, Seventh-day Adventism, Christian Science, and a host of minor foulnesses too numerous to mention.

"And, more and more, a spirit, traitor to God and to His Word, has sprung up in Christendom, a spirit which calls itself 'Tolerance,' 'Charity,' and other kindred words, forgetting that God has declared, *'Hereby know ye the Spirit of God: every spirit that confesseth Jesus Christ is come in the flesh, is of God: And every spirit that confesseth not that Jesus Christ is come in the flesh, is not of God, and this is the spirit of Antichrist, whereof ye have heard that it should come, and even now, already, it is in the world.'*

"And the *spirit* of Antichrist is preparing the way for Antichrist himself.   Whether there will be anything like a coming-out movement from Christendom, of the real and actual Believers, before He comes, it is impossible to say, but I am well assured that there are hundreds of godly men in our British pulpits, and thousands of loving-hearted loyal Believers, who feel that where they are is no place for them.   For there is the *'Voice from Heaven saying:* 'COME OUT OF HER, MY PEOPLE, *that ye be not partakers of her sins, and that ye receive not of her plagues.'*

---

*See "The Lure of a Soul," by Sydney Watson, "The Firs," Vernham Dean, Hungerford, Berks, or of Messrs. W. Nicholson & Sons, Limited, 26, Paternoster Square, London. E. C. 1s. 6d. Nett, Postage 4d. extra.

"Everywhere there is a call for union of the varying shades of thought, of belief, of profession, into one great universal church. And the book of Revelation shows such an union. The trend of things is all that way, and the throwing over of the doctrine of the Virgin-Birth of our Lord Jesus Christ, will make it possible, and easy, for Christendom to unite with Mohammedanism, Hinduism, Judaism, and, practically every other ism of the world. The fact that, broadly, Christendom accepts the Unitarian, points its own moral, in the direction in which I am now speaking.

"The final result of this union of all bodies of religious thought— the Re-union of Christendom, as it is sometimes called—will be the formation of the 'Great World Religion.' Of course, to accomplish this, the 'Salt of the Earth,' God's own true Believing children (and some of these are to be found in every section of the Christian Church, and some even *outside* all church organizations) will have to be taken away out of the existing church organizations. This will happen at the first stage of the Second Advent of our Lord—His coming into the air for *His* Church.

"Then, with the Church of Christ gone, and only Christendom left, the way for absolute unification of all creeds and no creed, will be easy and rapid. Then shall come to pass the prophecy of Revelation seventeen. The woman, '*Mystery, Babylon the Great, the mother of the harlots and the abominations of the earth,*' will ride the Beast—in other words, the newly-unified body of ecclesiasticism, will be supreme *for* a *time.*—'The Church' will rule the State.* But only for a time will this Apostate Church rule. Antichrist will use the foul harlot to help his purposes, then, when she can no longer be of service to him, he will easily arrange, with his 'ten horns'—ten kingdoms—to sweep her out of existence. Listen, friends, to the language that describes her destruction: *'And the ten horns which thou sawest upon the Beast, these shall hate the whore, and shall make her desolate and naked, and shall eat her flesh, and burn her with fire.'*

"Yes, yes, a thousands times yes, friends, *the* Lie is already at work. The way is being made easy for the Apostasy to be brought about. As if as a commentary upon all I have long thought and said, and have—more or less fragmentarily—said to you, tonight, I took up a Hampshire local paper, only this very morning, and under the Signature of a 'B. A.', 'B. D.' I read an article entitled 'The religion of the Future.' Here are a few of the marks, set down in that article as part of 'The Religion of the *Future*': *'It will be based upon nature, and* HER *divine laws, as discovered by science,* NOT THE SUPER-NATÚRAL *as handed down by tradition. . . . It will recognize the immanent God within man—not the* PERSONAL *God* WITHOUT . . . . *Its two chief sources of instruction and inspiration will be the revelations of science and human experience, and the instruction of* SPIRIT SPHERES, *through an universal mediumship. . . . Its ministers . . will be ministers of* NATURE'S *own ordination,* SPIRIT-CALLED *and* SPIRIT-BAPTISED, *and*

*See "The Mark of the Beast," Biola Book Room, Los Angeles.

SPIRIT-LED, *the channels of the grace and inspiration of the* SPIRIT-SPHERE.'

"Let me, friends, here interpolate the question, *'What spirit?'* There are but two Spirits revealed in the world.—*The Spirit of God,* and the *Spirit of Satan.* The *Personal* God has been ruled out by the writer of this article I am quoting from, then the ministers of the *future* religion, must be *called* and *baptized,* and *led* of Satan.

"The writer does not knowingly mean that, but the true Believer, the Student of God's Word, knows that the energiser, leader, etc. of the great future religion is to be Satan, *through* Antichrist, and the False Prophet. Thus, this will be Great Apostasy in full blossom.

"But listen again to this candid exponent of the coming Great Apostasy: 'Hither I see all nations, and kindred, and tribes, and people gathering.'

"That, friends, is what John saw in God's Revelation, *'the whole world wandering after the Beast.'*

"Yes, the days of the fulness of the great Apostasy draw very near, and Christendom is preparing to resolve herself wholesale into that great universal apostasy. Truly, friends, the days of signs of 'the coming of the Son of Man' are here, and the signs are abounding on every hand.

"But I promised, at the beginning, that I would leave time for *interviewing* anyone who might wish to ask any questions, as it is manifestly impossible that, in so huge an audience as this, we could expect to hear and be heard by shuttle-cock query and response. I am not an Encyclopedia on these topics.

I am simply a poor Japanese heathen who has been converted to God, and who, from prophecy and promise of the Christian New Testament, has learned the blessedness of looking for the Saviour, from Heaven; and, anxious to arouse others to the need of conversion, to see also the signs of the coming of Christ, I have painted my picture: 'Scarlet and Purple,' and I have, to-night, been trying to show you my picture-lesson in the realm of Christendom.

"There will need to be a second meeting like this; the date and all particulars will be announced in the Daily Press, when the arrangements have been completed."

The meeting closed with prayer, after which many came to the platform. Some to thank the speaker, some to question him. The last to speak to him was a gentleman who introduced himself as the Secretary of a great London "Brotherhood" meeting. "Only as I left home, to come to this meeting," he explained, "I received a wire from Sir Charles Wyndhameton, M.P. for West Blankshire, who was to have addressed our men next Sunday afternoon, but who has met with rather a serious accident, and therefore cannot come. I *must* get someone, I have very little time to secure anyone, and even if I had weeks to spare, I should still ask you, sir. Will you come to us next Sunday afternoon? You have a God-given message, come then to us. I can promise you a thousand men, probably nearer seventeen hundred than a thousand."

Tom promised.

CHAPTER XXII.

"BROTHERHOOD WITH CHRIST."

MOST of the leading London morning papers reported the meeting recorded in our last chapter, some of the papers entered very fully into the subject. An enormous amount of newspaper discussion was the result.

In response to his promise to the *first* meeting, and in answer to some of the newspaper criticism of his utterances at that meeting, Tom advertised the date of his second meeting, to be held in the same Hall as the first one.

Meanwhile, he went on Sunday to fulfil his engagement at the "Brotherhood" meeting. The preliminaries were characterised by the heartiness usual at these gatherings, then, just before he was to speak the chairman announced that

"Miss Cora Castlehayes would now sing 'To all Eternity.'"

The meeting roared with laughter at the droll way of putting it, and the Secretary whispered to Tom, "If she sings to all Eternity, Mr. Itoi, I am sure I don't know when you'll get a chance to speak."

But the chairman, wondering at the laughter, was asking the Secretary, "What are they laughing at?" A rapid whispered explanation followed, and the chairman laughingly put himself right with the meeting, and with the lady.

The singing was gracious and beautiful, and full
of feeling. Then "Mr. Tomassi Itoi," was announced to speak. He was received with a storm
of applause.

Quietly, modestly, consciously in the fear of God,
he began to speak:

"Brothers, friends! As far as I have been permitted to study this great movement of the 'Brother-
hoods,' I have decided that it holds within it all
the factors for becoming the most potent force in
the world, for the purifying of the nations where it
is found. It could easily, also, become a hideous
danger and menace to the nation. I mean this, let
every member of every brotherhood, become a true
Christian, a man born again of the Spirit of God;
indwelt by Christ, actuated, and energised by the
Holy Spirit, in all his thought, speech, and act, and
there is no limit to the power for God and for
humanity, to which such a true "Brotherhood" could
be used.

"But, mark you, my Brothers, every man must
be a *true* Christian, after the only source, and only pattern ever given by God, the pattern and source laid
down in the New Testament.

"There is a false, misleading, soul-damning talk,
which is heard sometimes, even in Brotherhood
meetings, as to every man being *a potential Christ,*
and, linked with this, is much mischievous, misleading talk, about a Fatherhood of God, and a Brotherhood of man in Jesus Christ, which has not so much
true substance as the soap-bubbles the children blow
on the Washing-Day.

"The *Creation* does not make God the *Father* of all men, in the Bible sense. • No man can call God, 'Father,' in the saving, eternal sense, save as he has been brought into a new relationship with God, by the New Birth—'*Ye must be born again,*' has never been repealed, and it is the law of entrance into the family of God, to-day, as it was in the day of Nicodemus. *To as many as received Him* (*The Lord Jesus Christ*) *gave He the right to become the Sons of God,*' *and* when—and only then—a man becomes a *Son of God,* can he call God: 'Father.' And there is but one way in which any man, (no matter his rank, wealth, learning, *virtue,* or aught else) can receive this Sonship in God, and that is by receiving Christ, as His Saviour. I say '*no other way,*' advisedly, for though *false* teachers have many *man*-made, fine theories, of how a man may be a Christian, no one has any right to propound any way, other than God Himself, and He has told the way in the New Testament. Let me illustrate what I mean, what God's Word says:

"In one of your glorious English wooded counties, where I stayed a few months ago, I was the guest of an English family who have shown me, a foreigner, much disinterested kindness. About a mile from the house where I was staying, was a very fine old mansion, that, for hundreds of years, had been in the occupancy of a very aristocratic family. The latest branch of this family had fallen on evil times, and the place was sold by them.

"The people who purchased the place, were enormously wealthy, but what Society (Society with a

big capital S, I mean) called 'Shoddy.' They had
sprung from the 'commonest of the common,' was
said of them.   They set up a magnificent establish-
ment; extensive stables for hunters, etc.; several
eight hundred, and thousand pound motor cars, in
fact, to sum the whole matter, the Hodgsons (we
will call them that, though the real name was not
so pretty) did things in a princely way.

"But none of the gentry called upon them, they
were 'cut dead' as Society would say. I was sitting
in my room, in the home of my friends, one morning,
with my window wide open, for though it was
November, it was as mild as May.   Presently two
men, close under my window, began to talk.   One
was a groom in the stables of the Hodgsons, the
other a gardener in the employ of my host. I soon
gathered that the topic between the two men was
the isolation of the rich Hodgsons.

"'Yes, they're rich enuff,' said the groom, 'but
money don't count a morsel among the gentry, it's
birth an' blood.'

"'What do yer mean by blood?' the gardener asked.

"'Well, the regerlar *haristocracy* is said to have
"*blue*" blood in their veins,' the groom explained,
'an' nobody ain't nobody among 'em unless they've
got great birth—some great family, you know, an'
have got the blue blood as makes 'em real *haristo-*
crats. There's books all about it, "Debrett," an'
"Burke," an' "Who's who?" I've looked into some o'
these, an' it tells you where the family sprung from;
an' the nobs are as proud as can be o' all that sort

o' thing, an' won't mix with people who ain't *born* right.'

" 'But how's these aristocrats to know who's shoddy as they calls it, when they all dresses alike, so to speak, an' all that sort o' thing?'

"From where I sat I could see the two men, and I saw a smile cross the face of the groom, and twisting with his tongue the piece of straw he held in his mouth, he said: 'Well, as a rule, however rich folks may be, who's only shoddy, they've only got to open their mouths, and your regular gent knows 'em at once.   Fur instance, I heard two swells a larfing the other day about my missus (an' I must say a betterer, kinderer, or more generouser missus never breathed,) but these two swells were larfin' about her talk, an' one o' 'em said, "I never felt so inclined to laugh right out in my life as when she said to me, '*H*only fancy,' captain 'Artley, *h*eight 'untin' 'orses *h*in the stables *h*eatin' their 'eads *h*off'." O'course I knew what the gent meant, it was about them 'aithches, an I knows it takes some doin' to manage them, an' that's one thing as my missus can't do.   Well, I 'spose it's 'ardly to be expectit, fur I've 'eard that thirty years ago she used to serve in her 'usband's ready-made clothes shop, somewheres in Whitechapel.   Now they're wuth a million o' money if they's wuth a cent; yet, becos they ain't *born right,* ain't got the right kind of blood in 'em, all the rest ain't wuth anythink.'

"The two men parted a moment later with a 'So long.' But I sat on, thinking over the words 'Ye *must be born again,*' for the illustration that I had just listened to, was really a wonderful one. No, no, brothers! Nothing can make us Sons of God, save the New Birth. It must be a BLOOD relationship, to make God our Father; and it is the Blood of the Christ, of the Saviour of the World that alone can give us the new life.

"The same *principles* apply with regard to setting up the relationship of brother with Jesus Christ. There is no brotherhood of Christ in Adam, nor yet in the 'Incarnation.' The Brotherhood of Christ to us, and us to Christ, *begins* only at Calvary, and is completed in the Resurrection. *'Christ died for our Sins, and rose again for our justification.'*

"No, friends, it is not in Humanity, merely, that the Brotherhood of Jesus is set up with us. In Hebrews two eleven, the Apostle says: 'For which *cause He is not ashamed to call us brethren.'* For *what* cause? What makes the true link? The Apostle tells us it is in that separation ('sanctification') of ourselves unto Him (Jesus) Who was Himself separated unto God. And the man among us who will be separate from the world, and unto God, is linked on to Christ Jesus in the only Brotherhood with Him that God knows.

"Jesus Christ is our Representative Brother, not our Brother in the Race that is fallen, but of the New Race that is made by Redemption. Thus it is the New Birth that gives us kinship with Jesus Christ.

"We must know God by the New Birth, and the new life, the Eternal Life of Jesus Christ, must be in us. This means that we not only have a new *life,* but that we move in a new atmosphere, we shall have a new mental and spiritual environment. The atmosphere and environment of merely religious services, of Brotherhood meetings, and the like, without an actual life in God, will only make a man a formalist or a Pharisee.

"Do not, my brothers, be deceived by any man or teacher, however high he may stand in name, fame, or scholarship, who would attempt to subvert, in the smallest degree, the statements of God's Word. Do not mistake civilization for Christianity. What is, to-day, often termed 'Progress,' is, from beginning to end, the glorification of man, of his talent, his business success—which is often only another name for consummate scheming. Human progress, merely, and the true *Christ*-life, are as wide as the Poles. The *Christ*-life lives and works only for the glory of God; 'Progress,'—which is another name for advanced civilization—lives for self, self-glory, self-aggrandisement.

"A deep thinker and a man of God whose works are very popular, these last few years, has well said: 'The first act of the leaders of this age (this age in a sense, began at Calvary) was to crucify the Lord of glory. This was a forcible expression of the policy of the "prince of this world" (Satan.) It was a declaration not only that the world did not need Christ, and that it desired nothing of His doctrine or of Himself, but that *the principles of His Kingdom, as stated in His teaching, were hostile to and destructive of those of the world.* Those age-leaders comprehended the situation fully, and they dealt with it accordingly.

They did not entertain an exaggerated view of the danger which, in the person of this Man, threatened the institutions of the world, its government, its religion, and wisdom.

" 'They charged that He was a menace to the throne of Cæsar, which was the throne of the world. They had heard Him disputing with, and silencing the Sadducees, *rationalists* of that day. He had also, in unmeasured terms, denounced the religious leaders of the time, charging upon them what those who set themselves up to be religious leaders of the age have ever since been doing, namely, making the Word of God of none effect through their tradition.'*

"His teachings, moreover, were a menace to the progress of the world, which depends upon the fierce struggle of competition for the riches and honours of the world. The universal application of the 'Golden Rule,' and of the principles set forth in what is called the 'Sermon on the Mount,' would bring the *progress* of the world to a standstill. Those leaders of the age instinctively felt the danger; and though they may not have understood it in detail, doubtless the 'prince of this world,' whose bidding they were doing, comprehended it fully. This Man was a menace to the world, and to all its institutions, and He must be disposed of.

"My brothers, I speak to you as an Eastern, an Oriental, one whom your Missionaries and Teachers would have called a 'Heathen,' but a little while ago, and I am bound to confess that what I saw in

---

*"The Number of Man," Philip Mauro. Biola Book Room, Los Angeles. Paper, 25 cents.

professed 'Christian' England during the years before my conversion, compelled me to think that beautiful as is the Christian ideal set up in the New Testament, yet the professing English Christians never made any attempt to fulfil that ideal. Since my conversion I have found some notable exceptions.

"I must be closing. I thank both you and your Secretary for allowing me ten full minutes beyond the usual time for the address. I thank you all for your patience and kindness in listening to me. I have spoken frankly, fearlessly, because the times need straight, frank speech, and whether you all agree with me or not, you would not be what you profess to be—A Brotherhood meeting—if you did not welcome frank outspokenness."

A tremendous burst of applause greeted this statement. Then, only waiting to be heard again, he added:

"Let my last word be an appeal, as an *'Ambassador for Christ, as though God did beseech you by me, I pray you, in Christ's stead, be reconciled to God.'*"

The meeting was one never to be forgotten, for more than a score of men, that afternoon, took the decisive step, *"into* Christ."

CHAPTER XXIII.

"DISCERNING THE SIGNS."

TO Jack Quentin and Maggie, this sudden and remarkable development of Tom into so convincing a public speaker, was a great surprise.

In response to their urgent pressing he had quite made his home with them, and, day by day, as they lived in contact with him, they realised how very wondrously the Christ-life was being lived out by him.

But they could not hide from themselves that the loss of Millicent Burn out of his life cast its shadow upon his spirit, at times. And, together, they sometimes talked as to how far they would be justified in seeking a second love for him. Among their few acquaintances there was one very sweet, cultured woman, an artist of some promise, who was intensely interested in Tom, partly because she had lived in Japan for a couple of years, and had acquired a great respect for his race. But she was evidently deeply interested in the man himself, as well, too, as in the artist. She was not, as yet, a decided Christian, though, brought under the influence of Maggie especially, her soul had become awakened to God's claims, and, as Maggie had remarked to Jack, "He *Who has begun the good work will finish it.*"

With all this in their minds, they sought opportunities to throw Tom, and the lady of their thought, into each other's company.

Tom recognised their kindly intention, but with a little quiet smile told them that it would be no use, for though Liberty Hindmarsh was a splendid woman, and he enjoyed her friendship, he knew, in his innermost soul, that she could never be a mate to him. He repeated, too, what he had said before, "I doubt if I shall ever marry, for, of course, I should not marry without love, and love hardly ever comes the second time."

"Not the same kind of love, perhaps, Tom," Maggie had replied, "but I am sure that love of a deeper, soberer character is often given as some compensation for the loss of a first and more romantic love. But we cannot force these things, and, if our Lord tarry, God may have His own fashion of mating you, some day, to some good woman."

On the morning of the morrow after this talk had taken place, Tom was in his studio, not feeling particularly workish. There was a half-formed idea roaming round in his mind, to take a day off, and have a run into the country.

Then the maid came to say that a lady wished to see him. The card which lay upon the salver held by the maid bore the name "Mrs. D. Moore."

"Show her up into the ante-room, please, Phœbe," he said.

As the maid left the room, Tom passed into the ante-room—a heavy plush curtain only divided this room from the studio.

A moment or two later "Mrs. Moore" was ushered in. She was a tall, graceful woman, handsomely, but not showily dressed. Her face, her form, her manner

all betokened good breeding, and there was a charm
and grace about her that won upon Tom the moment
that she spoke and smiled.

"You will pardon, I hope, Mr. Itoi, my coming in
upon you in this very unceremonious fashion," she
began.   "Yes, I am sure you will when I tell you
that I have but this one day left in Town, and it
was only last night that I saw some of your work
at Mrs. Enyon Davies', and I felt that I must come
and see you, to try to get you to undertake a special
commission for me."

Tom assured her that he was only too pleased to
give audience to any friend of Mrs. Enyon Davies',
and that if he found it in his power to execute any
commission for Mrs. Moore he would be delighted
to do so.

In a very few moments the pair were quite at
their ease, and were chattering as though they had
been friends for years.

"Are you engaged for this week-end?" she presently asked. "I mean, could you run down to my
place on Friday or Saturday—just which would suit
you best—and stay until Monday or Tuesday, when
I could show you certain things, and explain fully
what I want?"

She laughed a little gaily, as she said:

"I wonder if, in your heart, you are saying:
'What consummate impudence belongs to woman in
general, and to this woman in particular, that she
can suppose that I, a rising and successful young
artist, can drop all my studio work to go globe-trot-
ting for her, like some itinerant, who combines the

callings of photographer, barber, and watch and clock mender.'"

He laughed with her, and, falling in with her merry mood, replied:

"Faint heart never won an artist to peripatetics."

"And so you put a premium upon impudence, Mr. Itoi," she laughed.

"Upon promptness and adroitness I do," he answered, "for *I* could not dare use the word *impudence* to a lady."

"And you will really come?" she asked, adding in the same breath, "*When* will you come?"

"On Saturday, in time for a cup of afternoon tea," he replied, then with a merry laugh, he went on:

"There must surely be a shadow of impudence in artists in general, and this one in particular, in actually asking for his afternoon tea. It is akin to the London charwoman, Mrs. Moore, who *hints* that '*ho*win' to the dust, wot is that there orkard an' contrary that it will *persist* in gittin' inter the brunk-chual toobs, one gits 'orribly firstly at charin' work'."

Though strangers until half-an-hour before, the pair talked freely and merrily, both being in that mood when reciprocation becomes easy. For it is a fact, perhaps too little thought of, that in making acquaintance with people who have hitherto been strangers, the mood in which each person may happen to be, at the time, has often more to do with getting at home with each other than anything else.

"Send me a card, or a wire," Mrs. Moore said, as they parted, "telling me the time of your train arrival, and I will have something at the station to meet you."

As this beautiful, strong-souled woman—for she was all this, and more—went her way, she said to herself: "Truly manhood knows no race. Japanese, as he is—though I should have taken him for a Spaniard, more than a Jap—he is a true man, a man, though a stranger an hour ago, whom I could trust, implicity, under all circumstances. And of his Christianity there is no room for doubt."

And Tom was communing on very similar lines with himself: "What a cheery ring there is about that woman. It is a positive relief to meet a woman so fresh and frank, so full of common-sense. Her remarks, too, about painting, were full of real knowledge and worth. And yet she was as humble as possible about the same knowledge. Some folks, with not one-hundredth part of her understanding of art, would swell like pouter pigeons, and talk as bumptuously as though the very foundations of Art rested upon their precepts and verdicts."

Saturday afternoon at four-forty-five, found Tom sitting in the handsome drawing-room of "The Crest," taking a cup of deliciously-creamed tea from the hand of Mrs. Moore.

The next few hours were registered in his memory ever afterwards, as among the pleasantest he ever spent with a new acquaintance.

Seen at close quarters, in her own home, and in indoor attire, he decided that Mrs. Moore was an even more charming woman than he had first thought—high as his estimate had been.

And she found herself rendering a similar verdict of him.

They talked of many things, each new topic arising in some way out of the previous one, and each becoming a kind of mental tentacle flung out prehensory fashion, with a view of ascertaining how much more their two minds had in common.

But perhaps the two chief bonds of communion between them was, *first*, their oneness in God; and, *second*, the fact that both had suffered deeply.

Tom enjoyed the quiet Sunday, then, on the Monday morning he accompanied his hostess to the several spots she was desirous of having painted. He himself was so charmed with them that he undertook the commission to transfer their beauties to canvas, and that, too, at the earliest opportunity

In the evening he went back again to Town, engaged to spend the next week-end at "The Crest."

The Wednesday after his return from his visit, was the day fixed for the second great meeting at the West End Hall. The place was, if possible, more packed than on the previous occasion. The excitement was tremendous, and the whole place seemed electrically-charged.

The preliminaries were much as before; then Tom rose to speak, receiving a perfect ovation, which, close watchers saw, he received with closed eyes, knit brows, and face bowed.

"If," he began, "I was not absolutely convinced, in my own soul, that the return of the Lord Jesus

Christ was very, very near, I should not be so keen
on drawing your attention (and through the Press
that may report my utterances) to the combination
of circumstances that leads me to see the signs of
that *near* return.

"First let me quote from Dr. McKilliam, in a recent issue of 'The Morning Star.'—'Amongst many
of us,' he says, 'there is the deepest conviction growing day by day, that *the end of the age is upon us*
. . . If the Holy Ghost is doing one thing more
than another to-day, it is this. There is going on
quietly, almost imperceptibly to some under its influence, a spiritual movement of *heart* separation
from the visible and tangible to the unseen Presence
of the Lord Himself, and eternal realities. . . . .
To those who are capable of discerning it, this
movement—*entirely spiritual*—is the *proof*, transcend-
ing all others, that *our Lord's coming is imminent.*'

"In this connection, friends, let me remind you
how Jesus Christ taught, that when things were
blackest, i. e. *'At Midnight,'* the cry should be
heard, 'Behold, the Bridegroom cometh.' For hundreds of years of the church's history, the fact, the
promise, the hope of the Lord's Return, was practically lost sight of. During the first few centuries the
whole of the true Church of God was not only pre-
millennial in view, but looking for the Return in
their practice.

"Then as the centuries moved on, in proportion
as Roman Papal Catholicism advanced, the looking
for Christ's return died down; in other words, 'when
the Church became a *harlot* she ceased to be a

bride who goes to meet her Bridegroom.' The centuries of the almost absolutism of Roman Catholicism, were as a deep, wide, black chasm, in which
the Hope of our Lord's Return was engulfed and
hidden.

"The Reformers, especially the Waldensian Church,
and notably, the great Wickliffe, Tyndale, Latimer,
and others, believed in it and preached it. In the
seventeenth Century the doctrine arose again into
much prominence. Again, in the eighteenth century,
and the middle of the nineteenth century, was as
the very midnight cry: *'Behold, the Bridegroom
cometh.'*

"But now, in this year of nineteen hundred and
twelve, the signs abound so, that, but for the fact
that many of our Pastors and Teachers and ordinary
Christians have blinded themselves with prejudice, or
some preconceived notion, it would be inevitable, that
they would hear *'The Cry'* in the events transpiring
all about us.

"Would you know how to discern these signs,
there are myriads of books upon the market to-day,
which will help you. But all the *'signs'* about us,
are more striking and arrestive than even their mention in print.

"But *when will* He come? is the continual question of some. 'SUDDENLY, *when ye think not!'* is the
Bible reply. And, again: *'Of that day and hour
knoweth no man.'*

"But God does not say that we shall not know
the period, approximately. In Daniel twelve, four,
(dealing with the last days) God says:

" 'Thou, Daniel, shut up the words, and seal the book, even TO THE TIME OF THE END.' And in the ninth and tenth verses of that same chapter He says: 'Go thy way, Daniel; for the words are closed up and sealed, till the time of the end . . . none of the wicked shall understand; BUT THE WISE SHALL UNDERSTAND.' And even the superficial observer of our times, if he would compare present-day events with Scripture, would see how near this age draws to its end.

"Internationally, 'rumours of wars.' Nations armed to the teeth as never before, so that when the war dogs are let loose, there shall come a war that shall change all the map of Europe. Even as we are gathered here, to-night, the news-boys are crying the special editions, with the latest news from the Balkans. This may easily be the match that shall fire the train so long laid in Europe. Or, it may blow over for a time, as it has done before; but the explosion cannot be long delayed.

"When the great Near East War has come and gone, there will be brought about that confederacy of nations that will bolster up the Anti-christ. In a remarkable little shilling book, by Rev. R. Middleton, of Norwich, entitled 'Not far off!' he says:

" 'Many no doubt will enquire, and rightly so, What kingdoms are they which are represented as the final power? . . . To this I reply that it is not at all easy or possible to dogmatise, but one thing is certain, i. e., formed on the model of the old Roman power, it will comprise five Eastern, and five Western kingdoms. An ingenious, and I think reasonable suggestion, has been made by Dr.

Rutledge, in his book entitled: "Christ, Anti-christ, and the Millennium." He says:—

" ' "Our opinion is that the five kingdoms representing the Roman Empire of the West will be—(1.) England. (2.) France, either as a republic, or a monarchy once more, a very likely event considering the late trend of affairs in that country, and the volatile character of the French people. (3.) Austro-Germany. (4.) Italy. And (5.) the Peninsula under one king, i. e. Spain and Portugal.

" ' "The five kingdoms of the Eastern Roman Empire, we believe, will be (1.) Russia, at Constantinople. (2.) An enlarged kingdom, comprising, perhaps, Hungary, Roumania, Bosnia, and Servia. (3.) Greece, with enlarged dominion, including Crete, Macedonia, Albania, Roumelia and Bulgaria, to act as a buffer against the further encroachment of Russia, southwards. (4.) Egypt. And (5.) Syria, including Persia." '

"You will notice, friends," Tom went on, "that Ireland is not mentioned in connection with England. The reason is doubtless this, Ireland was never part of the *old* Roman Empire, and will probably not be included in the *new*. If politicians would only study past history in the light of the Bible, and Bible prophecy, there would come many new views as regards Home Rule for Ireland. But I am not dealing with Irish or British politics, but with the Signs of the near return of the Lord Jesus Christ.

"Of many of the more superficial signs of His coming, the pamphlets and books on the subject, which now abound in the Book Market, treat so fully, that I need but to *mention* a few, and then *detail* some of the lesser emphasised, and, in some cases, more recent signs.

"The Jewish question, as it seems to me, exhibits one of the most notable signs of the preparation for the closing up of this Age.   In the book I referred to, once before, '*In the Twinkling of an Eye,*' you will find many of the more *superficial* signs of Jewish preparedness for the end of the age.   But since that book was written many very wonderful signs in the Jewish realm have developed, and many others have come to the surface.   There are strange workings and internal divisions among the Jews themselves, all of which, taken in connection with the fact, that all the countries in which the Jews live in any large numbers, are getting tired of their presence—and their success, for they are amazingly successful—will result in a wholesale ejection of the Jews. Ejection, I mean, where the Jews themselves do not take the initiative.   The Rev. A. Zimmerman, Missionary in Warsaw, for the 'London Society for the Promotion of Christianity among the Jews,' told an interviewer, recently: 'Personally, I am convinced that the signs of the times point to the question becoming so acute that the nations will be compelled to take up the matter of assisting the return of the Jews to Palestine, as the one means of getting rid of the puzzle which has troubled them (the nations) so long.

" 'Look at Russia.   Why are there so many Jews in Poland? It is because Russia is gradually pushing them towards her frontiers.   If, one day, she decides to expel them, then the problem will become still more serious for other nations.'

"A curious fact concerning the return of the Jews to the 'Promised Land' is found in the movement among the present inhabitants of the soil. Whether or not the natives there see the shadow cast before of a coming event, it is a fact that they are emigrating in ship-loads to, mainly, South America. Local conditions have, no doubt, something to do with it, but these people, too, certainly fear the coming of the Jew. They are passing through Marseilles in thousands and thousands, bound for the great continent which has such a stupendous future.

"And there is another very important consideration. Look at the map of the world and note the position of Palestine. It is the corner-stone of three continents. The Mediterranean nations are stirring as they have never done in modern history. The Near East, and the Middle East, present European statesmen with great problems. There is the Bagdad Railway; there is the Cape to Cairo railway, to the very door of Palestine. For that part of the world which has Palestine, to speak broadly, as its centre, there must, in the immediate future, be a great awakening.

"All the powers in Europe will either be directly or indirectly interested in that happening, and I cannot see that it would be to the common advantage, if, indeed, it were permitted, that anyone of them should have a pre-eminent position, a predominant power, in Palestine, the key to vast lands now stirring in their slumber, the corner stone to countries with the

undeveloped 'Wealth of Ormus and of Ind.' One
can scarcely see, too, how that country can be left
in the state of confusion and neglect in which it
now is.

"What is required there is a buffer state, and the
enterprises which will be engaged in and around
Palestine appear to suggest that in that state we require the brains, the business acumen, the wealth of
the Jews, that there will be a favourable outlet for
all three, and that advantageous use of them can be
made for all concerned. All these, to my mind, are
the irresistible circumstances which are tending to
hasten the great solution of the Jewish Problem.
The rulers and peoples of Europe will, I feel sure,
eventually find it to their advantage, and to that of
the most remarkable race in the world, to make
easy—nay, to assist and subsidise—the return of the
Jew to Palestine.

"This return of the Jew to his 'Home-land,' bears
also an intimate relation to the wonder-work now
being performed in Mesopotamia. Pastor D. M.
Panton, of Norwich, writing in the 'Christian,' in
July of this very year (1912) says: 'We are con-
fronted with the revival of Babylon: and to-day, it
begins slowly to crystallize before our eyes. The
awakening of the East, with the profound upheavals
of Japan and China, is shifting the gravity of nations
eastward. Egypt, which has its part in the prophetic
role, has already, under a miracle of British restoration, leapt back into the rank of nations; and Asia
Minor, the cradle of mankind, that holds both Jeru-
salem and Babylon, is once again becoming the pivot

of the world.   But it is Mesopotamia, the land of
Shinar, which is now the crux of revival.   The Tigris
and   Euphrates   together   deposit   a   black,   alluvial
mould,   said   to   be   the   finest   corn   producing   soil   in
the   world.   But,   unless   guided   by   the   human   hand
these   rivers   either   make   a   desert   by   the   rarity   of
their   overflow,   or,   breaking   their   banks,   create   vast
marshes.

"The   secret   of   Babylonian   wealth   lay   in   a   huge
system   of   irrigation,   brought   to   light   by   recent   ex-
cavations,   and   extending   over   the   land   like   a   vast
spider's   web.   Now   what   is   happening?   For   three
years   Sir   William   Willcocks   worked   among   the
countless   ruined   cities   and   villages   of   Babylonia,
and   he   says:

"'I   have   traced   out   hundreds   of   the   old   canals.
The   headworks   were   at   Babylon,   Bagdad,   Seleucia,
Ctesiphon,   and   Opis,   and   formed   the   greatest   irriga-
tion   scheme   ever   carried   out.   The   problem   of   per-
ennial   irrigation   was   entirely   solved   by   the   Chaldean
Sages   of   old.'

"Some   four   or   five   thousand   labourers   are   already
at   work   on   the   reconstruction   of   dams,   etc.,   and
within   a   comparatively   short   period   the   great   desert
will   blossom   as   a   rose,   and   a   mightier   wealth   than
has   ever   been   known   from   any   district   of   the   world,
will   accrue   from   all   this   reconstructive   work.

"But   the   restoration   of   Mesopotamia   covers   the
site   of   Babylon,   *inevitably   entailing   the   resuscitation,
in   modern   shape,   of   Babylon   and   Nineveh.*'   The   maps
of   Sir   William   Willcocks   mark   out   certain   large
districts   capable   of   early   redemption   and   develop-

ment; and in the very heart of these districts is
the site of Babylon.

"Vast agricultural wealth would demand a new
commercial centre. Bagdad is now the centre of
Mesopotamian trade; but its population is already
large, and, resting on a site liable to inundation
when the Tigris is in flood, it would be difficult to
extend.

"Military reasons will also compel a rebuilt Babylon. The whole region is strategic. When Alexander
I. strove to get permission from Napoleon to take
Constantinople, Napoleon called for a map, and after
looking at it intently, rolled it up again, saying:
'No! Constantinople is the sovereignty of the
World.' And it was among the papers of Napoleon
himself, so fruitful in schemes which will be the
achievement of a greater than Napoleon, that actual
plans were found for the rebuilding of Babylon, with
quays, rivers, wharves, and all the equipment of a
great commercial city.

"Nor is it without dread significance, that the
modern mind is losing its recoil against the concen-
trated iniquity summed up in the word BABYLON—
'The Queen of Cities,' says Sir William Willcocks,
'the Capital of the World, the finest city man ever
built. Christian man, and Jewish man before him, has
cast over it the ban of superstitious loathing: only
the evil of Belshazzar is remembered. My hopes,
my ambitions, my work, are bound up with the re-
creation of Chaldea.'

"Yet Chaldea remains one of the moral plague-
spots of the world. It is not only that Mesopo-

tamia is the home of the fiercest Mohammedanism, itself the most uncompromising antagonist of the Christian faith—it is even more Satanic. 'I spent a week,' says Dr. Hume Griffith, medical missionary in Nineveh, 'With the Yezdi sheikh, in his mountain castle near the ruins of Nineveh. The priests of these Devil-worshippers are all clad in white and carry with them a wand of office, surmounted by a brass peacock. At the entrance to their chief temple is the figure of a serpent. This is looked upon with great veneration, and is kept black by means of charcoal. Each worshipper kisses the serpent before entering the temple. Their religious rites, which include the use of hypnotism, are kept very secret, and are only practised between sunset and sunrise.

"Babylon will re-erect her head in the one region of open Satanic worship, and amid the most purely Satanic environment in the world. It is fitting that such should be the case, since Babylon will be the 'Seat of Antichrist.'

" 'Where are the signs of His coming?' cry the scoffers, alluding to the Second Coming of Christ. Everywhere! This wondrous movement in Mesopotamia, is surely an unmistakable sign.

"The very desirability of an universal religion, a religion that will suit all shades of thought—and *no* thought—of all tastes, of all peoples, is continually being suggested in these days. Among certain schools of Theosophy, it is stated that there have been *eleven* Messiahs, as Moses, Mohammed, Jesus, etc. but there is to be a twelfth, and 'the Twelfth is to harmonise into one the perverted teachings of the mighty ones who have preceded him. He will establish an Universal Religion.'

"I spoke to you, friends, the other night on, among other things, what a man of 'Degrees,' had said the religion of the future would be. And the conditions of the world all point to the fact that is fast ripening for Antichrist, and since, as it seems to me, from Scripture, that Jesus Christ will come for His Church, before Antichrist is actually manifested, then the Coming of our Lord must be very, very nigh.

"The latest, world-wide movement of Theosophy: 'The Order of the Star in the East,' is but another of the preparings for the coming of 'The Man of Sin.' Last year in this very month, (October, 1912) ministers of all denominations in Britain, received a circular letter from Lady Emily Lutyens, drawing attention to the new Order, and enclosing a leaflet by Mrs. Annie Besant, which gave this note of explanation, amongst others:

"'This Order has been founded to draw together those, who, whether inside or outside the Theosophical Society, believe in the near coming of a great Spiritual Teacher for the helping of the world. It is thought that its members may, on the physical plane, do something to prepare public opinion for His coming, and to create an atmosphere of welcome and of reverence, and on the higher planes, may unite in forming an instrument of service ready for his use. The Declaration of Principles, acceptance of which is all that is necessary for admission to the Order, is as follows:—'

"Then there follow, in the circular the Declaration of Principles, beautiful enough in a vague way, but without a hint of God, of Christ, of The Holy Spirit, or the Word of God.   No truly Spiritually-minded devoted Christian, steeped in the Word of God—*as* the Word of God—could by any means be taken in with the whole fabrication.   But souls *ill*-taught, and *un*-taught in the Word of God might be easily ensnared by the glamour of the thing.

"The *world is* looking for a Great One, a Superman, but the World is not looking for Christ Jesus the Lord. They don't want Him. They would not have Him when He came before, they would not have Him if He came again now.   '*The whole* WORLD (every soul out of Christ) *lieth in the arms of the wicked One.*' And he, that wicked one, will see to it that none of his should welcome Christ, if He did come to earth again.   As a matter of fact He will not come to the earth again, until He has taken His own true ones out of the earth.

"Then *after* that, when He does come to the earth, it will be to take vengeance upon all who loved not His Appearing.   Instead of welcoming Him, they will so dread Him that they will '*call upon the rocks and the hills to fall upon them and hide them from the wrath of the Lamb.*'

"Friends, I must close, but let me close with an earnest appeal first to you that are Christians, that you search your scriptures, and see what God says as to the final events, and the final state of the Religious world previous to the Coming of our Lord Jesus Christ. Don't be deluded by the oft-repeated fallacy that the world is getting better and better, and that when it is converted to God, and fit for the coming of Christ, He will come to reign upon the earth.

"Men quote your poet Browning, most glibly:

> " 'God's in His Heaven,
> All's right with His world.'

"It is true that God is in His Heaven, but it is all wrong with the world. Because this is 'Man's Day,' and has been for nearly two thousand years, and the world is under *Satan's* rule.

"You point, some of you, to the ever-increasing betterment of the world's condition from the Hygienic, the Educational, the Philanthropic, and other stand-points, but these things are of the nature of *human* Progress, of Reform, all of which, of themselves merely, will manufacture Pharisees, but never give birth to sons of God.

"Listen, friends, to the great and good Lord Shaftesbury, one of the most untiring, indefatigable workers for the amelioration of the woes of the world, who ever lived; he gave this as his experience: 'I have been identified with a great number of humanising influences and activities during the last half-century, I have seen *humanity improve*d, and classes being drawn together; but the more I have seen them getting improved in those ways, *the further they have got from God.*'

"No, friends, instead of our expecting, and talking of the world getting better—save from the mere humanity point of view—we should face the fact that God definitely declares that it will *'wax worse*

and worse.' 'This know also, that in the last days
perilous times shall come. Evil men and seducers shall
wax worse and worse, deceiving and being deceived.'

"Note that, friends, such men are deceived themselves,
as well as deceiving others. There are many good men,
teachers, and preachers, and writers, who firmly believe, because they see so many signs of physical,
social, and educational betterment, that this proves that
men are getting nearer God. They forget that God
has said that the world will not get better. In this
connection, it is well to remember that there is not
a single text in the Bible, nor a hint, even, given
that the world is to be converted before the Return
of the Lord Jesus Christ.

"Many devout souls put God's Word upside down,
because they fail to realize the separate truths of
the separate dispensations. 'The knowledge of God
SHALL cover the earth, as the waters cover the sea,'
that is perfectly true. Men will not have to say
one to the other 'Know the Lord; for they shall ALL
know Me, from the least of them unto the greatest.'
But those, and similar passages refer to the time
after the Lord has taken away His people into
the air, and after the tribulation, when the world
will be rapidly converted to God, so that, practically,
'a nation shall be born in a day.'

"Then, many friends who do not see the dispen-
sational character of God's Word, and therefore put
things upside down, take those seven wonderful
parables in the thirteenth of Matthew, and point to
the parable of the 'mustard seed' and of the 'leaven'
and say, 'Do not those parables point to the mighty

growth of the Gospel?' And, most emphatically
we say, they do *not*, they point all the other way,
for they point to *the spread of evil*, and not the
triumph of good. In the parable of the 'Mustard-
seed,' the mustard tree makes lodgment in its
branches for the 'fowls,' 'the birds of the air,' both
of which Christ, in His explanation of the parables,
declared as signifying evil — Satan. And, truly,
Christendom, like some abnormal growth, has made
lodgment in its branches for every foul heresy under
the sun—Spiritualism;* Christian Science; Theosophy;
Unitarianism   Universalism;   Christadelphianism;
Seventh Day Adventism; Millennial Dawnism; and
foulest of all, because the most subtle, 'The New
Theology.'

"Then take again the parable of the 'Leaven,'
with the utterly false application so often given to
it, that the 'Leaven' hid in the meal, is the silent
secret working of the Gospel. When Leaven, in
itself is corruption, and in its symbol it represents
the same—corruption. Satan's agents began to mix
the leaven of error in the good meal of God, very
early in the history of the Christian Church, he hid
it, covered it over with fine flour, made it to appear
all fine flour, and secretly it has worked, until now,
our grieved Lord cries, 'When I come, shall I find
The Faith upon the earth?' In no single place in
Scripture does Leaven stand for good, but always for

*See "The Lure of a Soul," by Sydney Watson. Biola Book
Room, Los Angeles. $1.25 postpaid.

evil. God never changes His figures, He does not
juggle with His symbols, if He did we should never
know what He meant, unless God the *Holy Ghost*
affixed, to the change of figure, some explanatory
note for reason of the change.

"Now, finally, friends, I would make my last word
an appeal to every man and woman here to-night,
who has not passed from death to life, who has
never been born again of the Spirit of God, who
knows nothing of Redemption through the Blood—
the atonement—of Jesus Christ. Be warned, friends!
Christ will come soon, very soon, and the fate of the
unsaved, who are *left behind*, when He comes, is too
awful to conceive."*

With a word or two more of pointed appeal, he
closed.   Here and there, there had been, occasionally
through the evening, murmurs of dissent, but nothing
to disturb the meeting or the speaker. The strange,
divine mysterious influence called "The Unction of
the Holy One," had rested so manifestly upon the
earnest young Japanese, that even the occasional
murmurers were held dumb, after their first dissent.

For over an hour Tom heard and answered questions. Again and again people would say to him,
"Dr. so and so," or "Professor so and so says."
But to one and all he would reply, as he turned the
leaves of his little Bible, "But GOD says—"   He
would read the passage, and get the questioner to

---

*Some effort has been made to show a little of these dread
happenings in "The Mark of the Beast," by Sydney Watson.
Biola Book Room, Los Angeles. $1.25 postpaid.

read it, then quietly add: "We must believe God, even though clever men make blunders in their statements."

Scores of Christian people were led into the light of a deeper knowledge of God, and of His Word, that night. Some few men and woman trusted God for the first time. And so closed a most memorable time.

CHAPTER XXIV.

LOVE AS A SPECIALIST.

THE acquaintance begun between Tom and Mrs. Moore, under the power of a mutual attraction, grew into a very rapid and close friendship. Both had known comparatively recent deep sorrow, and found comfort in the strength of friendship existing between them.

The week-end visits of Tom to "The Crest," became an established institution, and Jack Quentin and Maggie, wise in their generation, talked and smiled hopefully to each other, as to the probable whither of these repeated visits.

To Tom there had come a vision of a more wonderful future than could ever have been his with Millicent Burn, for Marie Moore seemed, mentally, intellectually, as the other half of himself. No word of love had ever passed between them, yet each knew that theirs was more than an ordinary friendship. Things were in this position when, on a certain Thursday morning, Tom, who was busy in his studio, was interrupted by the arrival of letters.

One of these bore the familiar handwriting of Mrs. Moore, though Tom was startled at the shakiness of the writing. Ripping open the envelope hastily, he read:

"DEAR TOM,

"I would not wire you for fear of alarming you needlessly, but, if you can, I wish you would come to me the moment that you receive this. I am far from well: I feel very strange, and would like to see you.

"Yours, waiting,
MARIE."

Without a moment's delay, working indeed with a feverish haste, he went to his dressing-room, carrying the remainder of his unopened letters with him. Rapidly changing his clothes for a travelling suit, he thrust the unread letters into his pocket and only pausing, downstairs, long enough to explain to Maggie (Jack was out) the reason of his hurried departure, he left the house, caught a passing taxi, and in another moment he was whirling along to the station.

Ten minutes after he left the house a telegram arrived, urging him to come instantly to "The Crest." Of this, of course, he was quite ignorant, until his arrival, later, at the great house whose mistress was lying with the shadow of death hanging over her.

The high mail-cart was awaiting his arrival at the station, and it was from the groom that he heard of the deadliness of Mrs. Moore's illness.

The mare in the shafts of the mail-cart covered the ground at a racing pace, yet it seemed but a crawl to the feverish eager spirit of the almost impatient Tom.

Immediately on his arrival the doctor met him, and, confirming all that the groom had said, added:

"She cannot last twenty-four hours, sir. But come up to her room, at once, for she asks for you continually."

Tom was startled at the change, as his eyes fell upon her.

"Oh, Marie!" it was all he could find voice to say, but all the deep love of his soul was held in the tenderness of his tones.

Her eyes literally blazed with a sudden delight, as they rested upon his face. She stretched her arms upwards, and clasped him as he bent over her. Her gaze was full of deepest, tenderest yearning, and, with a feeble strength she held his face close to hers, for a moment.

"My Darling!" she whispered, at last, as, her strength failing her, she was obliged to let her arms fall back from the clasp of his neck.

She had never used an endearing term to him before, but now, somehow, it seemed perfectly natural. It was the tenderness of a death-hour.

"It was very sudden, dear," she murmured. "My only fear was that you would not have been in time, and I seem to have so much to say to you."

A slight movement at the foot of the bed caused her to look around. She caught the anxious expression on the faces of the doctor and nurse. She signed for the doctor to draw nearer.

He was at her side in a moment.

"I may lose consciousness any moment, eh, doctor?" she asked.

"Yes, it *is* possible!" he replied.

"Then let me be quite alone with my friend, for I have many things to say to him."

The medico acquiesced, only stipulating that if excessive faintness came over her, that he should be summoned, at once. He gave her a strengthening draught, and left the glass of the same cordial mixed

ready, which Tom should give her to sip, should
occasion require.

The next moment Tom and the dying woman
were quite alone.

"Sit close to me, dear," she whispered, and her
eyes never wandered from his face, as she watched
him fetch a chair, and, placing it beside the bed,
seat himself in it.

He took her hand in his, and her fingers closed
around his in a tight, passionate clasp. He began
to question her about her illness, but she checked
him with a sad little smile, and with the whispered
words:

"All that matters little, dear, since the doctor says
that nothing can save me, and I want all my strength
to talk to you. Yesterday I made a will, it was a
very short one, only a few lines. I have no single
soul belonging to me in the shape of relatives. I
have left everything I have, unreservedly to you
and——"

Her speech had been broken by weakness and
breathlessness, now she paused altogether.

Rising to his feet, he bent over her, a look of un-
speakable gentleness and sympathy in his face.

"Lift me, dear Tom, just a little higher on the
pillows," she gasped.

He put his strong arms about her, and lifted her
into a more comfortable position. She smiled up
into his eyes, and a quick colour came into her
pale cheeks, as his arms enwrapped her.

She nestled her flushed cheek against the back of
one of his hands, and the colour deepened in her
face, as she said:

"How restfully you hold me.   Let me lie thus,
a little while, while we talk, dear."

Her eyes were still fixed upon his, as she said:

"Repeat those lovely words of Suso's, the 'At
last,' which you repeated to me the other day."

He did her bidding, though he found it hard at
first, to command his voice. He went right through
that delicious poem, and, as line after line fell from
his lips, her face grew brighter, her eye reflected more
of the light of Heaven. It was absolutely transformed
when he reached the concluding lines:

> "Draw Thou my soul to Thee * * *
>   * * * Yea; Thou hast broken the enchanter's
>   spells,
>   And I am free.
> Now in the haven of untroubled rest,
>   I land at last;
> The hunger, and the thirst, and weary quest,
>   For ever past.
> There, Lord, to lose, in bliss of Thine embrace
>   The recreant will;
> There, in the radiance of Thy Blessed Face,
>   Be hushed and still;
> There, speechless at Thy pierced Feet,
>   See none and nought beside.
> And know but this—that Thou art sweet,
>   That I am satisfied."

As his voice ceased, she softly murmured:

"All that *has* been made true, in part, down here,
through His precious, pardoning, cleansing, keeping
Blood. But presently, I shall see His face!"

A look of rapture filled her upturned eyes, as she
whispered, in ecstatic tones:

"See His face, dear! Oh the wonder of the thought; of the prospect!"

In her delight, as if she was leaping to meet her Lord, she lifted herself slightly in Tom's arms. "Sit me up!" she murmured.

He lifted her into a sitting posture. There came a quick flush into her face, from the slight exertion, then she paled again as quickly. Her spirit was stronger than her body.

The better to support her, he had seated himself on the edge of the bed. His arms were about her. She leant against him, her head resting aginst his breast.

For a moment there was silence between them, then she spoke:

"Tom, dear," she whispered. "We have been very happy in our friendship together!"

"We have, Marie!" His voice choked.

"God was very good to let you come into my broken, lonely life," she said. "I wonder if you can know all that your friendship has meant to me?"

"I can gauge all that it meant, Marie," he sighed, "by all that your friendship has meant to me."

She smiled very sweetly, and there was an expression in her eyes he had never seen there before, and one which puzzled him, for the time, exceedingly.

"I want," she began again, brokenly, "to tell you, dear Tom, that I too believe what your dear dead Millicent told you, that you will yet meet the woman who will not only command all the love of your heart, but who will be permitted to share your life, cheering it with her presence, gladdening it with her love, strengthening it with her wisdom and counsel. Your nature, dear, and I think your art, requires all that such an one, in your life, will be, for all true art needs feeling thrown into it, to give life to it."

She paused a moment, her eyes drooped wearily, and she whispered:

"If I tire you, darling, lay me down. I am drowsy, and would sleep a moment or two."

Her eyes closed, but he did not lay her down. Her face nestled closer to his breast, and her spasmodic breathing became more regular. She slept.

She looked wondrously beautiful as she lay in his arms, and as he silently took in every feature of her beautiful face, he was struck by a strange renewal of youth in it. She was seven years older than himself, yet now she did not look an hour over twenty-four. He recalled the fact which he had heard and read, often, that *before* as well as *after* death, Nature will sometimes thus rejuvenate the face of the passer from Time to Eternity.

She was sleeping soundly now, with that quick, deep slumber that, though it may last but a few moments, is often so sound, in the experience of persons very ill.

He was full of deep, sorrowful thoughts, as he watched her. "To love but to lose!" he murmured to himself.

Suddenly her lips parted, and she began to murmur in her sleep: "My darling—you will never know—how—have—loved you! And if—only—you had—loved me—but—but."

The confession had slipped brokenly from her lips, and Tom's soul yearned to wake her, to pour out all his own deep love for her, But why intrude his love upon the dying, he asked himself.

Suddenly, a soft little sigh broke from her, and she opened her eyes.

"I think I dreamt," she whispered, "dreamt of you, Tom, dear."

"And talked in your sleep, Marie," he replied, "and gave me your dear secret. I love you, darling, as I have never loved. You love me. Would that God would give you back your strength."

Her face flushed at the mention of her sleep-confession of her love. A look swept into her face transfiguring every feature, making it like unto an angel's.

"I think—I think," she murmured, brokenly, "this is the Home-call. I must not keep Him waiting now that He calls. But I am glad you know my secret, dearest."

Her eyes held him by the strength of her adoring gaze; the intensity of her love burned into his very being, and he poured forth all the love that burned in his own heart.

Then for a moment or two there was silence between them, until, softly, she whispered:

"Lift me in your arms, and kiss me good-bye, dear Tom."

Tenderly he lifted her and laid his lips upon hers.

"You must not grieve, dearest, when I am gone—."

Hoarsely, huskily, for his emotion choked him, he cried: "I cannot, cannot think that this is to be the end, Marie. I am going to plead with God, that, if it can be, for His glory, and our true well-being, that He will spare you."

She smiled bravely back into his eyes, then her eye-lids drooped, and she murmured: "Lay me down, dear,—so sleepy."

He laid her back upon her pillows, and, instantly she slept.

Love and faith have worked miracles many times before, in the world. But surely no greater miracle ever accompanied love and faith than that of the recovery of Marie Moore. The doctors were staggered. According to every law of the faculty she could not live, yet, she not only recovered, but regained her old glorious strength.

The marriage of Tom and Marie Moore, gave an infinite satisfaction to Jack Quentin and Maggie, and the quartette became fast friends.

Three months after the marriage, Marie having told Tom of her great desire to see Japan, and proposed that Jack and Maggie should be invited, as their guests, to accompany them, the quartette started for the East.

After six months in the "Land of the Chrysanthemums," Jack and Maggie returned to England.

"Till He come!" cried Jack, when they parted. "If we do not meet here again, we shall meet in the air."